Ethan Was a Stranger . . . and a Strange Man . . .

Ethan regarded her intently. "I'm here because I want you."

Deborah stiffened . . . Panic and turmoil threatened to seize her again.

"Just tell me to leave and I will," he murmured.

It should have been simple for her to say, "Please leave," then, but even in the near-blackness of the room she was captivated by the intensity of his eyes. He filled the room with his presence, animated it, and with sudden understanding she knew how very alone she would be if he were to leave . . .

All the muscles of her throat seemed to have thickened so that it was hard to speak. "I don't want you to leave," she managed finally. He kissed her . . .

Sharon B. Pape

PUBLISHED BY POCKET BOOKS NEW YORK

Another *Original* publication of POCKET BOOKS

POCKET BOOKS, a division of Simon & Schuster, Inc.
1230 Avenue of the Americas, New York, N.Y. 10020

Copyright © 1983 by Sharon Pape

ISBN: 0-671-43350-4

First Pocket Books printing September, 1983

10 9 8 7 6 5 4 3 2 1

For everything there is a season
And a time to every purpose under heaven.

Ecclesiastes 3:1

September 12, 1692

A hammer rises and falls. A man is making repairs on a roof. Ben Purvey's form comes into focus, too awkward with age and weight for the work. One knee bent against the upward slope of the roof, one stretched behind him, the foot against the ledge. He wheezes, his breathing becoming more labored with each thrust of the hammer. Again he raises it in a high arc over his head. Suddenly he's overbalanced. His knee lifts off the roof. His foot slips along the lip. He totters drunkenly. For a long moment he struggles with gravity. Finally, hammer still clutched in his hand, he topples. With a scream like the rush of wind, his body slams into the hard earth.

Emily's head flew off the pillow, eyes wide with the terror of it. She pulled herself to a sitting position on trembling arms. Her heart was beating out of control, her mouth and nose so dry it hurt to breathe. The dream had been too real, too close. Never before had her dreams scared her so. Never had they presaged such tragedy. They had always dealt with the gentler rhythms of life: the gender of an unborn child, the time of the season's first snow, the coming together of a couple in marriage. And even these Annie had counseled her to keep to herself since the eruption of the hideous witch trials. "For far less than dreams they would have you hanged," she'd told her firmly. Emily knew she was right. Yet if she told no one of this dream, a man was likely to die. A friendly man who always had a smile for you when your path crossed his. She could be discreet, warn him and his wife alone in their house. But she'd have to hurry. The dream had been very clear, and that meant it was close to happening.

Suddenly Emily feared she might already be too late. The dull thudding of a hammer vibrated in the early morning stillness. Images from the dream flashed through her mind again and propelled her out of bed, the bedclothes tangling about her legs, tripping her. All caution evaporated. She flung her warm cloak over her nightgown, thrust her feet into shoes and ran for the door.

The morning was crisp and breezy, the sun burning through a haze just above the eastern horizon. Emily's stockingless feet chafed inside her shoes. She made a peculiar picture, an old lady half-running, half-hobbling along the mud-packed street, her gray hair and black cloak whipping about her.

She followed the steady pounding of the hammer up to the Purvey house. There on the roof, as in the dream, labored Ben Purvey. Even his position was the same. He wore only breeches and a soiled old shirt open at the throat, in spite of the chill in the air.

Bess Purvey stood outside the house looking up at her husband, an apron fluttering between the open folds of a coarse cloak much like Emily's. She turned at the sound of footsteps.

"Why, good day, Emily Hawkins. What is it that has you up and about this early of a morning?"

Emily shook her head breathlessly, eyes riveted on the roof and Ben. She wasn't too late after all. But he was swinging the hammer again. She fought for air and cupped her hands to her mouth.

"Ben. Don't. Come down. You must come down at once. Don't swing that hammer, you'll fall. I saw it in a dream."

Ben's arm was already extended well over his shoulder when the shrill, frightened voice carried up to him. He jerked his head quickly around to place the voice. His left knee lifted off the slope of the roof. Groping for balance his right foot slid along the ledge. For a dream-like moment he struggled to stay upright, then he fell with a hollow scream. Bess and Emily watched in open-mouthed horror. Emily felt the earth recoil under his impact, heard his skull crack as it hit the large, jagged rock. She wished it was the dream again so that she could wake and find it gone.

Bess was bending over her husband, wiping with her apron at the blood that flowed in a dozen places from his shattered head.

"Ben, my poor Ben," she was whimpering. "He only just yesterday dug that boulder up out of his planting field. Oh Ben, my Ben." Then she turned on Emily, tears in her eyes, tight-lipped. "This is your doing. All yours. What did you come by here for anyway? Why'd you want to do this?" The last of her words were crushed between sobs.

Emily was still frozen in place. Her thoughts moved sluggishly as if they, too, were in shock. Why had she come, indeed? She had thought to save a man. Now that man was dead. If she could have seen beyond the house in her dream, would she have seen herself standing there?

Chapter One

March 1982

"According to this we should be coming up on our exit in about five miles," said Deborah, trying to fold the map back into its accordian pleats.

"Here, let me do that," Edith clucked. "You've got it all wrong."

Deborah relinquished the map to her sister without a word. There were many things worth fighting over; a map was not one of them.

Hal eased the car into the right lane. "Didn't take us as long as I expected."

"We're just fortunate there weren't too many icy spots," said Edith, pressing the map into a compact booklet.

"It's all in the skill of the driver."

"Hmm," Edith remarked, turning from her husband to Deborah. "I still think this whole thing is a terrible mistake. Why would you want to seclude yourself in a little two-horse town all summer playing counselor to kids when you spend all winter trying to teach them?"

"I like kids," Deborah replied evenly. "And a little fresh country air will be a nice change."

"There's fresh air on Long Island," Edith went on petulantly. "Why couldn't you spend the summer on the Island with us? Go to the club, be catered to, pampered a bit? Maybe you would meet someone."

"Didn't we go that route last year, and the year before that?" Deborah reminded her. "I was bored silly after one week. I'm just not the sun-worshipper type and I'm a horror at bridge and golf."

"You didn't really try."

"And whom did I meet? Alan Simms—dull, fortyish, and fat. Or Dean Cartwright—there was a winner—short, skinny, and fascinated with himself."

"And very wealthy. Don't forget that," Edith interrupted.

"I couldn't. He wouldn't let me."

"She's right, Edith. You've got to give her that," Hal said in the referee tone he adopted for such discussions.

"A girl your age shouldn't be quite so particular, Deborah. A Robert Redford isn't waiting around every corner," Edith pointed out.

"I don't think that means I should just settle," said Deborah. "I'd prefer my life the way it is, if it ever came to that."

"That's ridiculous. Besides, who's to say this wouldn't have been the summer you would have met someone?"

"If all my life has been building up to this summer, it will just have to find me in Rachael Crossing, because that's where I'll be."

"Bravo!" Hal cheered, and he slammed his palm against the steering wheel in applause.

"A lot you care," Edith said, turning on him. "She's not your sister. I promised our mother I'd watch out for her— see to it she was settled, had security and happiness."

"I'm sure Momma realizes you've tried," Deborah soothed. "After all, you can hardly promise to find happiness for someone else, now can you?"

Deborah looked out the side window hoping to end the discussion that had begun more than a month earlier. Even in January, with two long, dreary months of winter still ahead, she had started thinking about the coming summer, determined to do something different. Life had reached a standstill. She didn't mind her job, but that wasn't enough of a reason to exist. Her social life was on the downhill without ever having peaked. She'd been introduced to every friend's cousin's son Edith could scrounge up, but after a while the relationships had all fizzled out. And Deborah equitably laid most of the blame upon herself. If the prospects hadn't shown much interest, it was because she hadn't been much interested. Not that she was expecting Robert Redford to sweep her off her feet, as Edith had often accused. Or was she? No, she decided candidly, she didn't merit a Robert Redford. While she looked a good deal younger than her thirty-seven years, she didn't consider herself beautiful. Her nose was just a little too long and straight, and her small mouth didn't reveal enough of her teeth when she smiled, so that her smile always had a shy, tentative quality. She had spent her teen-age years aching for a nose that turned up and a smile full of teeth. With these, she had told herself, she could be beautiful, Hollywood beautiful, because she already had one extraordinary feature. Huge dark brown eyes fringed with thick, straight, black lashes that bore out of her pale skin. Even if no one had ever told Deborah that she was actually beautiful, many had commented on her magnificent eyes.

By the time she had entered her twenties, Deborah had come to accept her shortcomings. She had even grown tolerant of the fine, brown hair that stubbornly refused to hold a curl. And after several futile attempts at managing shorter, more mature styles, she had relented and wore it back in a large barrette at the nape of her neck.

No, she wasn't holding out for Robert Redford, but neither was she ready to settle for Alan Simms or Dean Cartwright. So she pored over the ads in the Sunday newspapers, not even sure what she was hunting for, until a tiny ad near the bottom of a page finally stirred her. A camp in Rachael Crossing, Massachusetts was looking for a counselor. Deborah had never heard of the town before, and it held the promise of a peaceful summer away from the city, away from Edith. That was enough. She sent a letter and her resume that afternoon.

An interview had been requested. She'd taken the train up there in February. She had decided not to mention the prospect of a job to Edith until it was a fait accompli. Deborah wasn't going to give her the opportunity to dissuade her.

Finally, contract in hand, she had confronted her sister and brother-in-law. Their reactions were predictable. Hal had smiled approvingly from behind Edith, who had at once begun to criticize the whole idea. Deborah had silently heard her out.

"I understand your concern, Edith," she said once she had the chance, "but the contract is signed. They're depending upon me. And to be perfectly honest, I'm looking forward to a summer away and completely on my own."

"It sounds really wonderful, Deborah," Hal said quickly. Some time to yourself."

Edith glared at him before turning back to Deborah. "Where are you going to live up there?"

"Well, that's the only loose end," Deborah admitted. "I'll have to go up there soon and find a place. The school can't provide housing."

"You take a job, make all kinds of plans and don't have a place to stay?" Edith exclaimed incredulously.

"Oh Edith, calm down. I'm sure there are plenty of summer cottages or bungalows to rent in a place like Rachael Crossing."

"Rachael Crossing? I've never even heard of it. Where is it?"

"It's small, not far from Salem, Massachusetts."

"Why don't we all take a ride up next weekend?" Hal suggested. "We can help Deborah find a place."

"Now that at least sounds like a good idea," Edith agreed, anxious to have some say in the matter.

"Thanks, that would be great," Deborah replied, thinking it might even be worth having Edith along if it meant no more long treks by railroad.

Now Deborah wasn't sure the decision had been wise after all. Edith's harassed voice was demanding her attention again.

"A teacher. Why did you have to become a teacher?"

Deborah shrugged her shoulders at the familiar remark. Hal shook his head in sympathy.

"Who can you hope to meet but grimy, little kids and other teachers?"

Deborah wondered briefly at her sister's dislike of children, though she was devoted to her own.

"You wouldn't even let me use my connections to land you a job for a big firm in the city. There at least you would have met the right people."

"What connections?" said Hal. "Your friend from high school whose father was the ex-vice president of Fielding Copper?"

"Don't underestimate these things," Edith retorted sharply. "One never knows."

"Oh? I had the feeling you always did," Hal said soberly.

Deborah suppressed a laugh. She supposed it was Hal's sense of humor that had seen him through these past sixteen years with Edith. Yet as different as they were in temperament, physically they were a close match. Both were neat and conservative in dress and wore their hair short. Recently they'd begun to thicken somewhat at the waist and sprout lines like spokes around their eyes from too many summers at the pool and on the golf links. Their years together were blurring what differences there had been.

They rode in silence until Deborah signalled their exit. At the end of the ramp a sign listed five towns, an arrow indicating each direction. After fifteen minutes on winding, narrow roads they arrived at the outskirts of Rachael Crossing. A sense of expectancy charged the silence; Deborah was as eager to see her summer home as Edith and Hal were.

A white sign nearly hidden behind an overgrown juniper bore the name "Rachael Crossing" in black letters. Hal had pulled to a stop to read it.

"You'd think they didn't want anyone knowing where they were, the way that sign is hidden," said Edith. "Little rural places like this always seem to be harboring some secret or other."

"She sees too much TV," Hal said sympathetically to Deborah. "Shall we move on, ladies?"

"Please." Deborah sighed.

Edith pressed her lips together and said nothing. As they followed a curve around the sign, Rachael Crossing unwound before them along a straight length of road, made marginally wider to provide curbside parking. Deborah could see from the beginning to the end of the town in one glance.

"It's so tiny," Edith exclaimed. "I know you said it was small, but I never expected . . ."

Deborah ignored the comment, enchanted with the shops they were passing. Each occupied the first floor of an old house, some with porches, others with awnings and flower boxes. Even the post office looked like an old church, its steeple now sporting a weather vane.

"Very picturesque," said Hal. "I wonder if there's a real estate office."

"Wait, there's one," Deborah said, pointing to a white bungalow nestled snugly between two stores, its only identification a small, square sign in the window that read: Rachael Real Estate Office.

Hal braked and pulled the car to the curb in front of the building. They climbed out, massaging backs and stretching cramped legs. The few people who were about in the town paused and stared openly at them. Two women across the street whispered to one another without once averting their eyes.

"They certainly are rude," Edith muttered under her breath.

"You're looking at them the same way they're looking at you," said Deborah. "They're probably just not used to strangers." She turned and marched into the office.

Edith looked up at the overcast sky and silently beseeched their mother for strength. Hal took her by the elbow and propelled her into the office.

The realtor was a small round woman with silver hair cut like a man's, sparkling blue eyes, and thick legs that gave her the appearance of having been planted wherever she stood. She greeted them with amiable curiosity, but as pleasant and eager to please as she was, she was sorry to inform them that there just wasn't anything available to rent.

"Nothing?" Deborah repeated lamely.

"Well, we're not much of a tourist town ourselves, don't ya know," said Mrs. Hopkins. "And the few families who come up in the summer regularly have already leased everything there is."

"What about a boarding house?" Deborah asked, unwilling to look at Edith's triumphant smile. "Would anyone be willing to take me in as a boarder?"

Mrs. Hopkins shook her head. "No, dear. Up here we don't take too much to outsiders. Never have. There ain't a person I can think of who would open his house up to a stranger. That's jest the way of it." She fixed Deborah with a smile, the sympathetic sort of smile one might give a slow child. Deborah sensed that the woman was keeping something from her, but before she could form a question, Mrs. Hopkins spoke again.

"Now there is one place comes t' mind since ya seem so desperate, the old place on Foxton Lane, a bit outside of town."

"Just what is this old place?" asked Hal.

"It's just an old house the bank took over when the last owners left. Can't say as how we've had too much success renting it lately, though. Place needs some work to be sure. But it can be made livable."

"Can we see it?"

"Why sure, glad to have come up with somethin'."

"I don't like the way she connected being desperate with this house," Edith said to Deborah as they filed outside and waited in the car for Mrs. Hopkins to lock up.

"Let's see it first," Deborah said patiently. She and Edith had taken the back seat. Mrs. Hopkins climbed in beside Hal and directed him north through town. Near the top of a hill, set well back from the road, stood the house.

"Oh Lord, Deborah, look at this place," Edith said, forgetting to be discreet.

Deborah had to suppress an involuntary shudder herself. It was an old house, dating back to the late eighteen hundreds at least, and looked as if it had lost every battle with winter since. The wood, once painted white, was now a disintegrating gray. The shutters hung at angles from the blank, grimy windows. Deborah forced herself to imagine how it might have looked in better days: Two stories, sparkling white with glossy black shutters. Stately in its simplicity, with only a crown of wooden icicles encircling the flat roof to mark its Victorian heritage. It was a large house, set upon quite a lot of land. Some wealthy family had probably had it built, had had servants and gardeners, held parties. There—the place didn't seem quite so dismal anymore. Deborah took a deep breath.

"I want to see the inside, then I'll decide," she said, to Edith's horror, and proceeded to get out of the car.

Mrs. Hopkins was already out, rummaging through her pocketbook, and produced a large ring with a dozen or more keys hanging from it. "Now let's see . . . which key. . . ." She laughed. "Got so many. Here, this should be it."

"What a godforsaken place," Edith chattered as they followed Mrs. Hopkins up the cracked, overgrown path to the front door.

The door hesitated, then shuddered inward, creaking upon warped hinges. Inside, the house was reminiscent of other turn-of-the-century homes Deborah had seen. It was dark, especially in the small entry hall where the staircase ran straight up to the second floor.

"Sorry ya can't get a better look, but the 'lectricity's off," Mrs. Hopkins apologized.

"You mean this place actually has electricity?" Edith muttered sarcastically.

Mrs. Hopkins led the way. The wooden floors protested under their weight. The few furnishings were draped in plastic and old sheets. Lacy webs hung from the corners and dust lay thickly upon the scatter rugs, obscuring their color. From the dining room they turned into the large kitchen at the rear of the house where even Deborah was surprised to see fairly modern appliances. She reminded herself sternly that the house had been occupied until five years ago, according to Mrs. Hopkins.

Once the tour of the main floor was completed in the study, Edith had seen enough and sent Hal one of her "do something!" looks. Hal in turn repeated halfheartedly, "and no one has a room to let or anything like that?"

"Not a one," Mrs. Hopkins smiled tolerantly.

Deborah was still looking around the study. More than any other feature, the bare shelves lining the walls proclaimed the nakedness of the house, and Deborah had to make an effort to suggest cheerfully, "Oh, it needs to be fixed up and all, but I'm sure it could be quite livable, as Mrs. Hopkins has said."

"Why certainly, m'dear," said Mrs. Hopkins, surprised herself that Deborah might seriously be considering the house. "I'd have Carl, he's our handyman, well, I'd have him come over in the spring—spruce up the place a bit."

"You're not really thinking of renting this house," Edith cried in astonishment.

"Why not?" Deborah said bravely. "I'm sure it'll be fine. And besides, I've got the job, so I'll need a place to live, won't I?"

"Rent's not much," Mrs. Hopkins interjected quickly. "Had to keep dropping it to get it rented."

"How much is not much?" inquired Hal.

"Let ya have it for three-fifty for the summer. That's July first through Labor Day. Ya woulda never found anythin' cheaper in this neck o' the woods."

"That I'd believe," Edith said miserably.

"Oh, Edith, you never see the potential of things," said Deborah, feeling strengthened by her own words.

"Now that's the spirit," Mrs. Hopkins encouraged gaily. "Shall we have a look around upstairs before we head back to the office to sign the lease?"

"Fine."

"See you in the car," Hal nodded as he followed Edith outside.

The upstairs had three bedrooms and a bath, in the same dilapidated condition as the other rooms. But Deborah had already made up her mind. She suggested they return to the office to sign the necessary papers.

Edith spoke only intermittently on the way to the hotel in Lynn. Deborah found her silence strangely unnerving. She watched the wintry landscape rush by, bleak and gray, skeletal tree limbs reaching toward them in the wind. Had Edith really sensed something ominous back there in Rachael Crossing, or had it just been an act, a last effort to draw her home for the summer?

September 12, 1692

Emily had gone home. She was sitting in the kitchen in her nightgown and cloak, staring at the cold hearth when Anne Thorndike found her. A damp chill circulated around the room from the front door that had been left ajar.

Annie looked at her old friend and with a tearing at her heart knew that it was true. Emily had been at the Purvey's that morning. But beyond that she believed nothing of what was being whispered from ear to ear.

"Are you all right?" Annie asked gently.

At the familiar voice Emily blinked and looked up, tears brimming in her eyes.

"Come back with me to my house," said Annie. "There's a fire going. I'll make you a cup of hot tea."

Emily shook her head. "Ben Purvey is dead." Her voice was small and hoarse, as if she were strangling inwardly.

"I know."

"I dreamt it would happen. I went there to warn him. And now he's dead because of me."

Annie put her hand on Emily's shoulder. "Perhaps not because of you, but in spite of you," she said.

21

A small hopeful glow flared in Emily's eyes. "Do you believe that?"

"I believe you could never cause anyone sorrow or pain, Emily Hawkins. I would stake my life on it. Now you come along with me." Taking her by the arm she started to raise Emily from the chair. "It was an accident. A tragedy, to be sure. But we've gotten through worse together. And we'll weather this too."

She linked her arm through Emily's and guided her to the front door. She stopped abruptly at the doorway, pulling Emily to the side out of sight of the street.

A crowd of townspeople were marching purposefully toward the house. The sheriff was in the lead, followed by twelve-year-old Sarah Danby and the other half-dozen fickle, murderous girls who had more than twenty deaths on their collective consciences already.

Annie's face went ashen. She stifled the cry of despair that rose like bile in her throat. The witch hunters were after Emily.

Emily pushed past her friend and saw the mob descending upon the house. Annie grabbed her back.

"We must not let them see you. Let them think you ran away. I'll hide you in my house. We'll find a way," she rambled feverishly, tugging at Emily to follow.

"Annie, it's no use, don't you see that? If they don't find me here, your house is the very next place they'd look." She slipped her wrist out of Annie's grasp. "There's nowhere to hide and nowhere to run. I'm too old for that."

Annie looked stricken. "You're not just going to surrender yourself to that pack of murderers, are you?"

Emily drew herself up straight. She and Annie had always been strong for each other. And in Annie's fear she found new courage.

"I'll explain to them exactly what happened, how I meant to warn him," she said calmly. "They'll listen. After all, I've known most of them all their lives."

"Those folks out there, they're not what they were. They're not the same people we knew."

Emily peered around the door jamb again. The crowd was advancing in silence like a dark, menacing cloud, their features distorted with feral anger, making strangers of them.

Tricks of the mind, Emily told herself to calm her rising panic. She turned back to Annie, who stood quaking in the shadows.

"Go Annie. Get out of here. They'll take you, too, if they find you here with me."

"No, I cannot."

"They're almost here. Leave now!"

"Dear friend," Annie put her arms around Emily and drew her into a desperate embrace. Emily clung to her for a moment, feeling with a rush of emotion all the years and memories that bound them. Then she pushed herself away.

"You must make me one solemn vow," she said, engaging Annie's eyes.

"I swear it, no matter what it is."

"Say nothing in my defense."

Chapter Two

July 1982

"It's incredible what a difference a few months can make," Deborah remarked enthusiastically. Trees and bushes hugged the edges of the highway, each a different, luxurious shade of green. Birches, maples, oaks, elms, well watered in early spring, then nourished by weeks of sunshine, nodded like approving sentries as their car sped beneath them.

"The last time we were here everything was dead and covered with snow."

"I'll bet that house still looks just as bleak," Edith said. "Houses aren't rejuvenated by the spring like trees are, you know."

"How can you be so pessimistic?" Deborah chided her gently. "Everything's so beautiful, so full of life."

Edith ignored the comment and turned to look at Deborah on her right. "I just know that a few green leaves aren't going to do anything for that old dump you leased. I've always had to be the practical one, what with Momma dying and me left to care for you. I'm not the one with poetry floating around the brain. And don't go mistaking that for pessimism," she added. "I'm just a realist."

Deborah recognized the much-used line of defense and,

determined to keep the peace, said simply, "Well, at least enjoy the trip up there."

"I wonder if that Mrs. Hopkins will be there to let us in," Edith said after a few minutes.

"I'm sure she will," said Deborah. "I spoke with her just this past Wednesday."

"Well, we'll be on time anyway," Hal noted. "It's ten of and that's our exit coming up." He followed the ramp off the highway.

"Hal, stop," Edith demanded. "Stop here!"

"What the hell for?"

"Just do it."

Hal and Deborah exchanged bewildered glances over Edith's head. Hal slowed and pulled the car to a stop on the narrow shoulder, the tires on one side sinking into the muddy rut beyond it.

"Okay Edith, this had better be good."

Edith opened the glove compartment and withdrew the map. "I want to find a way to get to the house so we don't have to go through that town."

Hal groaned. Deborah choked on a giggle.

"You may think it's perfectly adorable," Edith remarked haughtily, "but I don't like it. Now you look here." She pointed to a line on the map. Hal bent to see it. "Won't this street bring us around into Foxton also?"

"Should. Anyway I don't think we'll get too lost. That is, if I can pull this car out of the mud."

The tires spun for a moment before getting traction, then the car lurched forward onto the road again.

"I've never seen you so unreasonable," Deborah said.

Edith was methodically refolding the map. "What's unreasonable about not liking to be stared at and whispered about?"

Twenty minutes later Hal made the right onto Foxton Lane. Deborah had felt the anxiety build in the pit of her stomach ever since they'd left the thruway. The house just had to look better than the last time they'd seen it. She swallowed hard as they rounded the last curve.

She didn't trust herself to look directly at the house, focusing instead on Mrs. Hopkins' car. Then she let her eyes follow the stone path slowly up to the house. The walkway was still cracked, but the grass had been nurtured and trimmed. The shrubbery needed clipping, but the flower beds appeared to have been turned and weeded. Hopefully, she looked up. The house was shining brightly against the sky, shutters rehung and glistening with new green paint. A loud sigh of relief escaped her lips.

"Look, Edith. They did a wonderful job. The house is beautiful."

"Well it looks better, anyway," Edith admitted as they emerged from the car.

The front door was open and they could see Mrs. Hopkins' round head appear from inside as they walked up the path. On closer inspection Deborah noted that the paint job was far from professional. Many areas needed a second or third coat where the dehydrated wood had sucked in the new paint. And the shutters hadn't been sufficiently scraped, giving them a rough, uneven appearance. Still, the total effect was such an improvement, she decided it would be less than generous to mention these few defects.

"Hello, hello," chirped Mrs. Hopkins. "Welcome home."

"Thank you," Deborah smiled. "You've done wonders with the house. I'm so grateful."

"Does look nice, don't it?" Mrs. Hopkins agreed, bobbing her head up and down merrily. "Pity it was left in such a state all them years. The whole neighborhood looks better for it. Come look around inside."

Deborah followed her through the rooms, Edith and Hal trailing. The covers had been removed from the furniture, the rugs cleaned and aired, the floors washed if not polished, the windows spic and span.

"The bank decided it was worth a few dollars to get the place rented. Shoulda done it long ago. Now maybe there'll be more tenants after you," Mrs. Hopkins commented. "Maybe we'll even get the place sold someday."

"Why does it smell so musty?" Edith complained.

"When a house's been closed up five years it takes a while to air," Mrs. Hopkins told her.

The bedrooms had been cleaned and freshened as well,

and after inspecting them Deborah felt considerably heartened.

"Shall I bring in your luggage?" Hal asked as they came back down to the living room.

"Sure, let me help you."

"Glad everythin's to your likin', dear," Mrs. Hopkins said. "Now here's the key. Same one for front and back doors, don't ya know." She handed Deborah the key on a chain.

"No double locks?" Edith exclaimed.

"This isn't the city, Edith," Hal laughed. "No one is going to steal Deborah. Don't be such a worrier."

"One lock's more 'n enough up here," said Mrs. Hopkins. "Plenty a' folks don't even bother with one."

"Still . . ."

"Edith, come on and help with my things," Deborah tugged at her arm.

Mrs. Hopkins followed them outside. "Well, I guess I'll be leaving ya for now. Enjoy your stay. Any trouble ya just gimme a call."

"Thank you very much," Deborah said shaking her hand warmly.

Edith and Hal added their good-byes.

"Oh, by the way," Mrs. Hopkins said, stopping by her car. "Carl'll be around to mow the lawn once a week. Any problems with the house, he can probably help ya."

"Okay. Thanks again," Deborah called back.

Once the suitcases were deposited inside, Edith, Hal and Deborah stood about not quite sure what to do next.

Hal spoke first. "I guess maybe Edith and I should be on our way and let you settle in, Deborah."

Deborah's stomach lurched a bit at the thought of actually being left alone in the strange house.

"We're not going anywhere," Edith said emphatically, unbuttoning her jacket and laying it over a nearby chair.

"Maybe we should leave it up to Deborah, then," Hal turned to his sister-in-law.

"I'd appreciate the company," she smiled. "Until I get used to the house and all."

Hal shrugged good-naturedly.

"There, it's settled," Edith said. "I'll help Deborah un-pack and you can see if that thing works," she nodded to the portable television resting incongruously on its plastic stand in a corner of the old living room. "I wonder if they even get more than one channel up here," she added as she followed Deborah up the stairs."

By the time Edith and Hal left, the sky was darkening, the house melting among the trees and hills in a monochrome of gray. Deborah waved them off. Then she went inside, clos-ing the door behind her. She looked around at the living room, gray too in the evening light. It was such a big house. So big and so quiet. It seemed to wrap itself around her. She turned on a lamp.

"Night fears," she laughed nervously. "Night fears, like when I was a kid." The sound of her voice was good and settling. A city girl needs time to adjust to this much quiet, she told herself, and she switched on the television for company.

September 14, 1692

"I am no witch!" Emily Hawkins cried out, jumping up from her seat. With wild eyes she searched the frightened, unsympathetic faces that packed the small courtroom. All friends, all strangers. Like a nightmare in which familiar objects assume alien forms.

"I am no witch," she repeated lamely, beseeching their help with trembling outstretched arms.

Rough hands grabbed at her and pulled her down again.

"Silence," roared the judge. "The verdict stands—guilty as charged. Emily Hawkins, you will be taken from this court of law and hanged for witchcraft this very day. Never again will your eyes cast spells upon our young nor your tongue foretell events that God would not have us know before time. Take her outside!"

Rumblings from the spectators crowded in on the judge's words, taunting the prisoner, demonstrating their repudiation of her, onetime neighbor, onetime friend. The noise mounted, echoing as the news was passed out through the open door to those waiting beyond. The air hummed with vengeance and relief.

"She accuses no one?" Anne Thorndike inquired hesitantly of a man who stood nearby.

"It seems she does not. The judge has ordered her out to be hanged."

Annie shook her head slowly, a shudder rippling the loose flesh about her neck. How could this be? It seemed as if she had known Emily Hawkins forever, back when she had still been Emily Saunders and in school. They had been as close as two girls could be without the same blood. Emily and Annie, one unbroken phrase. Emily had helped her give birth to her two sons and she had helped when Emily's only child had been born dead. Emily had comforted Annie when her husband had died. She and Emily had always been there for each other. Now Emily was about to be hanged for witchcraft, and where was she? Out of sight. She had kept her word to Emily, chafing at the constraint. Yet if she were to run in there, swearing on the Bible that no finer woman lived in Salem than Emily Hawkins, would it do any good? No one would listen to her. Or if they did, they would surely hang her, too. For in their frenzied logic only another witch would come to Emily's aid. So Annie remained outside, guilt and fear cutting her like a too tight corset, awaiting the inevitable verdict. Now that it was rendered, Annie started to turn away from the simple but forbidding building.

The crowd was surging out around her. She looked back. People were pushing out of the narrow doorway, forcing those immediately outside to step back. The sounds were becoming more distinct. One voice in particular, ordering everyone to "make way." Then she heard Emily's voice, "Oh God, Dear God, help me." Annie stood helplessly on the perimeter of the expanding crowd, unable to watch this atrocity but wanting to somehow ease Emily's anguish.

Emily was in the doorway, her pleas and supplications diluted into fitful whimperings. Her gray head was down, swaying like an October leaf before it falls. Annie fought the impulse to run. If she could not help, at least she could share the pain.

The procession was working its way up the path to the hill where the gallows had been erected five months earlier. At the head the minister marched, so haughty and sanctimonious that Annie could sooner see the devil at work in him than in all the poor innocents whom he had helped condemn. The judge followed. Then Emily. Dear Emily, with hands bound behind her, eyes riveted to the hardened mud path, unable to face the scaffold and rope that awaited her. She was being prodded along by a broad-shouldered ape of a man, illiterate and animal-like, who did the simple bidding of the judge.

He was watching Emily intently in case she might try to run, as if it would do her any good. And finally Sarah Danby and the girls passed. Oh, if Annie could just get her hands on one of them. . . . But she knew she couldn't. Wouldn't. Or she would be their next victim. As if they had heard her thoughts, two of the girls swung their heads toward Annie. Their eyes narrowed, locking on hers, freezing her like a mouse caught between the deadly claws of a cat. The exchange lasted only a brief moment. Not a step was lost in the sinister procession, but for Annie time had been arrested, bloating that moment with dread and frustrated rage that left her weak-limbed and breathless. Even after the girls had snapped their heads away, she could still see their cold, mocking smiles in profile as they marched along behind Emily.

The procession reached the gallows. The minister and judge stood to either side while the ape-man escorted Emily up the final steps like a grotesque parody of a wedding ceremony. Overhead, the sky was darkening with blue-black clouds that hung low as if heavy with the evil of the times.

Emily stood silhouetted against the sky, hope evaporated, body limp, as the thick, twisted rope was looped over her head and tightened under her chin. She looked so small and fragile up there.

You've got more strength inside of you than the lot of them, thought Annie. You wouldn't accuse others to try to save yourself. I don't know that I could be that strong. May the Lord give peace to your soul. If he hasn't already forsaken us. Annie could feel her throat working into hard, hot knots, tears forcing their way over her lower lids. She blinked them back lest someone notice she cried for a duly tried and convicted witch.

The minister was saying something and the spectators were applauding him. Then above all the noise, she heard Emily's voice, loud, strong and chillingly dispassionate.

"Listen to me," she said.

Annie looked back up at her. She had straightened her shoulders, her head was high, her voice carrying clearly and without strain to all of them. In a moment there was complete and surprised silence.

"Listen to me," she repeated. "You would hang me for witchcraft. I am not guilty. Nor were any of the others whom you have murdered before me. But I will not contribute to this hideous crime by pointing my finger at others in order to save my life. Yet I am human and I will have my revenge. You accuse me of foretelling the future. In this you are quite right. But I never used this gift, yes, gift from God, to hurt anyone in any way. Until now. For what you do to me here today and for what you have done before, you will be told. And you will suffer, long after I am dead."

Nervous mutterings were rising from the crowd.

"Listen to me," Emily ordered. There was uneasy quiet again. "If you believe I know of the future, then hear this. You who so diligently seek out evil shall find it, and regret it. There is one who lives among you who is the true instrument of the devil. From his line will spring a child who will summon destruction and horrors beyond your imagining. None of your progeny will be safe. This is not my own curse or spell, but the simple foretelling of what will come to pass." Her voice dropped a level. "Now you may go ahead and hang me. For I will never reveal his name and you will never be able to stop these events. You will tremble with this foreknowledge for all your living years."

For a moment the silence persisted. Then isolated shouts of "Hang her, hang the witch," erupted from the confused stillness. Quickly the cry was picked up, until the words lost shape and took on the rolling thunder of a drum. The minister and the judge, bewildered by Emily's outburst, hesitated numbly for a few moments. Then, yielding to the mounting pressure of the mob, they nodded to one another. The judge mouthed an unheard word to the ape-man, who pulled the planking from beneath Emily's feet. In an instant it was done. Emily's small form swung limply back and forth, slumped to one side as if she'd tired of this gathering and had taken a catnap.

Annie couldn't bear to watch the lifeless figure or hear the now satisfied ravings of the crowd winding down around her. She mumbled a last prayer for Emily and turned away, unable to deny the tears any longer. Before she had gone ten feet another voice, young and shrill, pierced the air. Annie looked distractedly over her shoulder. Sarah Danby had leaped up to the top of the scaffold, inches away from Emily's still swaying body. She was jumping up and down and screaming.

"I know who it is. I know who it is."

Once more the crowd hushed, watching the antics of the young girl with careful interest.

"I know who that old witch was talking about," she shrieked delightedly.

Annie could see the interest turn to panic on the faces around her. Who would be the next victim of Sarah Danby and her friends?

"My dear girl," said the minister, clambering hastily up the steps to her, "are you sure? How is it you come to have this knowledge?" He laid his hand upon Sarah's shoulder. "Calm down, please, and tell us everything."

Sarah allowed herself to be calmed down sufficiently to tell her story. Everyone strained to hear the words that would be uttered. Whose doom would be sealed by her lips in the next instant? Minds worked feverishly, trying to remember if Sarah had ever seen them in the company of Emily Hawkins. Only Annie listened without any real self-interest. Her own death could charge her with no more anguish than she had already spent on Emily's.

"Well, it was about a month ago," Sarah was saying. "Before we knew Emily was one of them," she turned up her nose distastefully at the defenseless corpse, "so I didn't pay it much mind. But I was up on that hill outside of town picking berries. You know, up where old Eli lived with his son. Well anyhow, I guess it was right after old Eli died, cause I saw Emily Hawkins coming up the hill toward the house. And I figured she was coming up to pay her respects to his son. Though it did seem a trifle strange—the way they always kept to themselves and all. Why should Emily Hawkins bother with them? Anyway, I picked my berries and I was just about to start for home when it came to me how long I'd been up there and I hadn't seen Emily leave yet. I walked over to the house, to make sure everything was all right, you know. I peeked in the front window and there was Emily sitting and talking to old Eli's son, as cozy as two kittens in a basket. And she must have been saying something important, because he was listening real hard, you could tell.

"Now, I couldn't make out what they were saying, but it was probably something to do with this prediction of hers. And maybe that wasn't the first time she went to see him. I'm sure those two are working together. They're both working for the devil himself," Sarah concluded triumphantly.

"Now Sarah," the judge said, frowning at her. "Those are strong words, strong accusations. And you never really heard what they were saying."

"But we know Emily Hawkins was a witch. Why else would she have bothered with those hermits, unless they're as evil as she was?" Sarah snarled at him.

The judge fell back a step, and averting his eyes from her, appeared to be considering this argument when the crowd started voicing its opinion.

"She's right."

"The girl speaks the truth."

With the support of their neighbors the cries grew fuller and more vengeful.

"Let's get him," someone shouted. "Let's hang him right here next to his evil companion."

The judge tried to say something about the necessity of a trial.

"No trial. Do it now," cried someone else.

And another, "Hang him!"

"Do it now!" Again the hollow rhythm of the crowd gained momentum. But more than anger or self-righteousness, what Annie read on their faces was relief. If a victim were taken, they would be spared another day. For a moment her sorrow was overshadowed by deep revulsion.

A young man had jumped to the platform. Andrew Marlowe. Annie was astonished. Was it possible? Shy, homely Andrew Marlowe who had grown up not a quarter of a mile from her home . . .

"I say we burn down his house and him with it!" Marlowe's face had gone purple with the effort of shouting above the general clamor. His eyes bulged from their sockets. "I say we burn it now!" The last word was elongated like a howl.

"Burn it now!" the crowd roared its approval.

"Burn it now!"

The minister held up his hand and opened his mouth, but what he said was drowned in the ocean of sound below him.

Marlowe leaped off the scaffold and, holding up his arms, ran through the crowd, past the courthouse and up onto the hillside in the direction of old Eli's farm. "Follow me," he commanded as he ran. The crowd started after him, flowing onto the hillside like the waters from a bursting dam.

Annie watched them until they had vanished over the first hill. She looked about her. The common was almost deserted. The minister and the judge stood a few feet away. Annie supposed they had felt it beneath their stations to take part in an unruly mob. The ape-man was taking down poor Emily's body. The minister and the judge were walking toward Annie now.

"You disapprove, Mrs. Thorndike?" the judge asked conversationally. He might have been asking if she'd found the winter too hard.

"Too old and tired to make the trip," she replied carefully, nodding toward the sounds that were still filtering back on the early evening breeze.

The judge nodded. The minister patted her shoulder indifferently. They walked on toward the judge's house. Annie gathered her cloak more closely about herself and went home.

Chapter Three

July 1982

Deborah had intended to get to bed early. She made up the bed with linens she'd brought from home. The room was no longer so austere with the familiar blue flowers swirling across the bedding. Her traveling alarm clock tick-tocked companionably from the night table. Like setting a stage with the necessary props, she reflected, as she crawled between the smooth, cool sheets.

A street light down the block cast a dim amber glow, outlining the windows and allowing her to distinguish between the general darkness and the blacker mounds that were the bureau and night table. She closed her eyes, but as tired as she was, her mind would not drift toward sleep. Restlessly she turned from side to side and then onto her back. She stared at the gray-black ceiling that seemed alive with glittery, moving things—tricks of the eye. How she longed for the humming engines and horn blasts of a city night.

Finally she gave up and put on the light. She remembered seeing several books in the study, left behind by the last tenants. Maybe reading would help her unwind. She padded barefoot down the wooden hallway to the stairs, flicking on lights as she went. What little comfort she'd managed to establish in the confines of the bedroom was quickly over-whelmed by the empty open spaces of the house. Instead of slumbering in darkness, the house seemed aware of her, registering her every move, absorbing her reactions. She knew the idea was preposterous, and yet the feeling of a presence was unmistakable. If the house wasn't watching her, *someone* was. Her breath caught in her throat and she glanced back over her shoulder, expecting to see a figure at the top of the stairs. But of course, there was no one there. She was troubled by the kind of uneasiness she always felt after watching occult movies late at night. But somehow this time the feeling was more focused. She twitched her shoulders as if to be rid of it and chided herself impatiently for such childishness.

In the study Deborah scanned the few volumes that sprawled along one of the shelves like discarded dominos: two poetry books, a copy of *Peyton Place*, a history of New England, a book on interior design and an anthology of mysteries. She blew the dust off the anthology and returned with it to the bedroom, turning off the lights behind her and determined not to look back at the darkness.

Six hours later she was awake. A beam of sunlight cut a swath across the bed, dust motes dancing and swirling before her eyes. As she glanced around the room, her heart tripped and started racing. The furniture had been moved. The windows were not in the right place. Then, Deborah let out a shrill, nervous laugh, embarrassed for having forgotten where she was. She pulled the light summer quilt up under her chin, luxuriating in its familiar softness.

She turned over to look at the clock. Six fifteen. The flimsy curtains that covered the large old windows couldn't keep out the sun's strong rays. She'd have to put up blinds or room-darkening shades if she ever hoped to sleep past dawn. She closed her eyes and tried to fall back to sleep, but after twenty futile minutes she sat up in defeat, rubbing her still-tired eyes.

A breeze blew in through the partially open window, fluttering the curtains. Deborah shivered and reached for the bathrobe she'd left at the foot of the bed, unaccustomed to the early morning chill. Summer mornings in Manhattan tended to be heavy with the heat and humidity that clung tenaciously through the night.

She came down the stairs feeling considerably less edgy than she had the night before. In the kitchen she put up water for coffee and sat down at the table to plan her first day in Rachael Crossing. It was Monday. Wednesday would be July Fourth. Since camp wasn't scheduled to open until Thursday, she would have a few days leisure to become acquainted with her summer home.

Deborah took her time dressing but was soon ready to go out. She threw a light sweater over her shoulders and locked the door behind her, hoping the town was stirring before ten. She intended to walk slowly; it was the kind of still summer morning of intense blues and greens that one wants to absorb through the pores and store up for other less perfect days.

She stepped back from the house to make a quick survey. Red flowers. Lots of bright red flowers. That was what the house needed. She started down the walk. She felt uneasy, and at the curb she stopped and looked back over her shoulder. No one was there. Funny, she had really thought . . . well at least in daylight the sensation of being watched that she'd felt since last night seemed less threatening. Her imaginings must be the result of unfamiliar surroundings, she thought.

The uneasy feeling began to dissipate as she moved away from the house. It seemed that most of the citizens of Rachael Crossing were early risers and the stores were all open. Without exception, the people she passed paused in their work to regard her, meeting her cheerful smiles with straight-lipped scrutiny.

Ahead of her, Deborah saw the hardware store with a large sign in the front window advertising its FULL LINE OF GARDEN SUPPLIES. She stepped inside. The store was small and, unable to move in the overcrowded aisles, Deborah sought a clerk or the owner to help her. She finally spied a counter, half-hidden behind paint cans, toward the rear of the store. Gingerly, she made her way to it.

"Excuse me," she ventured to the man dressed in coveralls. "I was wondering if you could help me pick out some flowering plants. I was thinking of bright red geraniums."

The man behind the counter looked her over. "New around here, aren't you." He said it as a statement of fact. After a brief pause, he stuck a hand out to her over the counter. "I'm Ed Schmidt."

"Oh, yes, well I am new," Deborah answered with a bright smile. "I'm Deborah Colby. I'm just here for the summer—camp counselor."

Schmidt seemed satisfied with that. He led her through the aisles of gardening equipment precariously perched on top of boxes and bags of fertilizer to a patio in back of the store where rows of shrubs and flowering plants were basking in the sun.

"These here are the geraniums," Schmidt said, pointing to pots of red, pink and fuchsia plants. "How many you think you'll be needing?"

Deborah hesitated, trying to visualize the front of the house again.

"Where is it you're staying, if you don't mind my asking, Miss Colby?"

"At the old house on Foxton Lane."

"You mean . . . that is . . . you say you're staying up on Foxton?"

"Yes. Mrs. Hopkins had the place fixed up. It's really quite nice now."

"Right. Well I'm sure it is," Schmidt said quickly.

"I think a dozen will do," said Deborah. "All red ones please."

"You living up there alone?" Schmidt pulled out twelve pots of red geraniums and placed them in a large carton that had been lying off to one side.

"Yes, I am," Deborah said uneasily. "Is something wrong with that?"

"No. No, just curious. Oughta mind my own business, I suppose. I thought maybe someone else was staying with you, it being such a big house."

"It was the only place for rent, and I had to stay somewhere," she said. "It's a little too far to commute here from New York every morning."

"Yeah, I guess it is at that."

"Well, I think these flowers will really help brighten up the place. Maybe doing the gardening will even make it seem like mine."

Schmidt laughed a tight, artificial laugh. "Yours? That house has never been anyone's. Not even the gent that had it built."

"What do you mean?" Deborah asked, both curious and disquieted.

Schmidt pursed his lips as if he regretted having said anything. "Oh nothing. Just that no one's ever lived there for very long. Now," he went on with a casual lift to his voice, "what shall we do with these fellers?" He nodded to the geraniums.

Deborah was still caught up in what he had said.

"You have a car?"

"Oh, no I don't," she said lamely. "I hadn't expected to be carrying more than a few packets of seed. I guess I could call a taxi."

"No need. I'll have my son drop 'em off around noon."

Deborah thanked him and paid for the plants. She emerged on the street again, her spirits dampened by his impromptu remark. He must have been surprised that a single woman would rent the old place, especially the way it had looked. He probably hadn't seen it since it had been refurbished. But what had he meant about it never belonging to anyone? The words gnawed at her like a half-forgotten dream as she walked on.

By the time Deborah finished her shopping the morning had turned quite warm. She had paused to put her packages down on a bench and pull off her sweater, when she heard the rumble of a bus a few blocks off. The walk back suddenly seemed very long and the packages cumbersome. The bus grated to a stop in front of her and she got on.

Deborah glanced around her. An elderly man occupied a seat near the rear of the bus, staring peacefully out the window at a landscape he had no doubt seen every day of his life. The only other passenger was a young boy of about eleven who sat across from her engaged in a comic book, noisily cracking his gum. Their commonness was reassuring. This could be any small town, she decided.

As the bus approached her neighborhood, Deborah stood up and made her way to the front door.

"Excuse me," she inquired of the driver, "Can you tell me the closest stop to Foxton Lane?"

He looked at her with the same curious expression she had come to expect from the residents of Rachael Crossing. "West Neck. Coming up now," he said flatly.

"Thank you," Deborah said, thinking that all bus drivers must take a course in monotone speaking. But then she heard him say in a more natural voice, "You visiting on Foxton?"

"No. I leased a house there for the summer."

The driver seemed puzzled. "There ain't nothing to rent up there, except the old. . . ."

"Yes, the old house," she interrupted testily. "It's been repainted and fixed over," she added more mildly.

He nodded and pulled the bus to the curb. "West Neck Road," he informed her in the monotone.

Deborah got her bearings, then started walking. As she came around the last curve to the house she stood looking up at it from the street. Why was everyone so surprised that she was staying here? It had begun to look bright and inviting to her. She felt drawn to it. As if she already belonged there.

September 14, 1692

The mob had reached old Eli's hill. Their shouting subsided, replaced by labored breathing and occasional mutterings. It was almost dark and the breeze had picked up. It had been a long day. They were tired. The crowd would have willingly disbanded, but no one dared be the first to turn and go home. If this matter were not settled today they would all remain vulnerable to Emily Hawkins' last words.

The house sat nakedly near the top of the rise. A fire cast a dim, changing light from one window. They stopped silently a few yards from the door. Andrew Marlowe stepped forward alone and knocked on the heavy wooden door.

"What do you want?" a voice came from within, deep, powerful, but muffled.

"We know what you are and we want you. Emily Hawkins has revealed your crimes."

"I have no idea what you are talking about."

"If you do not open this door we will force it down. We are on God's business." The crowd, freshly inspired, took up its chant once more.

"Get off my land. I have done nothing to invoke God's wrath nor yours. You're crazy. You're all crazy. Get off my property."

"You will not give us orders," Marlowe turned back to the crowd. "Break down this door," he commanded, perspiration beading on his forehead and upper lip.

Several of the larger men put their shoulders to the door. After a few moments it gave in with a splintering sound. The men lost their balance, scrambling to their feet as Marlowe marched in.

"Looks like he's run and hid. Find him." Marlowe waited in the small, sparsely furnished room. Near the fireplace, a narrow table that seemed to serve as a desk was strewn with papers and books.

"No doubt he was about some devil's work when we arrived," Marlowe said smugly, indicating the scene with a wave of his arm.

The crowd had begun to filter hesitantly into the room behind him, as if they'd expected to find all manner of devil's symbols and implements. The three burly door crashers returned from their search of the house.

"He's not here," one said breathlessly.

"You checked the pantry?"

"Everywhere."

"He must have gotten out the back. Come on."

Marlowe started out through the kitchen at a run, the other three behind him. The rest of the crowd followed less eagerly. Had Sarah Danby been mistaken? This looked like no devil's home—but neither had the others. They joined in reluctantly. No sense in putting one's life in jeopardy for a man who might well be a disciple of Satan.

The men were poking about in the wooded area behind the house. The sky was black except for the yellow glow of a half moon just coming up above the horizon.

"He's here somewhere," Marlowe called to the others. He turned to the crowd that waited at the back door. "Get me a lantern from inside," he shouted, running his tongue along his lips like a wolf stalking, almost tasting its prey.

A boy who was standing near the door ran in and reappeared a minute later with a flaming log. "This is all I could find," he said, running up the hill to Marlowe.

"That's good enough." Marlowe took the torch and held it up, straining to see into the darkness. He walked quickly in and out of the trees, the wind pulling the flame out in long scarves behind him.

Ten minutes passed and Marlowe emerged again. "He's not out there," his voice thundered. "Back to the house." The other men who had been searching came from the woods at a trot. Marlowe waited for them near the kitchen door, his eyes distorted and wild in the flickering light of the torch.

"He must have gotten away," said one of the big men who'd broken down the door.

"No, Lowry," said Marlowe stonily, "he couldn't have gotten away that fast. He didn't have time."

"But we searched the house," protested another.

Marlowe made no reply. He stood looking up at the house. There had to be someplace they hadn't looked. Then all at once he knew. He threw back his head with a gutteral laugh. "Okay, my friends," he howled. "We have him."

The crowd watched bewildered as Marlowe paced around the perimeter of the house until he'd come full circle back to the kitchen door.

"I know it's here somewhere," he muttered thickly. He turned away from the house and held the torch at arm's length so that it lit up the slope of the hill behind them. "There it is!" he exclaimed triumphantly. A few yards from the house the torchlight danced upon a wooden door that was set into the hillside. In the darkness it had been invisible, merging with the overgrowth that surrounded it. "The root cellar. That's where he is."

Marlowe ran up to it and stood over it for a moment, savoring his victory. "All right. You, Kravitt," he motioned to one of the men. "When I give the order, you pull open that door. The rest of you stand close. There will be no escape for him this time."

Once Marlowe was satisfied with the positioning of the men, he held the torch high to light the entire area and he nodded to Kravitt, "Now!" Kravitt grasped the handle and yanked. The door flew open. Marlow leaned forward into the dark cellar. A ladder leaned against one wall. He knelt at the edge of the opening and peered inside.

"We know you're down there," his voice rasped in the stillness. "Come on out, now!"

There was no sound. Nothing moved in the murky recesses of the cellar.

"Kravitt, Lowry, climb down there. Drag him up."

The two men exchanged uncomfortable glances. One after the other they climbed down the ladder. Immediately the mob heard angry shouts and scuffling, then the clap of fists on flesh. Lowry's voice drifted up to them, breathless but triumphant.

"We got 'im, Marlowe. We got 'im."

An anxious buzz of comments rose from the onlookers as Kravitt and Lowry struggled up the ladder, dragging the young man between them. They dropped him onto his knees before Marlowe.

"Bring him back inside," instructed Marlowe. "And let's be done with this."

As they pulled the young man to his feet and shoved him roughly toward the house, he stumbled and fell.

"Get up, you miserable scum," Marlowe snarled, kicking him viciously in the ribs.

"Would someone at least tell me of what crime I am accused," the young man groaned as he pulled himself to his feet, his face taut with pain.

"That's a good one. As if you didn't know," Marlowe laughed hollowly.

"Will I not even have benefit of a trial?"

"You were tried, as it were, in absentia," Marlowe informed him haughtily. "And convicted, I might add."

They had reentered the house and crossed the narrow kitchen into the living room, the crowd receding before them.

"Make him sit there," Marlowe motioned to the chair behind the desk. "Find something to bind him with." Moments later several leather thongs were held out to him. "Good. Now be sure to tie him securely." The men were silent.

"I don't understand," the young man said softly. "I simply don't understand."

"And I suppose you didn't know that Emily Hawkins was a witch either," Marlowe said, his thin lips twisting into a sarcastic smile.

"No, I didn't. And I doubt very much that it is true." The crowd broke out into nervous laughter.

"It was her that killed poor Ben Purvey," shouted a woman. "Her with her omens and spells."

"That's right," echoed a man. "Bess Purvey was right there. She saw it all."

"And Emily weren't nothing compared to the evil of you," hissed another woman.

"It's God's will that she's dead and that you die, too."

The young man shrunk back as if stricken. "Then it's true," he whispered seeing the confirmation on the uneasy faces of the crowd. "She has been hung."

"Quite. But *her* death was quick and painless." Marlowe assured him. He turned away abruptly. "Bring me everything that will burn. Put it here." Some firewood was dragged in, another table and two rough chairs, a footstool and bedposts from the half-room upstairs. "This will have to do," snapped Marlowe, growing impatient. He circled the prisoner, making sure the wood was carefully positioned. Taking one of the logs, he held it over the fire until it caught and then he began to ignite the pyre he had built.

"Death to evil," he screamed.

"Death to the devil," the crowd responded, the reflection of the flames leaping maniacally in their eyes.

The fire crackled and flashed from piece to piece, tightening the circle around the young man who sat in mute, wide-eyed horror. The small room was quickly choked with smoke and intense heat. The last of the spectators fell back, sputtering and coughing.

"It is done," Marlowe cried with exhilaration. "We can rejoice."

The crowd barely responded, but in his own enthusiasm, Marlowe didn't notice.

"Now we can return to our homes with the knowledge that we are safe. Our children and our children's children will be eternally indebted to us." He led the way jubilantly down the hill.

GHOSTFIRE

The crowd started silently after him. A few glanced back to see the whole of the little house engraved against the night sky in yellow-white flames that seemed to mock them. The acrid smell of burning hair and human flesh overtook them, stinging their nostrils and causing them to retch.

Chapter Four

July 1982

After lunch Deborah changed into her gardening clothes. She wrestled her way into her jeans and pulled on a loose T-shirt, then walked stiffly outside and eased herself down onto the grassy slope near the flower beds, waiting for Brad Schmidt to deliver her geraniums.

Birds chattered in the trees all around her. Deborah didn't remember ever hearing so many distinct calls. A fiery red cardinal perched in a fir tree a few yards from where she sat. Deborah watched it, engrossed in its intricate bobbing and the rapid movement of its black eyes. A dog barked nearby, an angry, threatening bark. The startled cardinal soared off into the sky; she watched it disappear behind the house.

Even before she turned back, Deborah knew the dog was on her lawn. He was moving in a slow, careful walk, black opaque eyes locked on her. She wasn't ordinarily afraid of dogs, but now she felt uneasy. The large shepherd had flattened back its ears and its tail was drawn between its legs. As it moved closer, Deborah's legs tingled with the urge to flee. Had she been standing she might have been able to reach the door before he could catch up with her. But sprawled on the lawn like this she knew she would never make it. She forced herself to remain still and breathe calmly though her heart seemed lodged in the base of her throat. Keeping her head immobile she searched the immediate area for a weapon of some kind but saw nothing.

The dog was a few feet away, pacing back and forth. She could hear a low, menacing growl through its bared teeth. Suddenly she remembered the flower beds behind her. Without taking her eyes off the dog, she snaked her hand slowly around until she felt the overturned soil. Her fingers brushed over several small stones and pebbles and finally closed on a rock the size of a flattened baseball.

She started to bring her hand forward. Her movements caught the dog's eye, and it hunched onto its hind legs and leaped. Deborah hurled the rock over her shoulder. In midair the dog twisted suddenly and changed direction. It landed off to Deborah's side and almost before its feet touched the ground, it charged off yelping wildly.

Trembling and bewildered, Deborah saw that the rock had landed too far left of its target. It couldn't have touched the dog.

A slamming door made her jump. "Hey, you okay?" Brad Schmidt was running up the hill. His small, crumpled truck was parked at the curb.

Deborah pushed herself up onto wobbling legs. "I think so." She took a deep breath. "Yes. Yes, I'm okay."

"I was just pulling up when that dog jumped at you. I reached for the horn to scare 'im off. But before I could hit it you walloped him good. He just about did a somersault in midair. That's some arm you got."

"But I never even hit him. I don't know why he ran away," Deborah said with a shaky laugh. "Did you recognize the dog? Does he belong around here?"

"Uh uh. Musta busted loose and wandered over here from somewhere else. I know just about all the dogs in Rachael Crossing."

"Well, I hope I don't have the pleasure of his company again."

"I don't think he'll be back. I've never seen a dog look that scared before." Brad stood shaking his head and looking down the hill the way the dog had gone.

"Thanks for bringing my flowers," Deborah said after a

few moments, to remind him why he was there. She needed to work off some of the nervous tension that was still zipping through her body like electrical charges. The gardening would help.

"Oh yeah, the flowers." Brad turned back to her. "They're in the pickup. I'll go get 'em."

He brought up the carton and set it beside the flower beds. "There you go."

"Do I just take them out of their pots and plop them right into the ground?"

"Pretty much. And water 'em. They should do fine." Brad raised his hand. "Bye now," and was off at a trot down the hill.

"Oh, wait a minute," Deborah called after him. "I'd like to give you something for delivering them. Would you come inside for a minute?"

"Uh, no, that's okay," he hesitated. "Not necessary. I promised my Dad I'd be right back."

Deborah watched as the truck stalled, shuddered and finally chugged off around the curves and she wondered why he was suddenly in such a hurry. She turned around and dropped to her knees beside the carton of geraniums and then realized with dismay that she had no gardening tools. She remembered seeing a disintegrating shack behind the house and hoped to find some there. Unlike the house, no attempt had been made to reclaim the shed, and its graying, splintered walls seemed to lean into one another for support. A dozen holes pitted what remained of the roof.

The door no longer had a handle or knob, and Deborah slipped her fingertips gingerly under one of the overlapping wooden planks and pulled. The door opened, releasing a mass of foul air smelling of mold, mildew, animal droppings, and decaying field mice. She peered reluctantly into the doorway.

Deborah took a cautious step inside. The shack was almost empty. A few filthy rags lay heaped at one end and there appeared to be some metallic objects in the corner beneath it. She nudged them out with her sneaker, and on examination they proved to be half of a broken rake, a small piece of chain, and a rusted trowel, its wooden handle broken and covered with small teeth marks. Carl, the handyman, must bring his own tools to take care of the lawn, she decided.

Deborah stooped to pick up the trowel. Holding its head between thumb and forefinger she stepped quickly out into full sunlight again and took her find into the house to clean it up. It was nearly two o'clock before she emerged to begin her gardening in earnest.

She dug until she had six nearly symmetrical holes in the beds on either side of the path. Then she began planting the geraniums, speaking to them softly as she worked them out of their pots and deposited them in the hollows she had made.

"There you go," Deborah cooed, patting the soil around one plant. "I'll have some water for you just as soon as I get all your little sisters and brothers settled. How does . . ." She stopped in midsentence, suddenly feeling very silly, as if someone other than the geraniums were listening. She turned to look over her shoulder, feeling foolish and knowing that she would see nothing but lawn and deserted street beyond. She was wrong.

A man stood in the street, one foot against the uphill slope of the lawn, arms crossed casually in front of him, head tilted to one side, watching her.

Deborah jumped to her feet, her pulse racing from surprise.

"Hello." His voice was smooth and strong. "I'm sorry if I startled you." He smiled disarmingly.

"Uh, no. No, that's okay," Deborah replied. "Hi." As she looked at him, her heart seemed to catch and come to an abrupt stop. She was sure she'd never seen a more magnificent face in her life. He was fair, with a squared jawline and sharply hewn cheekbones that underscored long, blue-green eyes. His hair, light brown and thick, fell onto his forehead where the breeze tugged at it.

With sudden embarrassment she realized she had been staring. From his amused expression, he had obviously noticed as well. She felt herself redden and wished she could think of something clever to say.

"My name is Ethan," he said, coming up the lawn to her. "Ethan Burke. He held out his hand and smiled again. The smile was subtle, just tugging at the corners of his mouth, while his eyes remained sober and intense.

Smiling back, Deborah brushed her dirty palm against her thigh before placing it in his. "I'm Deborah Colby," she said, looking up at him. She tried to guess his age now that he was closer, but soon gave up. He seemed neither particularly old nor young.

"Hello, Deborah." He closed his hand over hers for a moment, then released it. "I must apologize again for standing there staring at you. I'm not usually in the habit of sneaking up on people. It really was quite rude."

"Not at all. I guess I was just so engrossed in my planting I didn't hear you come along."

"Geraniums."

"Yes, beautiful, aren't they?"

He nodded, then stated simply, "You're new here."

"In a town this size everyone seems to know the minute an outsider arrives."

"I take it you come from a somewhat larger city."

"Somewhat. Manhattan."

This time the smile shimmered in his eyes as well, like sunlight on aquamarine waters. "Then you must be having a hard time adjusting to small town life."

"A little, though right now it's still novel. Are you from around here?"

"Originally, yes. But now I travel a lot on business. And you?"

"I teach history."

"In Manhattan."

"Yes," she responded, thinking that he had an odd habit of making questions into statements.

"Then you'll only be visiting here for the summer," he said thoughtfully.

"I'm afraid so," she said, then wondered why she had chosen those words. She certainly hadn't been made to feel welcome.

"You're not here with your family." Ethan's voice drew her attention back.

"No, by myself."

"There's no Mr. Colby, then."

"Only my father," Deborah replied, "but he died when I was ten."

There was a pause.

"Aren't you going to be astonished that I'm staying in this big old house all alone?" she asked in order to fill the growing silence.

"No, I don't see any reason to be."

"Good," she sighed. "I don't think I'm up to one more look of amazement today."

"The folks up here don't take easily to new ideas, or new people."

Deborah thought she detected a certain rancor in his voice, but when he spoke again it was gone.

"Now that the place has been cleaned up it looks rather inviting. I'm surprised no one bothered doing it before."

"I know. It seems such a pity to let lovely old houses like this one just decay and fall apart."

Ethan made no comment. He was staring at the house. He seemed so remote Deborah thought he had forgotten she was there.

"Is Rachael Crossing still your home when you're not traveling, Ethan?" she asked finally.

He turned to her and smiled, a bittersweet smile. "No. But this place used to belong to my family—a long time ago." His eyes traveled back to the house and beyond it.

"You mean you actually used to live here?" Deborah inquired, her interest aroused.

It seemed to take an enormous effort for Ethan to focus on the conversation again.

"Live here?" he repeated distantly. "No. No, I never lived right here. Yet it did, as I said, belong to my family at one time." He paused for a moment, then resumed more lightly. "Even as a boy living in Rachael Crossing, I used to love to come by the old place and look at it. I used to think that if I stared long enough and hard enough I would be able to see into the past and see my ancestors working about the house. It was a child's game, but one I guess I never outgrew. My folks and I moved away from Rachael Crossing when I was seven, but I still come by to see this house whenever business brings me in the general vicinity. And when I came along today and saw it all spruced up for the first time in ages, and you working so happily in the garden, for a moment there I couldn't help wondering if my little childhood game had finally come true."

"I like that," Deborah laughed gently.

"I'm glad," Ethan said soberly. "And I'm glad we met. But I must be going. Be well and enjoy the house." His eyes searched hers deeply for a moment. "Goodbye," he said and went back down the lawn in long, easy strides, disappearing quickly beyond the curve of the road.

Deborah stood there, as startled by his leaving as she had been by his arrival. She had been debating whether to offer him a cold drink, perhaps invite him inside for some iced tea. But with his sudden departure she scarcely had time to toss a hurried, "nice to have met you, come back anytime," after him. She wasn't even sure he heard her.

She felt strangely unsettled, as if she'd reached for something in a dream and awakened before she could grasp it. She knelt down distractedly beside the last few geraniums, placing them in the holes and tamping the soil down around them. The birds watching her were more raucous than ever and it occurred to her that she hadn't heard them at all when Ethan was there. The world around them had been as still as if time itself had paused. Or more likely, she laughed at herself, she'd just been too distracted by Ethan to notice anything else.

September 15, 1692

Annie lay in bed staring at the slanted boards that came to a peak directly above her. The town had settled down. Everyone had gone home. There was no more shouting. All that lingered of the day's affairs was the pungent, smoky odor that came through the window when the breeze shifted.

Annie's eyes filled with tears. Her broad chest heaved with silent, wrenching sobs. Emily was gone. She could barely grasp the reality of it. And yet time would soon begin filling in all the places that Emily had occupied, reducing her to an occasional memory. Annie didn't want that to happen. She owed it to her friend to remember as much as she could of her. But she knew how fragile memories were, as easily shattered and distorted as a mirror. She needed something concrete to bind them to, something that was uniquely Emily's.

Annie pushed herself upright. She knew what she had to do. Now, while the town was quiet she would steal next door to Emily's house. She dressed quickly, stooped beneath the low ceiling of the attic room that served as her bedroom. Coming down the stairs she clung to the bannister. Her fleshy legs, numb with fatique, were barely able to support her. She grabbed the lantern from the mantel, threw her cloak over her shoulders and went outside.

The streets were dark. No lamps burned in any of the houses. Annie picked her way carefully over the rutted streets, relying on only the dull light of the half moon. She dared not use her own lantern for fear of being spotted by someone unable to sleep. At Emily's door she hesitated, a new wave of sadness welling up inside of her. How many times had she come to this house, this door—several times a day for thousands of days. Emily had always been there to open the door. For a moment Annie thought she heard Emily's voice asking her to come in. The illusion was so strong that Annie's muscles tensed and she jerked her head from left to right expecting to see someone lurking in the shadows, mimicking Emily's voice. Her hand shaking badly, she opened the door. She stepped inside and shut it behind her. She lit her lantern, turning it down so that it gave off the faintest light possible and kept her body between the light and the windows as she moved through the house.

In the parlor she stopped, lowering herself onto her knees in front of the fireplace. She set the lantern down beside her. For several minutes she ran her hands over the stones that bordered the fireplace until she located the loose one. She pried up the edges with her blunt fingers and with her free hand reached underneath for the diary. She lifted it out of its dirt bed and eased the stone gently back into place. She pushed herself up, her knees threatening to give way, extinguished the lantern and tucked the diary under her cloak. At the door she checked to see if anyone was about. The town was still dark and quiet. She let herself out and hurried home.

She took the diary upstairs with her, undressed and crawled into bed. She was anxious to read it right then. It would be like talking to Emily again. But she didn't dare make the lamp bright enough to read by. Someone might wonder what an old woman was up to at such a late hour. She'd have to wait for morning. She knew pretty much what the diary said, although she'd never actually read it. Emily had told her. Aside from the ordinary daily happenings, Emily had recorded the incredible dreams that brought her visions of the future. Annie was the only one alive who knew about the diary. She had helped Emily find the hiding place when the witch trials began, so that no one would see it and accuse Emily of witchcraft. But it had happened even without the diary being found, Annie thought bitterly.

In the morning she'd have to find a new hiding place, in her own house this time and alone. Her eyelids closed, squeezing tears out between the lashes. She fell asleep close to dawn, the diary hugged tightly against her chest and awoke barely two hours later to shouting and movement on the street outside her house.

She bolted up and clambered out of bed and down the stairs, still gripping the diary. She stood to one side of the front window and peered out. Andrew Marlowe was standing on the street between her house and Emily's, confronting a growing crowd of townspeople.

"Today we must finish the work we started last night," he exhorted them. His voice was stronger, more powerful, as if nourished by the events of the previous day. "Today we must burn the witch's house. To the ground, as we did that demon's house. Let the flames purify this town!"

The crowd shouted back encouragement, its unity building. They had done such odious things already, that burning a vacant house was easy. Better to be a part of it than oppose it and be looked upon as an evil outsider.

Annie moved away from the window. She had to hide the diary. Someone might bang on her door at any moment to demand her assistance with the fire. She shuffled into the kitchen on bare feet, the cold floor sending chills like splinters up through her body.

There was a sudden crack outside, followed by a shattering, like a cascade of icicles falling onto hard ground. Annie froze where she stood, trying to place the sounds. They went on in a volley, cracking and shattering. Emily's windows. They were throwing rocks and breaking the leaded glass windows that had been Emily's pride. Tears flooded Annie's eyes again.

"Oh Emily," she whimpered. "The world's gone mad."

At that moment, as if to emphasize her thoughts, great whoops of exaltation erupted from the stone throwers as each projectile hit its target. Annie set herself to work, trying to blot out the hideous sounds of joy turned inside out.

Before falling asleep she'd decided where she would hide the diary. Now she wrapped it well in an old sugar sack. She emptied the barrel where she kept her flour and placed the sack at the bottom, dumping the flour back over it. After it was done she sank down onto one of the chairs at the small table, reaching around to massage her lower back.

The air was growing heavy with smoke and the smell of burning again, this time so much closer and stronger. It felt as if it were crowding all the air out of the house. Annie was having trouble breathing. She'd have to dress and go outside. If she made it through these awful times, she'd see to it that the diary survived, too. She'd find someone she could pass it on to. Someone she could trust. Maybe one of her sons or grandchildren. That much of Emily would go on forever.

Chapter Five

July 1982

Deborah marked her place with her index finger and rotated her head trying to relax the tense muscles in her neck. She looked at her watch. Almost eleven a.m. She had been sitting at the kitchen table for nearly two hours trying to concentrate on the new history text. There had only been one interruption, forty minutes earlier when the phone had rung.

Glad for the distraction, Deborah had jumped up and reached for the receiver before the second ring. It was Edith, who immediately launched into one of her lectures.

"You're not happy up there all by yourself in that dreadful old house, are you?" Edith accused immediately. "Tell me the truth, Deborah."

Deborah tried to sound more cheerful. "I'm happy," she said. "And everything's perfectly wonderful here. Including the house. I even planted some beautiful geraniums out front yesterday and enjoyed myself thoroughly."

"Hmmm," Edith remarked suspiciously. "You certainly sounded miserable when you answered the phone."

"No," Deborah insisted. "I was just distracted. I was working on the new history text for next year."

"Are they reimbursing you for working on that book?"

"No, of course not. This is something I'd have to do now or in September anyway. A teacher can't be very effective if she doesn't stay at least a chapter ahead of her students."

"Well, I just wanted to say hello and see if everything was all right. But I don't suppose you'd admit it even if it weren't. So try to have some fun and a happy Fourth tomorrow." She paused. "I still wish. . . ."

"Yes, I will," Deborah interrupted quickly. "And you have a good holiday with the family, too. Thanks for calling. Bye now."

"Okay, bye. Take care," Edith mumbled, trying to remember what she'd been about to say.

Deborah hung up the receiver as soon as Edith's last words had cleared the ear piece. Thinking about it again, Deborah had to admit that she hadn't been entirely honest with Edith about the work. During the last week of school, Joel McGregor, head of the history department, had asked if one of his teachers would be willing to go through the new text over the summer, outline it and suggest methods of implementing it. Deborah had raised a tentative hand. She had felt that she probably had fewer commitments than her colleagues, who were all married with families. And it would give her something to do during the long evenings after camp.

However, sitting there, that Tuesday morning, coaxing an unwilling mind to absorb yet another presentation of the nonracial issues leading to the Civil War, she found herself wondering why she had been so generous. Maybe she was just having a bad day. What with the first day of camp still ahead of her, it was understandable that she should be too restless to concentrate. She yielded eagerly to this possibility and, removing her finger from the book, let it fall closed. But her thoughts, once released, ran frivolously not to Thursday and the beginning of camp, but to Ethan Burke. Annoyed with herself, she stood up abruptly, nearly toppling her chair, and went outside to see if her plants needed watering.

The ground around the geraniums was still damp to the touch. She turned to go back inside. As her hand closed over the door knob she glanced sharply over her shoulder. That feeling again. But in daylight it was more disconcerting than frightening. And this time it was tinged with the hope that Ethan would be standing there as he had been yesterday. A hope which she instantly begrudged herself. No reason to assume he'd be back. When he'd left he'd told her to enjoy the house with a finality that said he would not return this summer.

Back inside, Deborah dropped onto the living room couch, sinking into its overly soft cushions. She wondered why she seemed to be succumbing to a schoolgirl crush at this late stage in her life. How often had she heard the twelve- and thirteen-year-olds she taught drooling and gushing over this boy's eyes and that one's smile. Were her rampaging thoughts any more sensible or realistic for all their supposed maturity? Yet she couldn't stop them. And she didn't really want to. It had been ten long, empty years since she had known anything close to the bittersweet ache and anticipation she felt when she thought of Ethan.

It was nearly noon before Deborah realized that she'd been daydreaming. She resolutely turned her thoughts to lunch and to planning for the afternoon. Mrs. Baily, principal of the school in Rachael Crossing and director of the summer camp program, had encouraged her to come in and meet some of the counselors and "get the feel of the place in summer before camp actually begins." With the afternoon looming barrenly ahead of her, Deborah determined to accept.

She walked along more quickly than she had the previous day. The sun was intense, but the air was clear and light and comfortable. She was so involved in her thoughts that she would have walked right on past the school had it not been for Mrs. Baily.

"Deborah. Deborah Colby," she called. "Hello."

Deborah looked around, startled to hear her name. "Oh, hi," she smiled, trying to dissimulate her confusion. She crossed over to the school grounds.

"Linda, this is Deborah Colby, the new counselor I was telling you about," Mrs. Baily said as Deborah approached. "Deborah, this is Linda O'Neil, an alumna as well as a two year veteran teacher here in Rachael Crossing.

Linda was about the same height as Deborah, but with a broader frame. Her dark blond hair was cut into a short wedge that emphasized a prominent jaw and short neck. But her eyes were appealing, round and soft, changing with the light from green to hazel.

"Glad to meet you," they said nearly in unison, and laughed.

"Linda, why don't you show Deborah around the school . . . camp grounds," she corrected herself with a deep chuckle. "Have to keep reminding myself what season we're in. I have some paperwork as usual. Stop by my office if you like before you leave, Deborah. We'll have a chat."

"It'll be good having someone young around for a change," Linda said as she and Deborah started walking.

Deborah smiled. "Thanks for the compliment, but I'm really not that close to your age."

"You're closer than the other women are," Linda assured her. "And I hear you come from New York. That gives us something else in common."

"Do you come from New York, too?"

"No, but I went to Boston University, and the experience sure took the small town out of me. I still feel at home here and all, but I'm seriously considering moving back to Boston to teach."

"Yeah, well I can understand how you must feel. This is a nice change of pace for me, but I don't think I would like it as a permanent way of life.

"There don't seem to be enough children in Rachael Crossing to keep even a few counselors busy," said Deborah once she and Linda had completed their tour.

"There aren't. But we have quite a few campers who come by bus from Salem and other neighboring towns. You'll see."

They navigated two short corridors and were in the diminutive teacher's cafeteria. Two older women were sipping coffee at one of the tables and Linda made the necessary introductions. Eleanor Sharpe was broad with a round bulb of a nose, overly rouged cheeks and dark hair teased and lacquered into wings on either side of her face. Rose Bennington was smaller boned; her hair, a natural mixture of auburn and gray, was curled into a neat bun at the nape of her neck. Her petite face was devoid of color except for brilliant blue eyes.

They sat with Eleanor and Rose for twenty minutes. Between swallows of the weak coffee, Eleanor pumped Deborah for information as courteously as possible.

"Are you staying right here in Rachael Crossing?" she asked, after having learned Deborah's permanent residence, occupation and marital status.

"Yes," said Deborah, wondering if she should just hand out a resume. Linda discreetly rolled her eyes in sympathy.

"Oh," Eleanor was saying. "I wasn't aware that there was anything available, were you Rose?"

"I've rented the old house on Foxton Lane," Deborah supplied, having decided that Eleanor would eventually drag the information from her anyway.

"The old house?" Eleanor repeated, her voice rising an octave. She shot a questioning glance at Rose, who looked like a stop-action picture with her coffee cup midway to her mouth.

"Yes, it's been fixed up of course," Deborah said dully, tired of defending her living quarters.

"Has it?" Eleanor remarked and then seemed at a loss for words.

Deborah stole a glance at Linda. She seemed to be trying to mask her own surprise.

"Is something wrong?" Deborah asked finally.

"No, no of course not," Linda broke into a smile. "I had just assumed they had given up even trying to rent that place anymore."

"Yes, so had I," Eleanor murmured under her breath.

There was an awkward pause. Then Linda said brightly, "Well, it's a good thing we were mistaken, because we're sure going to need Deborah's help, come Thursday."

Eleanor and Rose agreed heartily.

"Will you ladies be at the picnic tomorrow?" Linda continued, with forced effervescence.

"Certainly," Eleanor said, patting her stiff hair.

Rose nodded.

"How about you, Deborah? Do you know about our July Fourth picnic?"

"No," said Deborah, relieved that she was no longer the topic of conversation.

"It's one of the big town events," Eleanor explained. "Just about everyone shows up. It's really lovely."

Linda turned to Deborah. "Why don't you join me and my family," she offered.

"It sounds tempting. I think I will, thanks."

"Great. We'll pick you up about ten. Don't bring anything. My mother always packs enough for an army."

"We'll look for you there," said Eleanor. And Rose nodded.

"Well," Linda pushed back her chair. "I guess we should be going. Deborah wanted to stop in and see Mrs. Baily. See you tomorrow." She stood up.

Deborah stood too. "Nice meeting both of you."

Deborah and Linda walked down the long hallway toward the front of the building. Outside Mrs. Baily's office, Deborah put a hand on her friend's arm. "Linda, can I ask you something?"

"Sure, shoot."

"Just what is it about the house? Whenever someone hears that I'm staying there they react so strangely. Even you did."

Linda shrugged. "It's just that it's old. That's all. And it's been abandoned for a long time. But look, you said it's been fixed up. I'm sure it's fine now."

"Okay," Deborah sighed. "It's just so strange. Well, thanks. I'll see you tomorrow."

She watched as Linda walked away, still not thoroughly convinced that she had been told everything.

Chapter Six

"That's it," Bill O'Neil said, pointing with satisfaction at a large maple situated halfway down the slope of the common, its branches hanging low with overlapping, fanlike leaves. "That's the one. The best spot." He swung his head toward Deborah who was coming up beside him with Linda and Mrs. O'Neil. "We try to get here early every year just to get that tree. Great shade and a good view of everything that goes on."

"It really is beautiful here," Deborah said, admiring the tree-bordered meadow that sloped gently to a clear blue lake. Freshly painted peddle boats bobbed placidly on the surface, the reds, yellows, blues and greens gleaming in the brilliant sunlight. The sweet aroma of newly mowed grass still hung in the air tickling her nostrils. "It even smells beautiful."

"Okay, troops, onward!" Bill O'Neil commanded, and he plowed on across the field, a picnic hamper in each hand thumping against his thighs. The O'Neils came to a stop beneath the tree. Bill O'Neil lowered the baskets to the ground.

"I think this tree up and moved since last year," he said wearily, running his hand across his forehead.

"It couldn't just be that you're getting older, now could it, Dad?" Linda teased.

O'Neil chuckled. "You may blame it on the passing years, young lady, but I prefer to think that this tree just defied the laws of nature and backed up a ways."

Everyone laughed, and Deborah was glad she wasn't spending the day alone. They spread the huge old yellowed bedspread that Marge O'Neil had brought along and sat down to watch the rest of the town arrive.

Loud, friendly comments flew back and forth between groups as they staked out their territory and started to unpack. There were still many stares of curiosity cast in Deborah's direction, but there were also a number of genial greetings. Ed Schmidt and family set up a few yards away. Eleanor and Rose stopped by with their husbands, as did Mrs. Baily. Deborah felt warm and relaxed, as if she were becoming an accepted part of the community. But her sense of well-being was brief. As Eleanor and her husband were walking away, she heard him remark, "So, she's the one."

The ominous tone caught Deborah off guard. Suddenly all the other stunned expressions and cryptic remarks she'd encountered over the last few days tumbled back into her mind. She wondered if Eleanor and the others had stopped by out of friendship or merely to point her out as an oddity, a topic for speculation and gossip.

Linda was tapping her shoulder, laughing. "Hey, are you dreaming? Mrs. Hopkins is trying to get your attention. She's waving so hard, her whole body is shaking like jello."

Deborah followed her line of sight to where Mrs. Hopkins was sitting further down the slope. Having finally caught Deborah's eye, her waving changed to beckoning.

"I think she wants you to go over there," Linda prompted.

"Okay, I'll take a walk down and say hello," Deborah said dully. "Excuse me."

"Mom?" said Linda, once Deborah had moved away.

"Hmm?"

"Did I do the right thing by not telling her?"

"I think so."

"But she seems so disturbed when anyone makes a comment about the house."

"She hasn't noticed anything since she's been there, has she?"

"Not that she's mentioned."

"Then why create nightmares for her?"

Linda sighed. "I know you're right and it sounds logical. It's just that I really do like her, and I feel as if I'm deceiving her."

"Maybe protecting would be a better word for it."

"Protecting? Am I protecting her or leaving her completely vulnerable?"

"Oh c'mon now Linda. You don't really believe that, do you?"

Mrs. Hopkins introduced Deborah to her daughter and son-in-law and three noisy wide-eyed grandchildren. A cup of homemade lemonade was thrust into Deborah's hand and she was propelled into a lawn chair.

"Is everythin' goin' okay?" inquired Mrs. Hopkins.

"Fine," said Deborah, surprised to find herself smiling again.

"Glad to hear it."

Deborah tasted the lemonade. It was tart and refreshing. "Actually I do have a question that you may be able to help me with," she said between sips.

"Ask away and I'll see what I can do."

"It's just curiosity I guess, but I met someone the other day who claims his family once owned the old house where I'm staying. Would you by any chance remember a family named Burke living there?"

"Burke," Mrs. Hopkins repeated, pursing her lips. "Doesn't ring a bell. But my memory's not quite what it used to be, don't ya know. I can find out easy enough the next time I'm at the office. We keep records of that sorta thing."

"Oh don't bother," said Deborah, "it's not important. Just a whim really."

"No trouble. If it's there I'll find it quick as a wink."

Deborah thanked her and after a few more minutes of conversation excused herself and strolled back to the O'Neils.

Deborah helped put out plates and utensils. She wondered why she had made that inquiry of Mrs. Hopkins. Didn't she believe Ethan? What reason would he have to lie to her and what possible difference could it make even if he had?

After lunch Deborah and Linda sat aside, silently watching the peddle boats glide by. Suddenly Linda leaned forward, squinting into the sunlight.

"I don't believe it," she exclaimed.

"What don't you believe?" Deborah asked.

"Old man Darcy. I haven't seen him in years. I thought for sure he had died."

"Where?"

"Over there, near the playground. With that woman."

Deborah picked him out among the running, jumping forms of the children. He was walking so slowly, he appeared at first not to be moving at all. He was small and hunched over, balancing between a cane and the woman like a toddler just learning to walk.

"Who is he?"

"Just an old man. He used to tell stories to anyone who'd listen. Liked to frighten us kids with the scary ones." She turned to Deborah. "He's always been old. For as long as I've known him." She shuddered. "And he's always given me the creeps."

"He looks harmless enough now."

"Maybe so," Linda said with a short, nervous laugh. "But I'd still cross the street to avoid him."

The crack of thunder nearly threw Deborah out of the chair in which she was curled watching a summer rerun. She stood up and went to the window. There was no sound of rain. The sills were dry. A soft breeze drifted in. Then the thunder exploded again. Fireworks, Deborah reminded herself with a smile. Of course, Linda had mentioned there would be fireworks tonight. She pulled her bathrobe closed, shut off the television and hurried out the kitchen door just as the blue-green embers of another burst filtered down beyond the treetops.

She walked up the hillside behind the house wishing she'd had time to change back into her shoes. The grass was still saturated from the heavy rain that had surprised them late that afternoon and the moisture was already seeping through the thin material of her slippers. She heard the low *shush* as another rocket was launched, and she looked up expectantly. The storm clouds had passed and the sky was embroidered with stars. Then the stars were obliterated as the sizzling tentacles of color reached into the black sky. Deborah watched, as mesmerized by the spectacle as she had been when she was six. She waited until the last sparks of the reverberating finale had faded away. In the absolute silence that followed she could hear a low, moaning wind blowing through the trees. But there was no wind, she realized. Well, probably just some night animal.

She suddenly felt very much alone and vulnerable, so close to the densely wooded area up on the hill. She turned and started walking rapidly down toward the house. It looked comforting with the light shining in the living room. Like an oasis in the darkness. She had the eerie sensation again that someone was watching her.

Without turning to look back she started running, her feet slipping and sliding in the wet grass. Losing her balance, she toppled into a heap on the damp ground. She pulled herself up to a squat and rubbed her injured toes. She swept her free hand over the area searching for whatever had tripped her. Her palm hit a handle of sorts set into the hillside at an angle. She tugged at it, but it wouldn't budge. She let go of her throbbing foot and grasped the handle with both hands. She was about to pull again when she heard the phone ring inside the house. Dropping the handle, she pushed herself upright and limped inside in time to catch the receiver on the fourth ring.

"Hello," she said, her voice thin and breathless.

"Hello, m' dear, I didn't wake ya, did I?"

"Mrs. Hopkins, hello. No, of course not."

"I figured you'd be up to see the fireworks, don't ya know."

"Yes I was. They were beautiful."

"Always are. I was watching 'em myself. Went back to the common with my daughter's family. On our way home we stopped by the office here so's I could pick up my extra pair a' readin' glasses. Broke the others at the picnic today." She paused.

Deborah waited for her to continue.

"Well, see'n' as how I was right here, I took a minute to check out what ya asked me."

Deborah was suddenly alert. "Yes?"

"Maybe ya misunderstood yer friend. No one by the name a' Burke has ever owned that house."

"You're certain?" The question was just a reflex.

"It's all in the files, don't ya know," Mrs. Hopkins said crisply. "Ya can come by and see fer yerself, if you've a mind."

"Oh, no, I'm sure you checked thoroughly. Probably just a misunderstanding, as you said. Thank you for your trouble."

Mrs. Hopkins seemed placated. "No trouble, m'dear. Glad to help. Good night now."

"Good night," Deborah murmured and replaced the receiver. Why should Ethan have made up a story like that, she wondered, as she closed the living room window and went back into the kitchen to lock the door.

She climbed the stairs and got ready for bed, still mulling over the question. There didn't seem to be an answer. She reached over to turn off the lamp beside the bed. The clock stared back at her. With an acute flash of anxiety she remembered that the next morning camp would begin. She set the alarm for seven o'clock and turned off the light.

The house had cooled considerably She snuggled down under the covers. She hadn't realized how tired she was and her mind started to drift. At the very brink of sleep she recalled the handle in the ground and surfaced to full wakefulness. What had that been? A handle. A root cellar, possibly. Deborah yawned, too weary to speculate further.

Chapter Seven

"Don't they ever get tired?" Deborah groaned incredulously as the last minibus rolled out of the parking lot packed with babbling, red-faced children.

Linda forced a weary smile. "They're probably overtired. They just react differently than we old folks do. God, I never thought I'd be including myself in that category. But today I am really wiped out. Listen, do you have everything you need?"

Deborah checked for her pocketbook, group list and schedules. "Yeah, I think so."

"C'mon then, I'll give you a lift."

"I was going to walk back and forth for exercise, but today has definitely wrecked my willpower. I accept."

They slid into the red Pacer and Linda swung the car in a wide "U" heading out the way the buses had gone. Her hair bounced lightly from side to side when she checked the road for oncoming traffic. Deborah could feel her own hair lying limply in the barrette against her neck, and blowing in damp wisps around her face.

"You sure don't look as devastated as I feel," she remarked.

"Don't be fooled by appearances. Inside I'm wilted and

miserable. And I had the advantage of knowing what to expect."

"Here we are." Linda slowed as they approached the house.

"Would you like to come in for a while? I have some iced tea in the refrigerator."

She stopped abruptly, the car at an angle. "Oh, I uh, I, I promised my mom I'd bring the car back right after camp. She wants to do some shopping." Her words blurred together in a rush. Then she paused with a self-conscious smile. "Another time though. I'd like to have a chance to talk."

"Anytime. Thanks for the lift. You may have saved my determination as well as my life." Deborah got out and shut the door.

Linda mouthed a good-bye above the noise of the engine and pulled away.

In the bedroom, Deborah tossed her pocketbook and papers onto the dresser and slipped off the cotton shift that was still clinging to her back in spite of the car's air-conditioning. She left it in a heap at her feet, dropping her underwear onto it a moment later. She padded out toward the bathroom. In the middle of the hallway she hesitated, extremely uncomfortable with her nakedness. She hurried back to the bedroom and pulled on her robe. For some reason she felt self-conscious walking around here un-dressed. Once again it seemed almost as if the house itself was watching her. Irrational as it might be, she felt better with the robe closed tightly around her.

She made the shower lukewarm, almost cool, then shrugged off the robe and stepped in. The old nozzle spit the water out in a hard, stinging spray that stimulated her weary muscles. It had been a long, trying day that had begun with an intimidating introduction to one of the other counselors. Jeffrey Pomeroy. Tall, blond and tanned like a golden boy straight off the California beaches. Although more than fifteen years Deborah's junior, he had quickly stripped away her composure with his intent appraisal. Deborah had ig-nored him, or tried to. And mercifully there had only been fifteen minutes before the first bus arrived and the day had been swept off to its frenetic beginning.

He hadn't crossed her mind again until the shower had begun to revitalize her. Lathering her hair into a foamy mound she tried to define the way he had looked at her. Interested, but not attracted, surely not attracted. Maybe just curious, like everyone else. Or maybe when he'd heard that she was single—Mrs. Baily had said *Miss* Deborah Colby, hadn't she?—maybe he had visions of becoming the condescending young lover of a lonely, aging spinster. Deborah laughed at the image that sprang to mind. Jeffrey Pomeroy was definitely not her type, age not withstanding. He was handsome, but in an unremarkable way. His features too perfect, like a mannequin's, his eyes vacuous, devoid of character.

She leaned her head back under the shower, wishing she could dismiss another as easily from her thoughts. Ethan. Even during the chaos of the day his face had remained before her in sharper detail than she'd ever remembered anyone. It was as if the image of him had a peculiar strength of its own. As if it were visiting her rather than surfacing from her own memory.

Back in the bedroom she dressed in pants and a T-shirt. She had intended to go downstairs and fix herself an early dinner, but the bed looked too inviting. Just for fifteen minutes she promised herself and lay back against the pillows.

She didn't think she had fallen asleep, but the clock indicated that an hour had elapsed. Although it was light out, the house seemed enveloped in a nighttime stillness and shadowy fragments of a dream hovered in the corners of her mind. Their substance eluded her, leaving only a feeling of disquietude in their wake.

The sharp chime of the doorbell startled her. She pushed herself off the bed and headed for the stairs.

"Coming," she called, still feeling troubled and disoriented. Maybe Linda had decided to come back for that talk today after all. Or it could be Carl the handyman. He was due to mow the lawn any day now. She yawned as she pulled open the door and had to make a conscious effort to close her mouth. Framed in the doorway stood Ethan. He was wearing chino slacks and a white shirt open at the throat, the strong muscles of his neck outlined by the whiteness of the shirt.

His lips hitched up in a smile. "I'd almost given up on you. Were you sleeping?"

"Yes, well, not really," Deborah stammered, trying to compose herself. "I was just resting."

"I'd say sleeping if you didn't hear the bell till the second ring."

She shrugged and smiled. "Maybe. I did hear only one ring. I usually don't fall asleep in the middle of the day like that. I guess it was just the first day of camp and all."

"I'm sorry for coming at a bad time. I always seem to be apologizing to you."

"No need to, honestly," Deborah assured him. "I'd promised myself I wouldn't fall asleep anyway. A nap at this hour and I'll be up all night." She noticed for the first time that he had his hands behind his back as if he were holding something. Not to appear too inquisitive she moved her eyes back to his face. "I'm afraid I'm not being very polite. Won't you come in?" Edith would be appalled that she had invited a virtual stranger into her house.

"Thank you."

Deborah moved back from the door to let him in.

"I hope you haven't had dinner yet," Ethan said, bringing his hands forward with a bucket of fried chicken.

Deborah laughed. "No, I haven't. I was wondering what you were hiding back there."

"Would m'lady care to dine with me?" he inquired in a British accent.

"Why certainly. How kind of you to ask." Deborah did her best to imitate him.

"Are you sure?" he said, dropping the accent. "You don't have any other plans? I'm not interrupting anything?"

"My other plans would probably have been scrambled eggs."

"Great. But I really should explain why I, a near total

stranger, showed up at your door with a bucket of fried chicken at five fifteen on a Thursday evening."

"I'm dying to hear," said Deborah. "But why don't you sit down first. Make yourself comfortable in the living room while I put the chicken in the kitchen." She took the cardboard bucket out of his hands. "I'll only be a minute."

When she came into the living room the light was dim. She had left the curtains drawn all day to moderate the effects of the sun. Ethan was sitting on the couch, his long legs extended in front of him, his face in shadows.

"I put the chicken into the oven to warm," said Deborah. She turned on the old china lamp beside the couch.

"Fine. I meant to suggest that. The buses around here aren't exactly rapid transit."

"Sometimes it's nicer not to be rushing everywhere," she said, trying to decide whether to sit beside him on the couch. She was so strongly drawn to him that she was nervous about being too close. Afraid she'd be unable to shape thoughts into coherent words. Afraid her hands that ached to touch him, would reach out on their own. She chose one of the chairs across from him.

Ethan was watching her with a smile of amusement and steady, sober eyes. Deborah had the uncomfortable feeling he knew what she'd been thinking.

"All right," she said, trying to sound casual. "I'm ready for your explanation. What brings you here?"

"My car went dead on me a few miles past Salem this afternoon." He pulled his legs in and leaned forward. "I had to have it towed to a service station. The mechanic who looked it over said he could fix it, but it wouldn't be ready until closing time at eight. Hanging around there for four hours was out of the question. Then I remembered a certain young woman I'd met up at the old house. I said to myself, why not? The most she can do is tell you to get lost. And she probably won't even do that if you bring dinner along. So I stopped at the local chicken place, hopped on the first bus and here I am."

Deborah shook her head, smiling. "I guess you wouldn't have made up a story like that. What's wrong with the car?"

Ethan used his fingers to comb back the hair that was

edging down his forehead. "The carburetor, or something equally cryptic. I don't know the first thing about engines."

"I hope they don't rip you off."

His brows furrowed ever so slightly over the blue-green eyes, making them more intense.

Wasn't that expression common throughout the country? "I mean they may overcharge you. They're notorious for that."

The frown disappeared. "I'm afraid I wouldn't know it if they did. Let's hope I found an honest station." He paused just long enough to change subjects. "So, you're working at the camp here?"

"I started today. And I think I might have taken on more than I can handle."

"I doubt it."

"Is your business keeping you here over the summer too?" Deborah asked, astonished by her own boldness.

"I'll be in the New England area for a while."

"It is beautiful up here in the summer."

"Maybe better this year than most."

Deborah felt the color rising in her face. "I guess the chicken must be heated through by now," she said, jumping up.

Ethan stood too.

"You won't mind eating in the kitchen, will you? There's no dining room set. It's one of the few pieces the last owners took with them."

"I've always preferred kitchens."

Later, while they were clearing the table, Deborah promised to invite him back for her own fried chicken. They left the dishes to soak in the sink and went back into the living room. Deborah opened the curtains, letting in the gentler evening light. During dinner she had remembered Mrs. Hopkins' phone call and she was wondering how to reopen the subject of the house without appearing nosey and mistrustful. Ethan inadvertently helped her.

He was standing by the fireplace admiring the tile facing and the intricate woodwork along the mantel. "This is a marvelous house," he said.

Deborah seized the opportunity. "It was probably well

cared for when your ancestors lived here," she said, sitting on the couch and tucking her feet up under her.

Ethan turned from the fireplace and studied her carefully, as if he were trying to see beyond the words. Deborah found it difficult not to flinch under the intensity of his gaze. It was several long moments before he spoke.

"My ancestors never lived in this particular house. I guess you misunderstood me the other day. I only meant that the land had been in my family. Actually there was another house here before the present one. According to family history it was razed by fire."

Another, older house. That would explain why the name Burke hadn't been in Mrs. Hopkins' files on this house.

Ethan had come over to the couch. He sat down next to her, his body angled to the side so that he could look at her. Deborah stiffened, finding his closeness unsettling.

"Is something wrong?"

"No, I was, uh, just surprised. I wasn't aware that there had been another house here before this one," she said, looking down at her hands. She could feel Ethan's eyes on her.

"Tell me, Deborah," he said, "is it Miss by choice or quirk of fate?"

Deborah tried to smile naturally. She looked up. "A little of both, I imagine."

"Which is to say. . . ."

"I never liked what came along, and what I liked never came along."

"No one even came close?"

"I don't mean to imply that I'm impossibly picky," she explained. "Although Edith would disagree, I'm sure."

"Edith?"

"Edith," Deborah sighed. "Sister and surrogate mother. Actually I'm a terrible ingrate. It's just that we have different definitions of eligible."

"And what is yours?"

Deborah was about to answer, then changed her mind. "Time out," she said instead. It had occurred to her that she knew almost nothing about Ethan. She didn't even know if he were married. He wore no ring, but that wasn't a reliable sign. "Maybe you should have gone into detective work."

"I don't follow you."

"You've extracted a lot of information about me, but I know nothing about you."

"Well, I already know everything about myself, so I find you much more interesting. I didn't mean to be mysterious. What would you like to know?"

"Let's see. Where do you call home when you're not away on business? And what kind of business are you in? Are you married?"

Ethan threw back his head and laughed, long dimples cutting his cheeks. "I believe my character has been maligned. No, I'm not married and never have been. Do I seem like the type to have a wife and go out of my way to meet other women?"

"No," Deborah said lamely. "But then to be perfectly honest, I don't think I'd know the type even if I tripped over him."

"Then you'll just have to take my word for it, won't you?" he said still smiling. "As for the other questions, I sell medical equipment and I have a small apartment in Boston that I very rarely see."

"I'm sorry. I really didn't mean to give you the third degree either."

"No, you have a right to know. And although you didn't ask, I also never met the right person at the right time. Until very recently I thought I never would." He reached out and ran his fingers along the contours of her face.

The gesture had come so unexpectedly, Deborah's breath caught in her throat and it took all of her effort to maintain her composure and not look away.

"That may be a premature judgement," she said.

"I don't think so. Is something wrong with your foot?"

Deborah looked at him queerly, then realized that she'd been absently rubbing her injured toe. "Oh," she said, pulling her hand away. "I stubbed it last night. Nothing serious. It's just a little sore. I couldn't tell in the dark what I stumbled over, but I think it was a handle of some kind. Maybe from an old root cellar. How would you like to lend me some muscle and see if we can't get it open?"

Ethan's expression had hardened while she spoke, the cheekbones and jaw sharp and stonelike. His eyes were withdrawn, a strange mixture of pain and rage smoldering in their recesses.

"No," he said roughly. "There can't be anything out there worth seeing."

"Just curiosity," Deborah murmured, shaken by the abrupt change in him.

"The past is better left to itself."

Deborah didn't understand what he meant, but was afraid to pursue it, unwilling to antagonize him further. "Okay. I didn't mean anything by it, . . ."

Instantly his face softened and he was smiling brightly again. "Anyway," he said, glancing down at his watch, "I think it's about time for me to leave, or I won't make it back to that garage before eight."

Deborah walked him silently to the front door. She was confused and angry with herself for having mentioned the handle. She had inadvertently trespassed on something deep and painful and she feared he might never come back.

Ethan had stopped at the door. "I won't forget that home-fried chicken I was promised."

"Just tell me when you'll be back this way," she said, relief rushing through her.

"A week from Saturday."

"Done."

He opened the door. "Make it for lunch and we'll have a picnic."

"I hope the car's okay."

"So do I. Goodnight now." He leaned down to her and brushed his lips across her cheek and mouth.

"Goodnight." The words came as a whisper through the tightened muscles of her throat. She watched him until he was gone down the walk and around the curve of the road.

As she closed the door it occurred to her that she hadn't seen him with a car the first time. She went into the kitchen to wash the dishes, wondering if he really had a car, and if so, why he had come on foot to see the house that first day when he could have just driven by. He might have wanted the exercise. It had been a lovely day, she told herself, annoyed by her own suspicions. The service station in Salem. His story could be checked easily enough. There couldn't be that many stations in Salem. "No!" she said aloud and flung the dish towel angrily onto the drainboard. She was stunned by the intensity of her reaction. But all her reactions to Ethan were extreme. They overwhelmed her. Even as Ethan had been overwhelmed earlier, struggling with powerful emotions she couldn't understand. Had she imagined that metamorphosis, exaggerated it in her mind? Or was there a dark side of him that lay smoldering just beneath the surface? The possibility chilled her, but in no way diminished how irresistibly she felt drawn to him.

Chapter Eight

The screeching of an irritated blue jay wrenched her from a deep sleep. She stretched luxuriously and glanced at the clock. It was a few minutes past eight. Past eight! The thought echoed in her head, bringing her fully awake. The alarm hadn't rung! How could it? She'd never set it. Last night camp had been the farthest thing from her mind. She threw back the covers.

After a breathless walk she arrived at the camp with a minute to spare. The buses started arriving a little before nine. By nine fifteen Deborah had all of her campers and was leading them off to the softball field.

"Hang in there," Linda called after her.

Deborah looked back and smiled, "I will, don't worry."

To some degree the day was better than the first had been. By lunchtime Deborah had learned the girls' names and pinpointed those she could trust and those she had to keep a more watchful eye on. In general they were a good bunch of kids. There were a few who didn't want to swim at swim time and some who wanted ices instead of ice cream at snack time. One skinned knee, one upset stomach, several minor squabbles, but Deborah found she could smile with reasonable serenity when four o'clock finally rolled around. She was even able to give Jeffrey Pomeroy a disinterested "hello" when their paths had crossed on their way to the buses.

"Can I give you a lift home today?" Linda asked her once the children were on their way.

"Thanks, but I think I'll try to get a little exercise by walking," she said.

"Now that doesn't sound like the vanquished counselor I spoke with yesterday. Don't tell me it was that easy, and only on the second day?"

"Hardly," Deborah laughed. "I'm just feeling good."

"Anything illegal?"

"God, I hope not."

"Then you'll have to let me in on it."

"Sure, I'd like to."

"Okay, tomorrow's Saturday. Do you have any plans?"

"None."

"Let's do something. Maybe shop and have lunch?"

"Sounds perfect."

"I'll pick you up at eleven. I know a great little seafood place not far from here."

They said good-bye and Deborah walked down the lawn to the street.

She was at home, about to put on fresh clothes, when she heard a motor revving and sputtering. Then the noise stopped abruptly. She pulled on her robe and ran to the window that faced the front yard.

A man was standing on the lawn, bent over a power mower. He appeared to be in his forties, short and stocky, his T-shirted belly overhanging his belt. This had to be Carl, the handyman Mrs. Hopkins had mentioned. Deborah watched while he tinkered with the machine. After a few minutes he pulled the starter out. The motor caught, humming evenly. Satisfied, he straightened up and began to guide the mower across the lawn in long, even lanes.

There was something about the set of his body, the way he walked with sharp, harried movements that suggested to Deborah, even at this distance, that he didn't belong in Rachael Crossing.

From time to time he paused to mop his face with a gray-white handkerchief he kept stuffed into his pants pocket. Near the flower beds he came to a sudden stop and bent down to retrieve something. Deborah strained to see what it was. The trowel. She had never put it away after planting the geraniums. Lying there in the grass it reminded her again of the handle buried in the ground. Ethan's harsh expression flashed into her mind. And his admonition to leave the past to itself. But she couldn't imagine what harm could come of inspecting what was probably just an old root cellar. She'd go out and have another look at it in daylight. Maybe she could even persuade Carl to help her open it. She dressed and hurried outside.

Carl had deposited the trowel near the front door and returned to his mowing. When he looked up again he saw Deborah coming toward him.

"Hi," she said. "I'm Deborah Colby. I'm the one who's renting this house for the summer."

Carl choked off the motor. He nodded to her but didn't extend his hand. "I'm Carl, the handyman. Mrs. Hopkins tole ya about me?"

"Yes. Yes, she did," said Deborah, trying to place the familiar speech pattern.

"I left your trowel over by the door. It wouldna done my mower no good if she'da hit it," he informed her grimly.

"I know and I'm sorry. That's what comes of letting a city girl loose in the country."

"You're from the city, y'say?" Carl's narrow eyes lit up.

Deborah nodded. "Manhattan. Born and bred."

"Me too," he said, a broad grin stretching his black stubbled cheeks. He held out his hand. "Good to meet someone from back home."

Deborah shook his hand, finally placing the nasal Brooklynese that was so alien to Rachael Crossing.

"You'se stayin' up here all by your lonesome?" Carl asked, resting his tanned forearms on the mower handle.

"Yes."

He nodded and chewed on the inside of his cheek, as if he couldn't decide whether or not to say something.

"Why?" Deborah pressed.

"Nuthin', just wonderin'."

She was about to pursue it when Carl continued, "Look, it's been real nice meetin' ya and all, but I gotta get done here. I got another job t'do fore I can get home to dinner, so. . . ."

"Oh, can I ask you one small favor first?" Deborah said, switching priorities.

"What's 'at?"

"Well, if you could come around back for a minute I'll show you."

Carl sighed heavily and without a word followed Deborah to the rear of the house.

He watched with obvious impatience while Deborah hunted on hands and knees for the handle. He was on the verge of complaining that he had better things to do, when she cried, "Here it is. I knew it was around here."

Carl crouched beside her, studying the rusted handle barely visible beneath the grass and weeds. "What the hell's that?" he asked.

"I'm not sure," said Deborah, "but I think it might be an old root cellar."

"Ain't it pretty far from the house?"

"Well, that's what I thought at first. But there was supposedly another house on this land a long time ago. Maybe it belonged to that one."

"You say so. I'm no expert on that sorta thing," Carl said, scratching at his short, graying hair.

"Do you think you could help me get it open," Deborah said, smiling as sweetly as she could.

"What for? Even if ya get it open, there probably ain't nothin' down there but some ole roots," he remarked with a chuckle.

"I teach history. Old things interest me," Deborah tried to explain. "Please?"

Carl looked at her. "Yeah, awright. Go get me that there trowel I left by the front door."

When Deborah returned with the trowel Carl was already using his stubby fingers to dig away at the dirt and growth that were covering the area. Deborah knelt anxiously beside him. The wooden door was almost completely exposed. A large section of the old boards was blackened.

"This *was* from the original house," she exclaimed. "It must have been scorched when the house burned down."

Carl said nothing. He took the trowel from Deborah and worked it around the edges of the door to free it from the land that had encroached upon it. Then he put the trowel aside and pulled at the handle. The wood groaned and creaked as if it were about to break, but the door didn't move. Carl grunted and wiped his hands against his shirt before grasping the handle again. After a few more sharp tugs the door opened, pulling away at the hinges where the wood had rotted. A musty earth smell drifted up into their nostrils as they peered into the dark hole.

"Pheww!" Carl snorted. He pushed himself away and rose to his feet.

"Thanks for your help," Deborah smiled up at him.

He nodded. "Have fun. Just don' go fallin' in there," he told her. "I'm goin' back to work."

Deborah thanked him again and looked down into the root cellar. Even in the brilliant sunlight she couldn't make out anything but an old wooden ladder leaning against an inner wall. She ran into the house and returned with a flashlight. She shone it slowly around the inside of the cellar. All it revealed were the hard packed earthen walls. She held the light vertically to scan the bottom, sweeping it across the area in long, slow strokes. Just where the floor ran out of her line of sight, a small object glinted dully under the beam.

She debated climbing down the old ladder. It might not be safe, but that object down there, whatever it was, probably dated back hundreds of years. Impulsively Deborah backed toward the doorway. She placed a tentative foot on the first rung of the old ladder. It seemed sturdy enough. She shifted more of her weight onto the ladder until she was standing with both feet on the top step. Still holding the flashlight in her right hand, she cautiously lowered herself to the next step. There was an ominous grinding noise but it held. Deborah's heart was racing as she realized how dangerous a position she had placed herself in. If the ladder broke she would fall to the bottom. It wasn't a long drop, but she would have no way of getting out again. Carl might come around to say good-bye, but then he might not. She had made him late for his dinner already.

Deborah looked down in the direction of the object that had lured her. She released her right hand from its position against the ladder long enough to shine the flashlight on it. But it was no clearer than it had appeared from outside. She said a quick prayer that she would get safely out and moved down another rung. One more step, she estimated, and she should be at the bottom. She placed her foot where the last rung should have been. Suddenly she was falling, her arms wrenched from their hold on the ladder. The flashlight flew out of her hand. She landed half sitting, half lying on the floor of the root cellar.

She remained motionless for a minute, more out of fear than pain. She had fallen only a few feet, but the surprise of the fall had jarred her. She picked up the flashlight that had landed beside her, grateful that it was still working. She shone it on the ladder. The last rung was nothing more than two stumps attached to the sides, the middle no longer there. With rising panic she wondered if she would be able to pull herself up to the next rung when it came time to leave.

"First things first," she told herself sternly. She stood up and brushed herself off. She swung the flashlight over the ground and quickly located the object she was after. Kneeling down, she pushed the loose dirt away from it. She picked it up. A gold ring. By the size and weight she guessed it had been a man's ring, but it was impossible to make out any detail between the dirt encrusted in it and the darkness. Who had lost or hidden it, she wondered, standing here on the very spot where she now stood. She turned the ring over and over in her hand as if it might somehow yield its secrets. A piece of the past, part of a life long gone, with a story all its own. It was the type of historical link that had always fascinated her.

Finally she tucked it into the pocket of her pants and swept the light around once more, looking for any other objects that might have been left there. The cellar was small, ending only a few feet past where she had found the ring.

'Nothing else was immediately visible and she was afraid to stay and search longer. If she couldn't make it back up the ladder Carl might still be nearby to help her out.

She dropped the flashlight so that she could use both hands, and reached up as high as she could on the sides of the ladder. She took a deep breath and tried to pull herself up high enough for her foot to reach the first whole rung. Her foot skimmed it and missed. Splinters cut into the soft flesh of her palms as she slid back down. She shook her hands to ease the pain and fought against the tears that were threatening to blur her vision. She dried her sweating palms gently against her thighs. Then she grasped the posts tightly again, wincing as the splinters were pushed deeper into the tender skin. She swallowed, her throat dry and tight, and pulled herself up slowly until she was able to get first one foot and then the other onto the ladder. She relaxed for a moment, releasing a tremulous sigh, before continuing up to the top.

Once inside, Deborah performed minor surgery with a pair of tweezers. She soaked the ring in soapy water then scrubbed it with a toothbrush until the last of the dirt fell away. It looked like a signet ring. She held it directly under the kitchen light and rotated it between her fingers trying to decipher the engraving on the flat surface. Her eyes widened with surprise. There seemed to be two entwined initials and no matter which angle she looked at them from, they were the initials "E.B."

Chapter Nine

       Baynor's Inn was tucked off on a side road between Rachael Crossing and Salem. It was an oversized cottage, painted a gleaming white with yellow shutters and trim. Begonias in every shade of pink and red spilled out of the window boxes. Inside, ordinary and exotic plants hung from the beamed ceiling and filled the bay window. There was another dining area out back with yellow unbrellas fluttering over the tables and rock gardens bursting with pansies, firebrand, moss roses, and ageratum. But the humidity had made even umbrella shade uncomfortable and Deborah and Linda reluctantly chose a table indoors.

    They had spent several hours poking about in curio and antique shops crammed with every conceivable knickknack and dusty heirloom. Then they'd stopped at farm stands for fresh produce. "This restaurant is just so lovely," Deborah exclaimed. "How did you ever find it?"

    "Word of mouth. They don't advertise or anything, and you should see the crowd they draw Saturday nights. In fact, my first time here was on a Saturday night," Linda added with a wry smile. "Jeffrey brought me here."

    Deborah's eyebrows lifted in high arcs. "Jeffrey from camp?"

"One and the same. Surprised?"

"Well . . . yes."

Linda shook her head. "Just goes to show you how little we know ourselves. I met him last year at the camp. It was the first summer for both of us as counselors."

"Did he grow up in Rachael Crossing too?" Deborah asked.

"No. His family moved here about four years ago. I'd seen him around town. I mean he's the type who stands out even in a crowd, and there aren't too many crowds in Rachael Crossing. But I'd always figured he was too young for me." She paused to sip her wine. "I've since learned that age doesn't matter to Jeffrey. He considers himself an even match for anyone." She shrugged. "In a way I guess he is. Anyhow, the first day of camp he gave me that long, interested look of his. The one he gave you the other day."

Deborah nodded and swallowed. "I noticed. It was very disconcerting."

"All I can do is plead temporary insanity. I succumbed totally. And it wouldn't have been so awful if I'd gone into it sensibly and just for fun. But no, I draped all of my romantic fantasies around him and took my infatuation to heart." She put her fork down and pushed her empty plate away. "Needless to say, the more intense I became, the less interested he became, until we had an enormous fight. Not exactly what you'd call a lovers' quarrel, and it ended."

Deborah's smile had faded. She was seeing some very uncomfortable parallels between the way Linda had fallen for Jeffrey and her own uncontrollable feelings for Ethan. She had been more cautious than Linda so far, but then she had only seen Ethan twice. And romantic infatuation was surely an accurate label for what she was experiencing. She wondered if Linda had also felt the undeniable, almost magnetic tug she felt to Ethan.

Deborah looked across at her young friend. She liked Linda. She felt comfortable with her in spite of their age difference. And she would have liked to talk to someone about Ethan. But she always found it difficult to discuss her own emotions with anyone. She was the good listener, but the opening up process did not come easily to her. She took a deep breath and forced the first few words out slowly, self-consciously.

"I think I may have to cop that temporary insanity plea myself." She smiled a small, lopsided smile.

"You're kidding," said Linda. "Don't tell me you actually found an elligible man right here in Rachael Crossing!"

Deborah shook her head, rolling some bread crumbs under her finger. "I met him here, but he doesn't live here."

"I thought I knew all the people, transient or permanent in Rachael Crossing. My mother never lets a day pass without keeping me posted on the latest comings and goings."

"Well, does the name Ethan Burke sound familiar?" Deborah asked, feeling a strange excitement and relief at saying his name out loud for the first time.

Linda wagged her head. "No, not at all. Where did you find him?"

Deborah described her two meetings with Ethan. She tried to explain how she felt, the words coming more easily as she spoke. She even admitted checking out his story about the house and nearly doing the same with the car.

She paused to drink her coffee, then added lightly, "What do you think? Do I sound like a candidate for that temporary insanity clause?"

Linda pursed her lips, then smiled sympathetically. "Hey, did you ever ask Mrs. Hopkins about the other house?" she asked to change the subject. "The older one Ethan said burned down?"

Deborah shook her head. "I didn't want to bother her about it anymore. But I did rather literally stumble across an old root cellar up on the hill behind the house. And it appears to be charred as if it had been close to a fire." She didn't mention the ring she'd found. She wasn't sure what stopped her other than the fact that she wanted to show it to Ethan first.

"Now I'm curious myself," said Linda. "Let's ask Mrs. Hopkins again."

"Well, if you insist," Deborah grinned.

Linda took a last swallow of coffee and put the cup down. "How about now?"

It was past three o'clock when they arrived at the Rachael

Real Estate Office. A quiz show was blaring from a portable television on a stand behind the last desk. Mrs. Hopkins was wedged into a vinyl armchair, her back to the door. She didn't turn around when they entered and the door fell shut behind them.

"Hello, Mrs. Hopkins?" Linda called out. After a moment Mrs. Hopkins shifted in her chair and looked back over her shoulder at them.

"Hello there," she said, rubbing at her eyes with pudgy fingers. "Guess I musta dozed off for a minute. Hello, Deborah." She started to push herself out of the chair.

"Please don't get up," Deborah said. She and Linda walked around the desk so that they could face her.

"You can turn that thin' off if ya don't mind," Mrs. Hopkins pointed to the set. "The movie I was watchin' musta gone off whilst I was nappin'."

Deborah switched off the set.

"Now, what can I do fer ya?"

"Just satisfy some curiosity really," Linda began. "I've heard that the house where Deborah is living is not the original one on that land. That there was an earlier one that was destroyed in a fire."

Mrs. Hopkins' brows drew together, her eyes became pensive, as if she were looking through a trunk of memories for a particular item. "I seem to remember somethin' like that, but I can't quite put m'finger on it."

"Would your records go back that far?" Linda suggested.

"Might. I'll have a look-see."

"I'm sorry we had to disturb you," Deborah apologized.

"Don't worry yaself. This place is awful dull mosta the time," Mrs. Hopkins assured them, grunting as she came out of the chair. She shuffled over to a large filing cabinet, opened one drawer and after a minute withdrew a creased and dog-eared manilla folder. She pored over its contents, then looked up at them.

"All I can tell ya is that there was another foundation on that lot, dating quite a ways back," she said. "That'd be all we have in our files. No particular owner mentioned. When the present house was built, the land was bought from the town itself."

"That's pretty much a dead end," Linda sighed.

"Not really," Deborah pointed out. "We did find out there was another house, and that's technically all we wanted to know."

Mrs. Hopkins replaced the folder and closed the drawer.

"There is one place ya might go if you've a mind to findin' out more."

"Where's that?" Linda asked.

"Old Man Darcy. He must be ninety if he's a day. And knows everythin' that ever happened in Rachael Crossing. What didn't happen during his lifetime, he learnt of from his granddaddy, who learnt it from his granddaddy. That's the way that family's always been, don't ya know. Storytellers, town historians, ya might call 'em."

"Old Man Darcy, he's the one I pointed out to you at the picnic."

"Yup, he was there," nodded Mrs. Hopkins. "First time I'd seen him in a long while. Stays home mostly. I hear he's got arthritis bad now and his eyes are goin' on him. That's what comes of gettin' old," she added grimly, as one who knows. "He'd be your best bet for information, girls." She eased herself down in her chair.

Deborah and Linda thanked her and left. Back in the car Linda looked over at Deborah. "You game?"

Deborah shook her head and smiled. "Not really. And I know you're not. Besides, I already feel like an awful snoop." She didn't add that the mention of Darcy's name had inexplicably brought to mind the hazy, troubling dream she'd had two days before. Although she still remembered nothing specific about it, anxiety rose like a chilling mist inside of her.

She rode in silence until they pulled up in front of her house.

"Won't you come in for a while?" she asked.

"No, I can't. I . . . oh, okay," Linda agreed, seeing the hurt look on her face. "Just for a few minutes."

Later, Deborah walked her friend to the door and then went back to the kitchen. Linda had been so distant and uneasy, and so eager to leave. Fatigue had only been an excuse. Then she remembered Carl's reaction when she had invited him inside for some lemonade the day before, after she had finished cleaning off the ring she found in the root cellar. He had adamantly refused to set foot inside the door. And those expressions of surprise from everyone who heard she was staying in the old house. There had to be more to those startled looks. What was more, they were deliberately withholding that information from her. Deborah wondered if her own vague apprehensions about the house were more intuitive than she had been willing to believe. Was something happening around her, too elusive for her senses, but not for her more basic instincts?

That night she slept poorly, slipping in and out of fragmented dreams. The only one she remembered with any clarity was the last, in which she went to see Old Man Darcy. Based on her own distant view of him and Linda's remarks, her subconscious had conjured up a sinister image that remained with her even after she awakened. His withered form was hunched over in a chair in a dimly lit room and he was talking to her. She couldn't recall what he was saying, but a bleak and hopeless desperation lay over her like a heavy blanket.

Chapter Ten

"What's wrong with the house I'm staying in? What is everyone trying to keep from me?" Deborah asked bluntly and without preface. She and Linda were supervising their groups in a joint swimming period, their feet dangling in the churning pool that smelled overly of chlorine.

Linda did not appear as much surprised as disturbed by the question. She stared directly ahead of her at the pool and laughed. A thin, artificial laugh that ended too abruptly.

"Don't be silly, Deborah," she said. "What makes you ask a question like that?"

"Quite a lot of things," Deborah replied tersely, confused and irritated by Linda's reaction. The openness she had come to expect from her new friend was suddenly gone. "Most recently, the fact that you were so obviously uncomfortable in the house the other day."

There was a long pause. Still avoiding Deborah's eyes, Linda said, "I've never cared much for old houses. Especially after seeing *Psycho* at a very early age."

"That's not all there is to it."

"Of course it is. Why, do you want there to be more?"

"I want to know the truth, that's all. I'm not looking to be protected."

"Protected from what, Deborah? Do you really think that if there were something wrong with that house anyone would let you stay there?" Linda asked with convincing incredulity.

Deborah considered it. What reason would Linda have to lie to her? "I suppose not," she said lamely. "I just. . . ."

"Forget it," said Linda. She looked directly at Deborah. "Don't let people's attitudes or my quirks ruin the summer for you. You like the house; it's a fine house. Enjoy it. Don't be so suspicious of everything."

Deborah smiled vaguely. "I guess you're right," she said without conviction. And she let it rest, although she couldn't shake the gnawing certainty that some information was being withheld from her. Linda had become too tense at her questioning. As with an amateur bluffing at poker, her voice and face had betrayed her.

Her uneasiness was intensified all that evening by the persistent feeling that she was being watched, the same sensation she had experienced from the beginning, but somehow stronger. As if the watcher were closer. Just behind her. Just beyond the next doorway. She told herself it was no more than her imagination fired by Linda's evasiveness. But she knew only concrete answers would put her mind to rest, and Mrs. Hopkins would be the best one to talk to. She was not the furtive type. She would clear up this hocus-pocus about the house with a simple, logical sentence or two.

The decision to see Mrs. Hopkins calmed her for a while. But the uneasiness returned so powerfully when she was coming down the stairs to make herself dinner, that the flesh on her arms rose up in goose bumps and the tiny hairs on the nape of her neck prickled. It was only six o'clock and the house was still bathed in nearly full summer light. She heard only her own footsteps and the creaking of the old steps beneath them. Yet she was sure there was someone behind her. The air vibrated from the movement. Deborah broke into a run. Slipping, she took two steps at once and was thrown off balance. She landed in a heap at the bottom of the staircase. There was no one else on the stairs.

The phone rang some time after dark. Hearing Edith's

voice, Deborah felt homesick for the first time since she'd come to Rachael Crossing. She might have capitulated right then and left the old house forever, had it not been for Ethan. She pulled herself together and thanked her sister for calling. She was genuinely buoyed when she learned that Edith and Hal intended to take a trip up to see her toward midsummer. She replaced the receiver, heartened by the reminder that she still had ties to the outside world.

The next afternoon Deborah went straight from camp to the Rachael Real Estate office. She found Mrs. Hopkins once again seated in front of the television. This time she was awake. She looked over her shoulder when she heard the door open.

"Hello there," she said, pulling herself free from the armchair and switching off the set.

"Hello."

"I must say, I see more a' you than I do mosta the folks who live hereabouts," Mrs. Hopkins said amiably.

Deborah had come up to the desk. "I'm sorry to keep bothering you, I didn't. . . ."

"No, no, I didn't mean for ya to take offense, m'dear. Just makin' conversation is all." Mrs. Hopkins settled herself heavily into her chair again. "Glad to have your company."

Deborah relaxed and smiled.

"Here, sit yaself down," Mrs. Hopkins patted the top of her desk. "Or you can take a chair, if ya prefer."

"This is fine," said Deborah, sliding onto the edge of the desk. "As usual I'm here with a question."

"About the house?"

Deborah nodded.

"I'm afraid I won't be much help t'ya then. I've already told ya all that's in them files."

"No, this isn't anything that would be in your files. It's just something I thought you might know about."

"Ask away. I'll do ma best."

Encouraged Deborah went on. "It's just that I feel there's something about the house that I haven't been told. Whoever hears that I'm living there looks terribly startled, and no one seems to want to set foot inside the house. I simply want to be told what it is that everyone else around here already seems to know."

"I don' know, Deborah," she said, her face still passive and friendly. "*I* went inside with ya. Are you sure you're not building something out of all proportion?"

Deborah shrugged. The old woman didn't appear to be lying. And, she realized, Ethan, too, had had no qualms about entering the house. But that could have been out of an innocence like hers. "Maybe I am making more of this than there is," she conceded, "but I'm sure that there's something, however small, that's being kept from me. The funny thing is that I've really begun to feel welcome in this town, except for this business about the house. I'll tell you," she said, shaking her head, "it's really getting to me."

Mrs. Hopkins patted Deborah's knee. "I can see how it might. Look a here, old houses attract stories like lights attract moths. Just part a' bein' around so long. That's probably all 'tis."

"What kind of stories?" Deborah pounced on the word.

"Can't say. Never paid much mind to such things, don't ya know. The usual, I expect. Ghosts and noises and the like. But that's all poppycock, 'specially seein' as how you been livin' up there fer a couple weeks already, and you ain't seen or heard nothin', have ya?"

"No," Deborah said slowly. No, she couldn't actually say that she had. And yet how would she classify those feelings of being watched, of someone behind her on the stairs. She vacillated for a moment, wondering if she should relate these things to Mrs. Hopkins. She decided against it. They were feelings, nothing more. Chemical reactions triggered by an overactive imagination, one might say. She turned instead to a more realistic line of questioning.

"You never heard any of these stories from other tenants of the house?"

"It's possible, I s'ppose. But if I did, they went in one ear an' out the other. Like I said, I don't hold with such foolishness."

Deborah nodded with a small defeated sigh. She was on the verge of thanking Mrs. Hopkins and leaving, when she thought of one more question.

"Just one more thing, Mrs. Hopkins, if you don't mind, and then I'll be on my way. Have there been many different tenants or owners in the house since its construction?"

Mrs. Hopkins seemed to be tiring of the interrogation. Her smile had diminished to a bare curvature of the lips and her eyes had left Deborah and were flitting about the room. But her voice retained its amiable patience.

"I'd have to check the records to be certain of the number, but I know there have been a goodly few."

"Oh no, you needn't bother with the files," Deborah said, anxious not to irritate her source. "I was only interested in an estimate."

"About two dozen I'd say, give or take a couple."

Deborah had expected the number to be high—the house was well over a hundred years old—but twenty-four different tenants was more than she had anticipated. "Were there any long stretches during which the house was vacant?" she pursued.

Mrs. Hopkins yawned widely before replying. "Well now, a' course there been times it was empty. Not all that much call for houses up here, 'cept in summer. Mostly them that's been livin' here stays where they are, and them that's passin' through keep on movin', sooner 'n later. Yup, plenty a' times it's been empty. The wonder is more in findin' two dozen tenants at all up here, than in its stayin' empty."

"Then what you're saying is that even those two dozen or so tenants never stayed there very long," said Deborah, recalling the remark Ed Schmidt had made to her that day in his store: 'That house has never belonged to anyone. Not even the gent that had it built.'

Mrs. Hopkins was looking at the clock that hung on the wall above the desk. It was nearing five o'clock. "Hmmm?" she murmured, turning back to her.

Deborah repeated her question as she slid off the desk.

"I guess you could say that, but some stayed longer 'n others." Mrs. Hopkins' smile had expanded when she saw that Deborah was ready to leave.

"Thanks for satisfying my curiosity once more," said Deborah, moving toward the door. "I hope I haven't kept you from your dinner."

"That's okay, m'dear. Now you go on home and put that imagination of yours to rest before it gets the better a' ya."

Deborah walked home slowly. A refreshing breeze had sprung up, moderating the heat. At first she felt comforted by Mrs. Hopkins' homey, practical attitude. But as she walked further, the logic of their conversation became tangled in her memory, and by the time she reached the house, she found no solace in the fact that it had known so many occupants and had been vacant often and for long periods. That the people of Rachael Crossing kept their distance from it and were reluctant even to speak about it.

She stopped at the curb and looked up at the house. It sat nestled into the upper half of the hill, peaceful and innocuous in the softening light. The geraniums had taken well, their red blossoms bobbing cheerfully in the wind. It actually seemed welcoming to her. And to Ethan, she realized with a rush of excitement and relief. He had come by that first day, drawn to the house as she was. Either the town's fears were baseless, or she and Ethan were somehow blind to the truth.

Chapter Eleven

Deborah turned left on Carriage Drive. She paused in front of the first house, a brick and shingle split level like most of the others on the block, and searched for a number. Eleven was spelled out in black wrought iron script over the garage door. According to Mrs. Hopkins, Deborah needed number five. Toward the middle of the block she could see a few nineteenth-century frame houses, smaller versions of the one she was renting. They seemed huddled together as if for protection against the encroaching, newer models.

She still hadn't decided if she were just out for a stroll or if she really intended to ring the bell and try to speak to Old Man Darcy. Mr. Darcy, she corrected herself. She'd have to remember to use his proper name. If Mr. Darcy was the storyteller and town historian Linda and Mrs. Hopkins claimed he was, he would know more about the old house than anyone else.

She stopped in front of the first of the older houses. The mailbox at the curb was black and rusted in spots, its flap door hanging open like a beggar's hand. "Darcy" had been painted in large, uneven white letters on one side of the box. The house sat far back on a piece of lawn that had been burnt brown by the sun. Patches of dandelions and crab grass and a few scrawny bushes were all that remained green. The house itself seemed in good repair. It was white, like hers. Only the trim and window frames showed signs of peeling.

Deborah realized she'd been staring at the house for several minutes. If any of the neighbors were watching her they might think she was casing the place. Typical New York cynicism, she chided herself. Still, she had to make up her mind. March up to the front door and ring the bell or turn around and go home. Home was a house full of questions and dreams built on imagination. She smoothed back the loose, wispy ends of hair that had escaped her barrette, straightened her shoulders and started up the walk.

She took a deep breath and pressed the bell. She hated ringing doorbells at strangers' houses. It always made her feel small and vulnerable.

She waited and strained to hear footsteps from inside. There were no sounds. The old man might be hard of hearing. She put her hand up to the button again. Before she could press it, the door was pulled open. She stiffened and jerked her hand away from the bell as if she'd been caught doing something wrong.

A small, slender, middle-aged woman in a white uniform stood behind the screen door. She regarded Deborah through light blue rimmed glasses that magnified eyes of the same color. "Yes?" she said pleasantly.

"Hello," Deborah said. "Does Mr. Darcy live here?" That was stupid. Of course he did. Wasn't his name on the mailbox?

"Yes, he does. I'm his housekeeper. Can I help you?"

"My name is Deborah Colby. I was wondering if I might speak to Mr. Darcy, if it's convenient for him?"

"Can you tell me what it's in reference to?"

Deborah tried to explain who she was, and that being interested in history she had hoped Mr. Darcy could supply her with some additional information about the town and the house she was renting.

"Well Miss Colby, I can't guarantee how much information you'll be able to obtain, but I'm sure Mr. Darcy would be happy to have a visitor. He doesn't get many. It might perk him up a bit. We were sitting out back, if you'd like to come with me." She held open the screen door. "My name is Vera Brinks."

"Thank you." Deborah stepped inside and followed the petite Mrs. Brinks' silent rubber soles through several neat rooms to the back door and on outside. She was surprised to find herself on a green concrete patio, surrounded by a beautiful rose garden. Someone who didn't care much about lawns had certainly given these roses loving care.

Small bushes circled the patio, backed up by white trellises where climbing roses intertwined with the latticework. Red, pink, yellow and peach flowers, from buds to full ruffled blooms, filled the air with a sweet, heady perfume.

"Oh, this is wonderful," Deborah exclaimed.

"Thank you," Mrs. Brinks smiled proudly. "It's my hobby. Mr. Darcy seems to enjoy it also. I bring him out here whenever the weather permits." She nodded toward three rattan armchairs off to one side of the patio. The old man was sitting facing away from them.

Deborah had been so absorbed in the unexpected garden that she hadn't noticed the freckled, sun-browned pate with its tonsure of white hair rising above the back of the chair. He seemed almost grandfatherly. She was relieved. She had done the right thing by coming here.

"Come, Miss Colby," Mrs. Brinks was saying. "I'll introduce you to Mr. Darcy." They walked around so that they were standing in front of the old man. He was staring blankly at the rose bushes, his features nearly lost in the folds and creases of his skin. All the lines in his face were drawn down to where his lips puckered in over his gums, as if his mouth were a whirlpool sucking them in. He didn't move. He seemed unaware of their presence.

"He daydreams sometimes. At ninety-two he must have plenty of memories to get lost in," Mrs. Brinks explained with a tolerant smile.

Deborah nodded and wondered if her visit had resulted in another dead end. He was so oblivious to them.

"Mr. Darcy," Mrs. Brinks said, raising her voice. "Mr. Darcy." She leaned toward him and gently shook the gnarled hands that lay atop one another in his lap. "You have company. Someone's here to see you, Mr. Darcy."

The old man's eyes slowly came into focus. He tilted his head and looked up at them. He studied Deborah, his hairless eyebrows furrowing as he tried to place her.

"This is Miss Deborah Colby," Mrs. Brinks said. "She's new in Rachael Crossing. She wanted to meet you because she was told you know more about this town than anyone."

Deborah smiled.

Darcy nodded. "Nice to meet you," he said. The words were badly garbled.

"He isn't wearing his dentures today," Mrs. Brinks whispered to Deborah. "He doesn't bother when no one's coming."

"Sit down," Darcy mumbled, lifting a shaky hand to point to the chair beside his own.

"Thank you." Deborah sat.

"You two try to get acquainted. I'll go fix some lemonade, and find his teeth," Mrs. Brinks added with a wink for Deborah.

Deborah tried a couple of questions, but the old man's answers were nearly incomprehensible. She decided to smile and wait for Mrs. Brinks' return. When the housekeeper reappeared, she poured lemonade all around. Then, after a few firmly whispered words, as if she were disciplining a toddler, she helped Darcy insert his dentures.

Deborah sipped her lemonade and pretended a fascination with the bees that were darting between the plants.

"Darn things are a nuisance," Darcy said finally. "Always make my gums ache."

Deborah turned back to him. Vera Brinks had settled herself in the third chair a few feet away.

"They look very well on you, though," Deborah assured him. They filled out his jaw and cheeks to more normal dimensions. Even the lines in his skin seemed less deeply etched.

"I'm past lookin' for compliments. I was as handsome as any in my day." His voice was mildly irascible, as if he were testing her companionship, yet not too eager to discourage her company.

"Well Mr. Darcy," Deborah said, "I understand you're Rachael Crossing's town historian."

Darcy pursed his lips. They bulged unnaturally as if the teeth were somewhat too large. "I know a lot of stories, that I do. Some go back to the very beginnings of this town. Some even further. Heard 'em from my poppa an' from my granddaddy. Came down through all the men in the family. Minstrels of the New World they was." He laughed, a cackle that ended in a brittle cough.

"From father to son and so on down to me. And with me it dies." The laughter was gone from the bloodshot brown eyes, replaced by pain and anger.

"There was no one to pass it on to?" Deborah inquired kindly.

"Huh!" The old man grunted and fixed his eyes on the rose bushes again.

Deborah looked in bewilderment from him to Mrs. Brinks. She hadn't meant to say the wrong thing.

"Mr. Darcy has a son and a grandson, both lawyers in New York," Mrs. Brinks said softly.

Darcy turned abruptly back to Deborah. "And a great grandson who travels around the world looking for himself. Course it would never occur to the spoiled brat to look here in Rachael Crossing, which is where he belongs. Him and his father and his grandfather. I don't have a son anymore. I have a stranger in New York. A philanthropist. He pays my bills, pays Brinks here to nursemaid me. Comes to see me sometimes, when he can fit me in. Doesn't even like to hear the stories anymore. None of 'em do. Never really did. Television," he bared his teeth with disgust. "We never had television. Then the stories were an entertainment. Something to be treasured, looked forward to. All I ever hear now is, 'Oh, grandpa, not those again.' Progress. Progress will wipe out everything. Someday it'll wipe itself out, too."

"I'm a history teacher, Mr. Darcy," Deborah said when he paused finally. "Stories about the past fascinate me. I'd love to hear all of them, all you have to tell."

Darcy was eyeing her suspiciously. "No one cares anymore about what happened twenty years ago, let alone two or three hun'red. All they care for is now and tomorrow."

Deborah returned his gaze stubbornly. "Maybe I'm a throwback then, but I want to hear those stories."

He considered for a moment. Then, with childlike petulance, he said, "I don't know if I even remember most of 'em anymore. Shoulda been my son's job long before this. Or my grandson's. A man gets too old to hold detail and sequence. Some days I feel like I'm living those stories myself. Some days I can hardly remember my poppa's face." He sighed deeply. His shoulders hunched forward and his eyes seemed to submerge into the folds around them.

Mrs. Brinks stood up. "I think he's ready for a nap," she said politely but firmly. "Maybe if you came back another time."

Deborah nodded and rose.

The old man lifted his lids and looked up at her. "Deborah is it?"

"Deborah Colby. You rest now. I'll be back to see you soon. I promise."

"Where you say you was stayin'?"

"I didn't. But it's the old place on Foxton Lane."

"You shouldn't be stayin' there," he said, his face pinched into a frown.

"I've been fine there, really," Deborah assured him.

"They burned it. To the ground, they did."

"The first house. I know."

"To the ground. They did right. They did right. . . . But it weren't enough." He paused, licking his lips. "You ain't seen nothin' there?" he demanded.

"No. No, I haven't," said Deborah, startled by the sudden vehemence in his tone.

"What about that dog? Brinks here heard all about it from Schmidt's son. He sure as hell seen it, that dog that leapt at ya. Why do ya think he turned round in midair and run off yelpin'?" He fell silent, observing Deborah's bewildered expression. "Well, ya think yer what scared the dog off? Huh! Yer a fool, young lady. And ya oughta leave that place. Ya oughta . . . ya oughta . . ." His voice trailed off and his eyes closed.

Deborah wanted desperately to shake him awake and ask him what he thought had scared off the dog. But Vera Brinks had put her arm around Deborah's shoulders.

"He really is overtired," she said, motioning for Deborah to follow her. She led the way out of the garden and back through the house. At the front door she stopped.

"He often falls asleep in the middle of things like that, I'm afraid. And I wouldn't worry about what he said to you. He rambles sometimes. Gets his stories muddled. Mixes time by decades and centuries. Poor man." She smiled with affection. "He always expected to pass it on. But you can't blame the younger generations. They have to live their lives, too. His son was the first Darcy to leave Rachael Crossing, but it was his right."

Deborah nodded. "I'll be back. Tell him that, will you?"

"Sure. If he even remembers you were here when he wakes up."

Deborah walked home slowly, her head spinning with more questions than she'd had before. She hadn't given the incident with the dog more thought. But Darcy saw it as meaningful and ominous. What did he think had scared off the dog? She'd been there. So had Brad Schmidt. And they hadn't seen anything extraordinary. Perhaps Darcy was nothing but a lonely old man with an erratic memory and the burden of a heritage he couldn't pass on. But Deborah suspected there were truths to be unraveled there if she were patient. She knew she would go back to see him again.

Chapter Twelve

At night a blanket of hot, stagnant air settled over Rachael Crossing. Deborah awoke tangled in damp linens, her nightgown clinging to her body. The sky was sickly white from the thick haze of humidity and so low it seemed to hang on her shoulders, coating her skin with its moisture and making every movement a struggle.

Deborah was glad when the bus bounced to a stop near the camp grounds. Although the air outside was no cooler, at least it didn't reek of gasoline and oil.

The heat and humidity were having their effect. The most rambunctious of the boys were subdued and sullen. The power failed twice, shutting down the pool filters, darkening the cafeteria, and reducing the ice cream to milky puddles.

The temperature soared to ninety-eight before midday. Schedules were thrown out. By the time the day had ended, one camper had fainted and several others had been sent home.

Although Deborah had left the drapes and shades drawn in the house, it still felt as if all the air had been sucked out and the walls were pressing in on her. She needed to get outside and find a shady tree. She cooled herself off first in the shower, fastened her hair up on top of her head and was on her way to the door when she heard the drone of the lawn mower. She peered through the living room window. Carl was plodding across the front lawn behind the machine, his T-shirt stuck to his chest and back in wet, gray patches. Droplets of perspiration glistened in his hair and ran down his face.

Seeing him made Deborah forget about her own discomfort. Carl might be able to elaborate on the "stories" Mrs. Hopkins had mentioned. Like Linda, he had been reluctant to enter the house. He probably knew what the others knew. If she approached him properly he might just tell her. She went outside to say hello.

Carl looked up, his face strained and moody. "Lo," he said without stopping.

Deborah came up to him and kept pace alongside the mower.

"Watch yer feet," he grunted.

"How have you been?" she inquired, raising her voice so he could hear her over the motor.

"Hot."

"Yes, it sure is hot."

Carl glanced at her. "How d'you manage to stay lookin' so cool?" he asked accusingly.

"I took a shower when I got home."

"That's what I'm gonna do. Gonna sit in a cold tub. An I ain't comin' out 'til this here heat wave ends."

"It's no different than in New York. We've had some pretty hot summers there, too," said Deborah to remind him that they were both outsiders in Rachel Crossing.

"I s'ppose. Still, the city's one thing. You don't expect it up here."

"How about taking a break for some lemonade?"

"Sure could use somethin' wet," Carl agreed, wiping the back of his hand across his mouth. He shut off the mower. "You wouldn't happen t'have a cold beer lyin' around, wouldya?"

Deborah shook her head. "No, I'm sorry. The best I can do is lemonade or iced tea."

"That's okay. This belly's seen too many beers already,"

he said, patting the damp rolls at his waist. "Lemonade'll do fine."

"C'mon in,' Deborah said, anxious to hear his answer.

"How about we sit under that there maple. Prob'ly cooler than in the house anyways."

"Why sure," she forced a smile. "Go ahead and sit down. I'll only be a minute." There, she had given it one more try and it was obvious that he didn't want to go inside. Maybe now she would find out why.

She returned with the two glasses of lemonade. Carl was resting his back against the trunk of the maple, his short legs stuck out in front of him, his stomach spilling over onto his lap.

"Thanks, Deborah," he said, accepting a glass. "Not everyone's thoughtful enough t'offer ya a cold drink these days."

Deborah watched while Carl drained his glass in two long gulps.

"Can I get you some more?"

"Nope. That was perfect. Can't drink slow, never could. 'N if I have one more I'll be paying for it with cramps all night."

Deborah nodded and sipped her lemonade, wondering how to turn the conversation toward the house. "Carl," she said finally, "I feel we have something in common, if you know what I mean, up here among all these country people."

"Yeah, ya could say that," Carl nodded, plucking a wide blade of grass and tearing it into strips.

"So I thought you might help me with something."

Carl looked at her. "Ya found another root cellar ya want dug up?"

"No, no, just some information you might have."

"Information? Sure, that's easy 'nough. But what could I know that'd be of any interest to you?"

"Why are you afraid to come inside this house?" she asked, hoping to catch him off guard and insure an honest response.

"Afraid?" he growled. "Who says I'm afraid?"

"I'm sorry. I just assumed that was the reason you refused to come in last week and again today."

" 'Course not. It's just, uh, it just don't look right for me to go inside with a single lady. I don't want folks talkin', is all. A guy's gotta be careful up here."

"Come on," Deborah chided gently. "I can't find anyone else who'll level with me. But I know that you will."

Carl chewed on the inner wall of his cheek and scratched his head. "Awright, look, it's really nuthin' much. The kids bring home all kindsa stories from school. Some of 'em was about this old house."

"What kind of stories?" she prodded.

"Somethin' about someone dyin' here. Or somethin' like that. Don't remember for sure."

"People die in houses all the time. There must have been more to it to make you keep your distance."

"Listen, I just figure why look for trouble. It finds me all by itself anyways. So I drink my lemonade out here or in there. Whatsa difference? Why look for it?"

"Are you sure you can't tell me anything else?" Deborah pleaded. "It's really driving me crazy not knowing."

Carl put his pudgy hands on the ground and pushed himself up. "Don't know no more. If I did I'd tell ya. If ya'd like, I can ask the kids. That kind of thing they remember. Homework they forget, but stories like that they remember."

Deborah stood too. "Would you?" she said, picking up the empty glasses. "I'd really appreciate it."

"Sure, why not?"

"Thank you."

"Thanks for the drink," he said and started walking to his mower. "Hey," he turned back to her. "You ain't had no problems, have ya?"

"No, just curious," Deborah replied. "No problems." She went inside and put the glasses in the sink. She had expected to feel lighthearted and relieved knowing that her questions would soon be answered. But the oppressive air had dulled her spirits and instead she found herself fearful of learning those answers.

Chapter Thirteen

Deborah began to have shadowy dreams, disrupting her sleep and setting her on edge. Talking with the old man and with Carl seemed only to have aggravated the problem, providing her imagination with new fodder: Old Man Darcy presiding over a roomful of decomposing corpses, his own head mutating first into a dog's, then into a living skull.

Even the fresher air that had swept through Rachael Crossing during the early morning hours did nothing to dispel the heaviness and dread with which she awakened. Then she remembered that it was Saturday and she would soon be with Ethan. In moments the dark mood disintegrated like the dreams that had produced it.

Exhilarated, Deborah raced from room to room, cleaning and straightening up. She prepared the chicken she had promised him, giving the most meticulous attention to all the ingredients and measurements. She hurried upstairs to dress. It was nearly noon and she didn't know just what time to expect him. Or if he would come at all, a small voice whispered in her head. She pulled off her nightgown and tried to ignore the awful possibility that had been lurking in her thoughts all week.

He had never phoned to confirm their date, nor even to inquire how she was. Certainly he was busy traveling, and yet, weren't there times, in the evenings especially, that he would have the opportunity and hopefully the desire to speak to her? Edith would quickly have jumped upon this lapse to illustrate his poor character and lack of any real feelings for her.

"Well, I'm not Edith," she told herself firmly, slipping her pale yellow sundress over her head. Besides, he was probably so accustomed to traveling unhindered by responsibility and attachments, that it simply never occurred to him to call. He had made the date and she was certain he would honor it. Or nearly certain, she admitted, tying the bows that secured the dress at her shoulders.

Before leaving the bedroom she took the old ring from its place on the dresser and slipped it into one of the patch pockets on her dress. Then she went down to the living room to wait. She looked as good as she ever had, she assured herself. And without question she looked better than Ethan had ever seen her. That first day they had met she had been covered with dirt from head to toe from gardening. And the second time, tired and drawn from her first day of camp, hadn't been much of an improvement. She honestly wondered why he wanted to see her again. But he did. She was sure. Wasn't she? She glanced at her watch. It was after one o'clock already. He had said lunch. A picnic lunch. Disappointment began to form a hard lump in her stomach like drying cement. When the doorbell rang ten minutes later she jumped up from the couch. In the stillness that followed the chimes she could hear the blood pounding madly through her body. She forced herself to walk slowly to the door, trying to regain her composure. What if it was Carl or Linda or Mrs. Hopkins or anyone but Ethan? she wondered, nearly hysterical at the prospect. No. It's him, she told herself sternly. So calm down. She held her breath and opened the door.

He filled the doorway, making the rest of the world seem remote and less real. "Hello." His voice vibrated inside of her.

"Hi," she exhaled. Her relief felt tangible. She was sure

he could tell. "Come on in. I didn't know what time to expect you."

"I didn't know myself. I was up in Maine on business until late last night."

"Well anyway, everything's ready, so your timing was perfect." Even if she had nearly died waiting for him.

"Ummm," he murmured. "If that's the chicken I smell, you certainly seem to have kept your part of the bargain." He held out a bottle of white wine. "I hope this will compliment it properly."

"Oh, that'll be wonderful, she said, taking it. "Thank you. Would you like to relax in the living room or keep me company in the kitchen while I pack up the food?"

"The kitchen by all means. I didn't come all this way to stare at some old furniture. Why are you bothering to pack up the food?" he asked, following her into the kitchen.

"Aren't we going on a picnic?" Deborah asked.

"Sure, it's the best way to eat fried chicken. But why not picnic right here—out back I mean. No dragging blankets and bundles. No crowds."

Deborah backed up a few steps. Being so close to him distracted her and she had trouble thinking what to say. "Yeah, I guess so," she stumbled over her words.

"Hey now, you really want to go to a park or someplace, just say so. I didn't mean to dictate the terms."

"No," Deborah smiled. "Now that I think about it I agree with you." It would be better not to share their afternoon with whomever they might bump into at a public park. The day was too precious to allow the possibility of anyone infringing on it. As much as she would have liked to show him off, she preferred to keep him to herself.

In the back of a cabinet they found an old tray that was rusting through its enameled flowers. Ethan carried the food outside while Deborah hunted in a closet for one of the sheets that had draped the furniture before she moved in.

Ethan helped her to spread it in the coolest shadows of an old oak tree, but the thick, gnarled roots protruded uncomfortably through the thin sheet and they were forced to settle further from the trunk. There the sunlight winked at them through the leaves that shifted in the light breeze. Between mouthfuls they exchanged bits and pieces of conversation. Ethan explained a deal he was trying to work out with a California-based company. Deborah talked about the camp and the people she'd met in Rachael Crossing. She avoided telling him about her fears about the house. She didn't want to appear foolish.

"Do you have any family near here?" she asked.

Ethan finished chewing a piece of chicken and took a drink of wine. "No. My folks aren't around anymore and I never had any other family aside from them. Maybe a distant aunt or cousin. But no one I stay in touch with." He spoke evenly, as if the loss had been some time ago.

"Both of my parents are gone too," said Deborah.

"But you still have Edith," he reminded her with a broad smile, the long slash of dimples appearing in the planes of his cheeks.

"That's for sure," Deborah laughed. "That's for sure."

Ethan dropped the last chicken leg onto his plate, half-eaten. "Lady, you do make fantastic fried chicken."

"Thank you." She handed him a dampened cloth.

"And you think of everything." He wiped the grease from his hands.

"That's just Edith rubbing off on me. I'm really not all that efficient myself."

Ethan started to refill her empty glass. She covered it with her hand.

"No more for me. This has already gone to my head."

He shrugged and poured the remainder of the bottle into his own glass.

"Oh, I nearly forgot," said Deborah. "I have something to show you."

"What's that?" Ethan asked, reclining on his arm.

Deborah dug her hand into her pocket and withdrew the ring, extending it toward him in her open palm.

Ethan sat up, suddenly alert and reached for the ring. "Why that's my . . . that's my family's ring," he exclaimed.

"Yes, that's what I'd supposed," she said, bewildered by the intensity of his reaction. "It was in that old root cellar, the one I told you about," she said hesitantly, remembering his anger the last time she'd mentioned it.

Ethan didn't seem to be listening to her. He was turning the ring over and over in his fingers as if he could absorb the memories that had been buried with it.

"The cellar was probably from the original house," she went on. "The one your family owned. Being the history buff I am, I had to explore it. And that's where I found the ring. It was just lying inside, on the ground."

"It's remarkably well preserved."

"I cleaned it up a bit," said Deborah. "But what surprised me about it were the initials engraved on it."

Ethan studied the ring more closely. "Yes, I see them. E.B.," he said matter-of-factly.

"You don't seem at all surprised."

"No reason to be. This ring no doubt belonged to my great, great, great grandfather. Did I stick enough greats in there? Anyway, his name was Eli Burke."

Something about Ethan's explanation bothered her, something she couldn't quite put her finger on.

"Here." Ethan held the ring out to her.

"No, you keep it," she said. "It's yours by rights. I'm glad I was able to find it for you."

"If you're sure. Thank you." He tried it on the fourth finger of his right hand. It slid easily over the knuckle. "Look, it fits fairly well."

"Maybe you should have it sized properly, though," she said. "If it's a little loose it could slip off."

"Yeah, I'll have to see about that. Thank you again." Ethan laid his hand along her cheek. He leaned toward her and kissed her gently. "You're so lovely," he murmured, his lips still touching hers. Then he kissed her again, pulling her against him in strong, possessive arms.

Deborah was heady from the wine, her body weak and tingling as if it were no longer under her control. It seemed like forever that he held her, his mouth moving on hers, his tongue hot and probing. An intense warmth surged up from deep within her, spreading through her chest and down along her legs.

She felt herself moving backward, Ethan's large hand cushioning her head as it touched the ground. She was no longer on the sheet. Grass pricked at the nape of her neck.

She opened her eyes for a moment. Ethan's face was inches above hers against the leaf spangled sky. She wanted to say something, but he was kissing her again and whatever she had been thinking of was swept out of her mind.

His fingers were moving lightly on her shoulders. A moment later he slipped the top of her sun dress down to her waist. Startled, she tried to protest, but Ethan kept his mouth over hers until she had quieted. One of his hands still cradled her head. The other he ran over the smooth skin of her breasts. Then he was pushing up the hem of the sun dress, stroking the sensitive skin on the inside of her leg.

It was happening too fast. Deborah felt threatened, not only by his physical strength, but by his power over her. She tried to move her mouth away from his, to push his hand off her. But her breath was coming in short, inadequate gasps and her body was frighteningly unresponsive to her mental commands.

Ethan moved one leg over between hers and she could feel him hard and probing against her thigh. She fought harder to pull away from him.

"Deborah," he whispered heavily, "Deborah."

"No, not out here, like this. Someone might see us," she pleaded, seizing on the excuse and knowing it was a lame one.

"There's no one around here," he said, finding her mouth again.

He was right. The houses on the block were widely scattered and the woods that encircled the rear of the house were a natural screen. No one would come back there uninvited, except perhaps Carl, but he had been there the day before. It was incredibly still. She could almost believe they inhabited a private world which no one else could enter.

She felt defenseless and vulnerable, her fears neutralizing her desire for him. She put her palms against his chest and with one enormous effort she pushed him back, rolling over and away from him. She pulled herself to her knees no more than two feet from his reach, holding up the top of her sundress, ready to flee. But he made no move to grab for her. He remained half reclining on the arm that had been beneath her, looking up at her with a mixture of confusion and dismay.

She watched him carefully, trying to steady her breathing and the trembling of her hands.

"Deborah," he said in a voice constricted to a whisper, "I'm sorry."

She nodded almost imperceptibly.

Ethan moved his hand toward her. She started to jump up.

"No," he said and simply placed his hand over hers where it held up the front of her dress. "It won't ever happen again. It should never have happened this time. I just thought . . . I guess I was mistaken." His eyes were searching hers as if he were trying to read behind them.

She began to feel foolish. She couldn't think of anything to say, either accusing or forgiving. She could only wonder why she had panicked. There was not the slightest doubt in her mind that she had wanted him from the first moment she had seen him smiling up at her from the foot of the hill. What had held her back? Her stomach was in knots and she wanted to cry. Large, hot tears spilled over her lids and were weaving slowly, ridiculously down her cheeks, carrying her mascara with them. She must look like a disaster.

Ethan wiped the tears away with his hand, but others followed.

"Can I stay and we'll talk, or would you rather I left?" he asked.

Deborah supposed she should ask him to leave, but her panic had subsided. She let herself fall from her knees to a sitting position.

"I'd like you to stay," she murmured.

"Can I pour you some iced tea?"

She nodded, stifling the urge to sniffle. She retied the bows that held up the top of her dress, then sipped the tea, plucking absently at the grass beside her.

Ethan emptied his glass. He looked directly at her. "Don't you want me to make love to you, Deborah?"

She was startled. She had expected the conversation to turn to something trivial and nonthreatening. She had hardly thought he would pursue the topic. But the matter-of-fact way he was regarding her made her feel silly and schoolgirl-ish again. He was waiting for a response, and the longer she hesitated the more awkward that response became.

Finally she took a breath to steady her voice and forced herself to meet his gaze.

"Ethan, no one's ever made me feel the way I feel with you right now. But it's all so sudden, I'm afraid. These things haven't worked out very well for me in the past. I guess I'm just a silly old spinster."

"You're a bit too young to claim that title," said Ethan and he took her hand in his.

Deborah looked down. "I don't know why I said that. Your pity is the last thing I want."

"I never said you had it." After a moment he went on. "I can't love a woman and pity her at the same time."

Deborah felt the impact of his words in her stomach even before she had absorbed them completely. He had said love. And clearly he had meant her.

They sat under the oak tree until late in the afternoon. They didn't notice the sky changing, the thin filigree clouds routed by blacker ones bloated with rain.

The storm started sluggishly, heavy drops splattering onto the leaves above them. But within seconds it became a downpour. Deborah and Ethan jumped up, startled at the sound of the first drops. They piled everything into the center of the sheet, tied it into a clumsy bundle and half dragged, half carried it across to the back door. Inside they laughed and shook the water off their heads and arms.

"It's getting late anyway," Ethan said, "and I have some business calls to make. I'll try to see you again before I have to leave for L.A. If not, when I get back."

He kissed her tentatively, as if afraid she would pull away. "You know I haven't given up on you," he said, holding her close to him a moment before releasing her.

"I'm glad," she whispered, more to herself than to him.

She walked him to the door, wanting him back before he was even gone. He went down to the curb where a small, late model blue car was parked. She hadn't even noticed it when he'd arrived.

The elusive car, she thought and smiled. Another mystery solved by itself. She waited by the door, unwilling to close it until he had driven off and she could no longer see his profile through the open window of the car.

Chapter Fourteen

Deborah cleaned up after the picnic. She worked mechanically, absorbed in her thoughts, one minute overwhelmed by excitement and a longing ache remembering how she had felt encircled in Ethan's arms, the next, cringing inwardly with confusion and embarrassment when she recalled how she had panicked.

What did Ethan see in her? She tallied her attributes while she washed the chicken platter. She was pretty, thanks to her expressive eyes, fairly intelligent, and she'd maintained her figure, though it had never been a voluptuous one. What else? Oh, of course, she thought with a grimace, she was sweet. Isn't that what everyone had always said of her? She wondered if "sweet" was what interested Ethan. She hoped not.

She dried her hands on the dish towel and decided not to subject her good fortune to any further scrutiny. Perhaps, she mused, her turn had come at last and she didn't need to look beyond that.

She slumped into a chair in the living room, weary and drained from the day. It was only eight o'clock, and if she went to sleep this early she would probably be up at three a.m. She tried to read, to watch television. But she couldn't settle on anything. She considered calling Linda, thinking it would be nice to talk about Ethan. Just saying his name aloud gave her pleasure. But before she even reached for the receiver she realized she didn't really want to talk about her intimate feelings and questions. It didn't surprise her. That was the way it had always been.

After wandering aimlessly from room to room, she gave up. She checked the doors, shut the lights and went up to bed. She fell asleep immediately. For the second night in a row her dreams were distressing.

She was lying on a beach on a warm cloudless day, enjoying the way the sun was burrowing into all the deep places inside her. She was so relaxed she felt as if she were melting into the powdery sand, lulled by the lapping of a calm tide, the distant screeching of gulls. Then in an instant the sun was blotted out. The orange-gold light that had played against her closed lids went to black. She opened her eyes, expecting to see a cloud across the sun. What she saw was a tall man standing over her, completely dressed, even to his shoes, which were half submerged in the sand. She couldn't distinguish his features. He was standing with the sun behind him, but even so, the shadows that hid his face were peculiarly dark. The effect terrified Deborah, and although he said nothing and made no move toward her, she jumped up and started to run. She stumbled awkwardly through the sand, looking around her for help. Minutes before there had been small knots of people scattered along the sand, children digging tunnels and carrying splashing bucketfuls of water. Now the beach was deserted.

The man was following her. He was only walking, but somehow he was keeping pace with her. She ran down to the surf, hoping to find someone there. But the waves were breaking evenly, undisturbed by bathers. Even the gulls had flown away. It was unnaturally quiet. She ran along the edge of the water. He was still behind her. She didn't turn to look. In the silence she could hear the slap and crunch of his shoes on the hard-packed sand. She pushed herself to move faster, a small, sharp pain flaming in her right side. He was closer. She could feel his fingers hovering above the skin on her shoulder. Her body was clammy with fear. Perspiration ran between her breasts and down her legs. He was about to grab her. She swerved and ran into the water, hoping he wouldn't follow her. If he did, she knew he could easily drown her out there, completely unobserved. But there was nowhere else to run. She didn't stop until she was shoulder deep. Then her chest heaving, the pain like a knife slicing through her waist, she turned and looked behind her. He was gone. She scanned the beach slowly from horizon to horizon and saw no one anywhere. But before relief could settle over her, she felt the water swirling strangely, pulling her further from shore. She struggled against it but she couldn't make any headway. The tide had strengthened. Her throat was dry, her lungs aching. Just as suddenly, the water relaxed its grip on her. She started to swim frantically for shore. Then, looking back over her shoulder, she saw it. A huge green-black wall of water cresting just behind her.

The next time she opened her eyes she was lying on the beach again. The tall man was back too, staring down at her. She still couldn't see his face.

"Deborah, are you all right?" he said.

Deborah pushed herself up onto her elbows. She was in her bed. She recognized the voice. "Ethan?" she whispered hoarsely. Her heart was thumping painfully.

Ethan sat down on the edge of the bed. "I'm sorry if I scared you," he said, smoothing her hair back from her face.

Questions were flooding her mind too quickly to sort. "What are you doing . . . How did you get in? . . . I don't understand . . . Why?" she sputtered.

"Calm down first," he said softly.

Deborah took several deep breaths. "Okay," she said, her voice still trembling, "I'm okay now. Just tell me how you got in here and why."

"I wanted to see you again. But it was after midnight and I wasn't sure you'd be up. So I drove over and looked for a light. There was one in the living room. I figured you were watching television. I rang the bell and when you didn't answer I got worried and tried the door. It was open and here I am."

"No." Deborah was shaking her head. "No. I shut all the

lights and checked to make sure the doors were locked before I came upstairs."

"Maybe you thought you did. Things like that you do by habit, without thinking about them. It's possible that you forgot this once."

"No, I'm sure, I . . ."

"Then how do you explain me?" Ethan asked, his dimples fading in and out as he spoke.

"I don't know," Deborah said, weighing the possibility that she'd been so involved in her thoughts that she hadn't shut all the lights and locked all the doors. "I suppose it could be," she conceded halfheartedly.

"Are you feeling better now? When I walked in you were moaning and thrashing around as if you were having a nightmare."

Deborah shuddered at the memory. "Yes. I'm okay now. Why don't you go on down to the kitchen and I'll be down in two minutes to make us some coffee." She started to throw back the cover.

"Thank you, but I don't want any," said Ethan. "I didn't come back here at this hour for coffee." He paused and regarded her intently. "I'm here because I want you."

Deborah stiffened. She couldn't think of what to say. The panic and turmoil of the afternoon threatened to seize her again.

"There won't be any replay of this afternoon," he assured her. "Just tell me to leave and I will."

It should have been simple for her to say, "Please leave," then. With no other man would she have even considered the alternative. But in the near blackness of the room she was captivated by the fine angles of his face and the intensity of his eyes. He filled the room with his presence, animated it, and with sudden understanding she knew how very alone she would be if he were to leave. An emptiness of more than space, of opportunities forever lost.

All the muscles of her throat seemed to have thickened so that it was hard to speak. "I don't want you to leave," she managed finally. "But I don't think. . . ."

"Stop thinking so much," Ethan told her gently. "It isn't

always necessary. And don't be so afraid of being disappointed."

He kissed her, pressing her back against the pillows. Deborah reached up and put her arms around him. His shirt was taut across his back and her hands slid down along the smooth, hard muscles of his shoulders and arms. There was a tensile power to him. This strength coupled with his urgency had overwhelmed her this afternoon. Now the urgency was gone. She felt safe, even relaxed in his embrace. There was no threat in the gentle way his lips touched hers, then brushed across her cheek, her temple, the lobe of her ear and returned to her lips again. It was Deborah who opened her mouth to him, wanting to feel the warmth of his tongue, surprising even herself. And while he bent to caress her neck and the soft arc of skin above her nightgown, the sudden rush of pleasure made her shudder. He opened the tie that held the bodice of the nightgown, letting the gown slip down her shoulders. Unbuttoning his own shirt, he dropped it to the floor, and drew her against him with a patient tenderness that she trusted. If he had misjudged her that afternoon, she had perhaps misjudged him, too. Believing he would release her if she asked him to, the last of her anxieties slipped away. She arched closer to him, her body throbbing wherever it touched his. In response, his arms grew tighter around her, his mouth more demanding, insatiable, burning against her skin and quickening her desire with his own. She felt the room tumbling away and with it all that was real and rational, all that had bound her so solidly to earth. Lost in the consuming need for him she willingly let go. And when at last he drew the nightgown from her, she helped him, unable to bear even the thin fabric between them anymore.

She remained locked against him for a long time after, feeling their hearts slow in unison, marveling at how much she loved someone she hardly knew. And yet it was true.

Ethan moved his head back so that he could look at her.

"Are you all right?"

She wanted to tell him how much she loved him, how incredible he had made her feel. But she didn't seem able to say anything sensible or even coherent right then. So she smiled and nodded.

But Ethan wasn't smiling back. If anything, his eyes were sadder than she had ever seen them. As if he had just discovered some tragic loss.

She reached out and touched his cheek, the stubble of his beard rough against her palm. "What's wrong?"

"I really have fallen in love with you," he said, his voice a whisper.

"Is that so awful?"

His expression brightened, but mechanically, by sheer force of will. "No. No, I didn't mean to make it seem that way. It's my turn to be a little overwhelmed, that's all. I've never felt quite this way before."

"That's okay, neither have I."

His mouth drew up in a small, crooked smile and he hugged her close to him as if afraid she might slip away.

Deborah closed her eyes, but the contentment she'd known moments before was shattered. In spite of his protests she knew that Ethan was troubled. She couldn't fathom why and she sensed he wouldn't tell her. Not yet anyway. There were still so many closed doors to him, so much to unlock. But he had said he loved her and surely she would have the time she needed to understand it all. With this thought she drifted off to sleep.

She knew he was gone before she opened her eyes. The room was dim although the clock showed ten past ten. She recognized the gravelly sound of rain being driven against the windows. She put her hand out to touch the place where he had lain. Nothing of him lingered there. She looked around the room. Everything in its proper place. She pulled on her robe and padded downstairs barefoot. The lights were all off. She tried the doors. Both were locked. He'd probably taken care of them when he'd left. If he was really ever here. . . .

"Nonsense, of course he was," she chided herself and went into the kitchen to make a cup of coffee. But she was unable to shake the feeling that something was not quite right. That awful dream was the problem, and to have awakened to see Ethan there. It had all been a little hard to absorb. Still, she was glad he had come back. She had only imagined that nights like that were possible.

Chapter Fifteen

Ethan didn't call Monday. All week Deborah dragged through her camp routine, racing home to wait for a call that didn't come. Each night she went to bed more despondent than the last, trying to console herself with the hope that he would call the next day. By Friday she no longer believed herself. She remembered that he hadn't called the last time he'd been gone for ten days either. But she'd hardly known him then. She changed rationales. He was probably one of those people who didn't bother with telephones.

Twice during the week Linda had inquired if anything were the matter, but Deborah had insisted there was nothing wrong. Friday afternoon she and Linda were sitting alone in the cafeteria drinking sodas from a vending machine.

"At the risk of sounding nosey and monotonous, What's the matter? Maybe if you told someone you'd feel better."

Deborah opened her mouth intending to say that there was nothing wrong, but all her feelings and anxieties about Ethan poured out between embarrassing sobs. She wasn't any happier, but she did feel somewhat relieved, as if the tears had been a burden she'd been carrying around.

Linda shook her head. "I wish I knew what to say to you that would make a difference."

"That's okay." Deborah pulled a napkin out of the dispenser and dabbed at her eyes. "I don't know what to say to myself anymore either. I guess I just needed to let it out after all."

"It could be like you said, he just isn't one to pick up a phone unless there's an emergency."

Deborah sniffled. "But you'd think he would have called even once."

"Yeah, I guess I do. Look, he might just show up on your doorstep this weekend, that seems to be his style."

Deborah shrugged and tried to drink her soda, but her throat was constricted and the bubbles stung when she swallowed.

"Maybe you wouldn't be as depressed if you weren't home alone so much," Linda was saying. "Would you like me to stay—I mean would you like to stay with me and my family for a while?"

"There you go again!" Deborah jumped at her. "Why are you so damned afraid to be in my house?" She suddenly didn't feel like crying anymore.

Linda was startled by the anger in her voice. "I'm, "I'm not," she stammered. "I meant to invite you to my house to begin with. Come on, I'm not in the habit of inviting myself to other people's homes," she insisted.

"One minute I think you're my friend and confidant, and the next you're shoving a wedge between us. What is it with you? What is it with this weird little town? Why won't anyone tell me the truth?" Deborah banged the side of her fist on the formica tabletop. The soda cups shook. "I'm beginning to wonder how friendly this goddamned town really is!"

Linda put her hand on Deborah's arm. Her soft hazel eyes were troubled. She opened her mouth, but before she could say anything she was cut off by a masculine voice.

"Hey girls, would you two rather be alone or do you need a referee?" Jeffrey Pomeroy came over to their table grinning.

Linda glared up at him. "We don't need a referee and

besides, you'd be about as impartial as a Russian judge at a skating competition."

Jeffrey ignored the comment and looked at Deborah. "Do I go or stay?"

Deborah was concentrating on pleating a napkin. The last thing she needed was to have Mr. Ego around when she was hurt and angry and her nose was bright red. "Don't bother staying unless you've got some answers for me," she said bitterly.

"Question me, I'm yours," he said, throwing his leg over the chair beside her and folding himself into the seat.

"Do you know where I'm staying?" she asked, still studying the napkin.

"Yeah, the old haunted house on Foxton, right?"

Deborah snapped her head around to face him. "Did I hear the word haunted?"

"Yeah, everyone knows that," Jeffrey said good-naturedly. He looked across at Linda for confirmation, but received only an icy stare and an almost imperceptible wag of her head.

"Everyone but me obviously," Deborah muttered. "Just what happened in that house for it to have earned that title?"

"The usual," Jeffrey said vaguely, aware now that he had stumbled into forbidden territory.

"You'll have to be a little more specific. I'm a novice at this sort of thing."

Jeffrey shrugged and shifted in his chair. "I was never in there. I've only heard things secondhand."

"I'm listening."

"Well, you know, unexplained noises, apparitions, things that go bump in the night," he added, trying to lighten the mood.

"And these things went on with one of the tenants or with all of them?" Deborah pursued.

"All of them I guess," he said lamely.

Linda was shaking her head. "As long as old blabbermouth here has opened this Pandora's box, I might as well at least straighten out the facts a bit."

"It's about time, wouldn't you say?" Deborah rebuked her.

Linda looked levelly at her. "Yes, I lied. But not to cause you pain or trouble, only to spare you some unnecessary fears. I've known the stories about that house since I was a little girl, and from what I've heard they go back to its very beginning. No one's ever lived there for very long, not even the man who originally had it built. But let me add one important fact to that—no one has ever been harmed in that house either. They complained of noises and visions and objects moving, that sort of thing, nothing more. You've been there over a month now yourself, and nothing out of the ordinary has happened, right?"

Deborah shook her head slowly, Nothing concrete, she thought. Certainly nothing like what Linda and Jeffrey were describing.

"Maybe you've exorcised the ghosts," Jeffrey chuckled.

Deborah looked annoyed. Linda groaned.

"Well, I've got to be heading out now," he said, standing so quickly he toppled the chair. "Listen, Deborah, if you ever feel the need for protection, give me a call." He set the chair on its feet again and left.

Linda watched him go. "I should have known that big jerk would say something. Deborah, I'm sorry. My mom and I talked it over and we thought we'd be doing you a favor by not passing on those stories."

Deborah's expression had softened. "Okay," she sighed. "I might have done the same thing myself, I guess."

"Friends?" Linda smiled tentatively. "No more lies, I promise."

"Friends," Deborah agreed. She had to trust someone. She hoped she wasn't being naive.

"How about taking me up on my invitation?"

Deborah considered for a moment. "No, I don't think so. You never know, Ethan might decide he misses me. Besides, I didn't hear anything today that I hadn't already imagined. Not that I relish the idea of living in a haunted house, but I'd begun to think it had to be something more horrible and sinister, the way everyone was so secretive."

"In that case I'm glad it's out in the open now." Linda sucked the last of the soda out of the crushed ice. "Come on, I'll give you a lift."

At home Deborah looked in the mirror. It was obvious she'd been crying. Her eyes were still red-rimmed, her cheeks blotchy. She splashed cold water over her face and went outside to water the geraniums and wait for Carl.

The geraniums were growing nicely, filling out and producing new red blossoms almost daily. She plucked out the weeds that were sprouting between the plants. Maybe she hadn't been bothered by spirits because they liked her geraniums. She laughed, a short, nervous laugh, more like a hiccough, and chewed absently on her lower lip.

Carl's pickup truck ground to a stop against the curb. Carl pushed himself out of the cab and lumbered around to the back of the truck. He raised his arm to Deborah.

She waved back. She watched him open the tailgate, set up the ramp and guide the mower down. His chest and belly, covered in the customary gray T-shirt jiggled with his efforts. She wondered if Carl's wife ever used bleach.

Carl dragged the mower up the lawn to her. "How you doin'?" He leaned his arms on the mower's handle.

"Fine, and you?" Deborah was still gripping the watering can.

"Can't complain. Heat wave broke, thank God."

"Yeah, it's been lovely all week."

"Listen," Carl said, his voice lower, confidential, "I asked my kids about them stories. The ones about this house?"

Deborah nodded. Part of her wanted to hear, but another part wanted to run away and cover her ears.

Carl scratched his head. "You sure you wanna know this here stuff?"

She shrugged. "If I don't find out I'll just conjure up something worse," she said, hoping she was right.

"Well okay. The kids say there's the usual, things flying around, noises, but that ain't nothin' compared to the visions."

"What makes them so awful?" Deborah's voice cracked.

"It's a fire. All a' them people that's lived here seen it. An' it looks real, like you think the whole place is gonna burn down. But a' course it don't. An' in the middle of all them flames there's a man. All black and burning and screaming."

Carl's voice had risen with the telling. When he'd finished, the silence was still vibrating with his words.

A chill rippled through Deborah's body like a wave, starting at her scalp and flowing down to her feet. "Is that the only thing anyone's ever seen?" she asked in a small thin voice.

"According to the kids that's what they all seen. The same exact thing. A' course kids tend to exaggerate," he added, seeing how pale she'd become. "You ain't seen nothin', have ya?"

Deborah shook her head.

"Eh." Carl waved his hand in the air. "Maybe whatever it was is gone."

Deborah's mouth bent up in a crooked smile. "I exorcised them with my geraniums," she murmured.

"Huh? What's that?"

"Nothing. A private joke. Thanks for remembering, Carl."

"I think maybe I didn't do ya such a great favor."

"A favor's a favor. Now, how about some iced tea before you get to work?"

"Sure. But under the maple?" Carl grinned.

Chapter Sixteen

The stories had spooked Deborah more than she cared to admit. Not so much what Jeffrey had said. That had been vague enough to be catalogued and forgotten. But she couldn't get out of her mind Carl's description of the fire and the man burning alive. Fires had always been particularly frightening to her. The thought that she might awake any night to see the house in flames, and not know if it were real or an illusion, terrified her.

Ethan had said the original house had been razed by fire. He'd never mentioned if anyone had perished in that blaze. Besides, she thought, even if someone had, what did any of it have to do with the new house? All that remained of the old one was that root cellar. She'd been down inside it and nothing had happened to her, nothing supernatural anyway. Still, she'd like to ask Ethan whether he knew if anyone had died in the fire. That was, if she ever saw him again. Tomorrow would be Saturday. A week had passed. Another week loomed ahead. Tears were building up in her eyes.

"I am not going to cry anymore," she told herself sternly. "I hardly know the man. It's only been a week that he hasn't called. I'm acting like an imbecile. And there's no point in worrying about the house either. It's a perfectly fine house.

Whatever bothered those other people is gone, if it was ever here." She pulled on rubber gloves and started scrubbing the dishes from her dinner. "I'm not going to worry about things unless they happen." She wouldn't be like Edith who always worried in advance.

The doorbell rang. Deborah shut the faucet and pulled off the rubber gloves with a snap. Her eyes shot to her watch. Seven o'clock. It was still light out, but who would come by at this hour? Mrs. Hopkins was no doubt comfortably ensconced in her favorite chair in front of the television. Linda had mentioned something about a family dinner. Ethan was the only other possibility. Her heart seemed to be beating in her throat.

She smoothed back her hair, and wet her lips. She didn't have time to do anything more about her appearance.

She stopped to peek out the living room window on her way to the front door. It looked like a man standing there, but he was just beyond her range of vision. The bell rang again. If it was Ethan he was impatient. She pulled open the door, her lips spreading into a welcoming smile.

"Hi," said Jeffrey Pomeroy. His teeth sparkled, white and even, against his tanned skin.

Deborah's smile collapsed. It felt as if a rock had crushed everything inside of her. "Oh hi."

"I was in the neighborhood and I thought I'd stop by. See how you were."

Deborah nodded. "I'm fine." Why did that line sound so much less believable coming from Jeffrey, than it had when Ethan had used it?

"I mean, you seemed so upset and all at camp today. About the house." He was shifting his weight from foot to foot like a little boy. It occurred to Deborah that the tables had turned. She was making him uneasy. If she weren't disappointed she would have found the situation amusing.

"I meant it when I offered my company today," Jeffrey was saying.

"I'm sure you did." Deborah tried to sound polite and serious.

"Can I come in just for a little while?"

"I guess so." She showed him into the living room wondering how soon she could ask him to leave.

They stood in the middle of the room like two actors who'd forgotten their lines.

"Can I get you a cold drink or some coffee?" Deborah offered finally.

"No, no that's okay. I really don't want anything."

Deborah sat on one of the chairs. "So, Jeffrey, you're not afraid of ghosts and things that go bump in the night?"

Jeffrey grinned and perched on an arm of the couch. "I'm here."

"Why *are* you here?" Deborah asked, in an effort to keep the upper hand. "Aside from being in the neighborhood. I mean, let's face it, Rachael Crossing isn't much more than a neighborhood itself."

Jeffrey regarded her evenly. "You're a pretty woman. There aren't many pretty women around here. What you see are mostly old ladies and girls."

Deborah was the one unsettled again. "Girls. You mean like Linda?"

"Yeah."

"You aren't exactly a middle-aged man yourself," she reminded him.

Jeffrey leaned toward her. He dropped his voice as if he were letting her in on a secret. "You know what they say about younger men and older women."

"It doesn't work."

"No, they say that they're the most sexually compatible. Women don't reach their peak until their thirties. And by then men have. . . ."

"I've read the same articles, Jeffrey," she interrupted. "I was only being facetious. But I really don't feel like discussing that research right now."

"Oh sure. I didn't mean to—hey, how about we sit, relax, get to know each other. I brought something." He stood up and dug his hand into his hip pocket. It got caught at the second knuckle.

"That's the trouble with skin tight jeans," Deborah said sarcastically. She realized she was trying to make him uncomfortable, the way he usually made her feel. It was silly. Like a game they were playing. Yet it seemed to be the only way she could react to him.

Jeffrey just grinned and sucked in his breath. Using his other hand to hold the pocket open he finally withdrew a joint of marijuana.

"You got a match around?"

"So, Rachael Crossing comes of age," Deborah said dryly. "But I don't smoke. Tobacco or grass."

"Aw, you must be kidding! It's great for loosening up."

"I like being tense."

Jeffrey laughed. "You don't mind if I . . .?"

"Yes, as a matter of fact I do," she said. "I can't stand the smell of those things. They remind me of gray tiled bathrooms with wet clumps of brown paper towels lying in the sinks."

"Where you teach?"

She nodded.

"Maybe if you made love stoned sometimes you'd forget those other associations."

"I'm not so sure I'd like the new ones any better."

"Okay, say no more." Jeffrey stuffed the joint back into his pocket and dropped down onto the couch. "I don't suppose you believe in booze either."

"As a matter of fact I like mixed drinks. But I don't happen to have any liquor around. Either the last tenants took their scotch with them or the spirits have been into the spirits." Deborah couldn't help smiling over the bad pun.

"You do have a sense of humor after all," Jeffrey chuckled. "A little warped . . ."

"That's what happens when you get old."

"You're not old," he said soberly. "I could prove it to you, if you'd let me."

Deborah shook her head. "You're tenacious anyway."

"I don't give up easily either."

"Very cute."

"No, seriously, you're up here all alone for the summer. I'm here. Why shouldn't we have a few good times together? I'm not talking about commitments. I'm talking about fun."

"I'm sure you are." Deborah wondered if he'd come up

with his truth in advertising speech since his involvement with Linda. He'd obviously never made the arrangements quite so clear to her in the beginning. She looked at his smooth tanned face and the self-assurance in the curve of his mouth. Talk about a positive self-image. When someone rejected him he was probably more put out than hurt. If anyone had ever rejected him. The possibility of being the first appealed to Deborah. It would be interesting to see the mask crumble. Or at least crack a little.

"You don't have to spend every night alone in this place," Jeffrey was saying.

"From what you told me today, I've already got company."

"It's easy to joke when someone's here with you. I'll bet you're not so flip in the middle of the night."

Deborah felt her composure unravel like a loose thread. He was right. "Look Jeffrey," she said, "I'm not in need of handouts."

"I don't believe in charities. Why can't you take the offer for what it is?"

"Why can't you take the refusal for what it is?" Deborah looked for a reaction. But his white smile was constant. He was staring straight at her.

"I asked you first."

"Whether you know it or not, I answered you." She could hear the exasperation in her voice. She hoped he could too. The game was grating on her nerves.

Jeffrey held up his hands. "Okay, okay. But if you don't mind I'll take that coffee, if you're still offering it."

"You're not going to give up?"

"Coffee?"

"Coffee." Deborah stood up. "All I have is instant. It'll just take a few minutes to boil the water."

"Instant's fine."

Jeffrey leaned back in the couch. She was going to be harder than he'd thought. Or Linda may have queered it for him completely. The two of them seemed pretty chummy. But she was worth the additional effort, an enigma that intrigued him. She was gentle, quiet, almost to the point of being shy, but at the core a woman, mature and self-possessed.

He sniffed the air. There was a peculiar smell. Like something burning. What the hell was she doing—did she forget to put water in the kettle? No, the smell was coming from the wrong direction, from behind him. He stood up and spun around. There was nothing there, yet the smell was stronger. And then he saw it. A flame flicking around the hinges of the front door. It moved like a hand seeking a way inside. Jeffrey stood motionless for a moment watching the prying, poking flames as if he didn't quite believe what he was seeing.

"Deborah. Hey, Deborah," he called, searching the room for something to smother the fire with. She didn't answer. He pulled open a closet near the door and grabbed an old sheet off a pile on the top shelf. Keeping it folded to protect his hands, he batted at the flames. It took only a minute and it was out. Only a thin wisp of smoke curled in the air. He let the sheet fall onto the floor and bent to examine the place where the fire had been. He couldn't find any damage.

His face was only inches away when the flames shot out at him. He jumped back, the heat singeing his eyebrows and lashes. He grabbed the sheet again and pressed it against the door jamb. But each time he removed it the fire was still there, crackling and dancing; it seemed to taunt him for his impotence. Suddenly it leaped out, flashing around the door frame, spewing gusts of heat and smoke into his face. He drew back, coughing, fear beginning to pump through his body. This was no ordinary fire.

He turned to the kitchen, calling for Deborah. She had to have heard him, but still she didn't answer. Where was she? Was he alone? He looked back at the fire. It had engulfed the whole of the entrance foyer, the flames reaching out long tentacles to the stairs, devouring the curtains at the living room window, closing in, stalking him. It didn't make sense, and yet he knew it was true. He started to run toward the kitchen, but the flames had crept up behind him. He was surrounded.

Clouds of thick black smoke billowed out, filling all the corners of the room. He could barely see and the smoke was crowding the air out of his lungs. He screamed, but the scream was swallowed by an even more piercing shriek and he froze. From between the waves of flame a blackened form was advancing on him. A man. Or what was left of a man. Charred flesh hung in ragged patches from its bones, fluids oozed from enormous blisters. Flames swept up and down its length. There was no way it could be alive and yet it screamed. Crazy, subhuman screams.

The smoke carried the smell of the burning flesh. It seared his nostrils. When he opened his mouth to breathe, he gagged on the putrefying taste of it. The burning mass reached out toward him, inches away, and Jeffrey saw the bitter agony still reflected in the ruined wells that had once been its eyes. Jeffrey bolted, crashing through the ring of fire, his own screams echoing like thunder in his head.

At the kitchen doorway he slammed into Deborah. The tray she was holding flew out of her hands. Cups and saucers shattered. Hot coffee, milk and sugar splashed onto the walls and ran across the floor in muddy, gritty rivulets.

"What the hell . . .?" she sputtered.

Jeffrey grabbed her arm. "We gotta get out the back way." He was yanking her along behind him.

She pulled herself free. Her wrist was red from his grip. "What's the matter with you?" she yelled. "What are you talking about? Look at this mess!"

"The whole goddamned house is on fire and you're worried about a mess?! Didn't you hear me screaming for you? C'mon, now!"

"Fire? What fire?" Deborah peered into the living room, then back at Jeffrey wild-eyed and disheveled, holding open the back door and motioning hysterically for her to follow.

"Did someone slip you some angel dust, Jeffrey?"

His hand dropped off the door knob and he sniffed the air. "That can't be. I don't smell it anymore." He walked cautiously back to Deborah.

"Smell what?"

"The fire. The whole front of the house was in flames." Jeffrey looked into the living room, his eyes wide and incredulous, his mouth gaping open. The room was as it had been when he'd arrived, except for a sheet lying on the entry floor.

"It's not possible," he gasped. "The fire, the man, the

screaming—you didn't hear anything, see anything?" He searched her face.

Deborah shook her head. Her initial anger was gone. A fire and a burning man. Jeffrey had seen it. Or was he pretending he had, to frighten her into accepting his company? No, she didn't think he could act that well. He was gripping the kitchen door frame so tightly that his knuckles were white and his breathing was erratic and noisy.

"It's true." He swallowed loudly and exhaled. "I didn't believe it before. But now *I've* seen it. That, that thing, was inches away from me. I could have touched it. It looked so real. This goddamned place *is* haunted!"

Deborah felt peculiar. She wanted to laugh. Jeffrey had finally been bettered. The mask had not only cracked, it had disintegrated. But she was frightened, too. She couldn't ignore the stories anymore. Jeffrey had seen the ghost fire and maybe that dog had seen it also. There *was* some power at work in the house. It had spared her so far. But for how much longer? Maybe it was toying with her. Or maybe she was somehow immune to it.

"Do you have someplace else you can go?" Jeffrey asked, his voice tight and agitated.

"No. I mean, yes. I guess I could go to Linda's."

"I'll take you. Go get a few things, but make it fast. I'll wait for you here."

At least he had the courtesy not to run off and leave her stranded. But if she did go, coming back would be worse. No, it would be impossible. She couldn't spend the summer at Linda's house.

"No thank you, Jeffrey. I'm staying. No one's ever been hurt here," she added, remembering Linda's words and praying they were honest. "And I've never even seen this grand illusion." She tried to make her voice sound light.

Jeffrey was frowning, his face screwed up as if she were speaking a language he didn't understand. "You've got to be kidding. You're not really going to stay here?!"

"Yes. For now at least. I really am."

He shook his head. "You want me to help clean up before I go?" he asked halfheartedly.

"No, that's okay. I'll probably get it done faster myself. You go on."

"You're sure?"

"I'll call Linda if I chicken out."

"Okay. I'm sorry about all this." He started to walk out toward the living room, changed his mind and came back through the kitchen. "I'll use the back door," he mumbled as he passed her.

The door closed. Deborah knelt down and began picking up the larger shards of china. Wherever she moved sugar crunched beneath her.

Well, at least I managed to get rid of Jeffrey, she thought with a wry smile.

Chapter Seventeen

"What did you think of it?" Linda asked. She and Deborah were walking out the side exit of the movie theater into the parking lot. It was late afternoon, overcast with a fine mist hanging in the air. The rain had stopped, but the trees were still shedding water whenever the breeze picked up, like wet dogs shaking themselves.

"It wasn't bad. I don't usually go for slapstick. But I guess I needed to laugh today," Deborah said, looking down to avoid the puddles.

"Yeah, I have to be in the mood for it, too. Did you remember your umbrella?"

Deborah raised her left hand with the old black umbrella. "I only lose new umbrellas. Never the ones with the bent spokes and tattered edges. That's why I packed this one."

"Let's hope that's the end of the rain for a while. I don't feel up to another camp trip to the bowling alley." They had reached the car. Linda unlocked the doors.

"Amen," said Deborah, sliding in. "The last time we went there the thud of falling bowling balls was echoing in my head all night."

Linda started the engine. "Home? Or is there someplace else you'd rather go?"

"Home is fine, and Linda—thank you."

Linda backed the car out of the space. "For what? Keeping me company this weekend?"

"I honestly don't know how I would have gotten through these last two days if it hadn't been for you. So please don't try to dodge the credit."

Linda didn't reply until they had left the parking lot and were headed back toward Rachael Crossing. Then she turned and smiled at Deborah. "I'm your friend. No special thanks required." She looked back at the road. "Besides, if you want to thank someone, thank Jeffrey. If he hadn't called to tell me what happened, you probably would have stuck it out all alone the entire weekend."

Deborah shrugged. "I've never been very good at asking for help."

"That's what I mean." A light patter of rain was dotting the windshield. Linda switched on the wipers. "Who would have thought Jeffrey Pomeroy would be man enough to put our personal cold war aside and call me in order to help someone else?"

"Not me. Deep down under that even tan and perfect smile there must be a real human being."

Linda laughed. "If someone has a knack for scrounging."

They rode quietly, the rain tapping on the roof of the car and splashing under the tires. Deborah stared at the concentric arcs the wipers were drawing across the windshield.

After a few minutes Linda broke the silence. "I don't know how you stood it alone there Friday night."

"I barely did," Deborah replied, shuddering. At first I tried keeping busy. At bedtime I didn't even change. I wanted to be ready in case I had to leave in a hurry. I lay down fully dressed. I only dozed off a few times. And everytime I woke up my heart was pounding and I expected to see the house in flames."

"Were you okay last night?"

"Better. I tried to keep my mind on Ethan. It's painful, but at least it's not scary. And after all, I never really saw anything. Jeffrey's the one who'll probably be having nightmares for a while. Who knows, maybe it was only his imagination working overtime anyway. In all the excitement," Deborah interrupted herself, "I forgot to tell you—I went to see Mr. Darcy last week."

"Old Man Darcy? Why?"

"Well, at the time I wasn't getting any answers from anyone else," Deborah said wryly. "So I thought he might help me."

"But you seemed so surprised when Jeffrey told you."

"I was. Darcy wasn't exactly a fountain of information. His mind wanders and he falls asleep in the middle of a sentence."

"He wasn't terrifying?" Linda asked incredulously.

"Not at all. Pathetic is the word that comes to mind. Disappointed?"

"I think so. You've just unmasked the Lone Ranger. You know how kids love to be scared and hate to be scared at the same time."

"Personally I'm glad he wasn't frightening. Nightmares come easily enough to me."

"Well at least you got that out of your system."

"I'm going back."

"Why?"

"Maybe he'll have a more lucid day. There's got to be a ton of information stored away in those old brain cells."

Deborah walked straight up to the front door without hesitation. She had tucked a small notebook and pen into her pocketbook before leaving her house, thinking that if she wrote down Darcy's ramblings to study later, she might get more out of her visit. She rang the bell and waited. They were probably out back in the rose garden.

Mrs. Brinks opened the door and smiled. "Hello, Miss Colby. How nice to see you again. Won't you come in?"

Deborah saw that she was wearing gardening gloves and a dirt-smudged apron over her uniform. "If you're sure I won't be disturbing you," she said.

"Oh, not at all. I was just puttering around with my roses."

Deborah followed her out to the garden. It was as beautiful and fragrant as she remembered. The soil between the bushes was freshly turned and lent a healthy, pungent odor to the air. She could see that Darcy was sitting in the same chair, his head, with its ring of white hair, rising above it.

"Have a seat," said Mrs. Brinks. Then she winked at Deborah and added. "I'll get the lemonade and his teeth."

Deborah came around to face the old man. He looked as if he hadn't moved at all during the past two weeks. As if he had sat right there in that chair in suspended animation waiting for her to return. A wax figure with a tape-recorded voice that spoke when the appropriate button was pushed. The illusion lasted only a minute. Then Darcy turned to her.

"Hello, Mr. Darcy," she said. "I'm Deborah Colby. Do you remember me? I came to see you two weeks ago."

His shirred lips effected a smile, but his eyes regarded her blankly.

"I've come back to hear some of those stories of yours," she said.

A flicker of memory lit his eyes.

"Yes, Deborah, right," he mumbled. "Have a seat. Where's Brinks with my teeth?" He twisted his head around to look for her.

She was coming onto the patio with the tray of lemonade. She set it on the table in front of them. "Here you go, Mr. Darcy." She helped him on with the dentures.

"Good," he said gruffly and waved her off.

She told Deborah to please help herself to the lemonade and went back to weeding her garden.

Deborah withdrew her notebook and pen and asked if Darcy minded her taking notes.

"Not at all," said the old man. His chest puffed out a bit and he seemed to sit up straighter in his chair.

"Can you tell me when and how Rachael Crossing was settled?" Deborah asked, hoping to lead him to talk of the first house on Foxton Lane.

Darcy's knobby shoulders lifted and dropped. "There ain't much to tell. Wasn't even a town 'til, let's see," he stared down at his lap, "the late eighteen hundreds," he said finally, satisfied with his memory.

Deborah had her hand poised to write, but she relaxed it. "I thought it was much older than that."

Darcy frowned at her. "You think I don't know what I'm talking about, Missy?"

Deborah checked herself. She'd have to be a lot more careful with her remarks if she planned on learning anything. "Oh no, Mr. Darcy, I was just surprised. That's all. I obviously have even more to learn that I'd thought."

"Hmmm," he grumbled and turned to watch Mrs. Brinks work.

"How did it get started at all?" she inquired.

He didn't respond right away, and Deborah wasn't sure if he had heard her or if he were ignoring her. She was about to repeat her question when he turned back to her.

"It started as a few houses that needed a grocery store closer than Salem. And it ain't a heck of a lot more 'n that today."

He appeared bored with the subject. Deborah knew she'd have to encourage him to choose his own topic, before he lost interest completely. But she had to ask one more question.

"When was the oldest house in Rachael Crossing built?"

Darcy nodded approvingly as if she were an errant student who had finally caught on. "Now that goes back quite a ways further 'n the town," he said. "The first house was up on the rise. They call it Foxton Lane now. Not the house you see there today. No, the first one went back to the seventeenth century, it did. A much smaller house to be sure."

From the way he was speaking, Deborah sensed he didn't remember that she was living there. But she didn't want to break his train of thought, so she said nothing.

"Burned it down to the ground they did. That witch thought she'd tricked them all with her black riddles. But she was wrong." He paused to lick his lips. "I'm getting awful dry."

Deborah had been jotting down notes, but she stopped abruptly. "Witch?" she echoed. "One of the Salem witches?"

"Brinks, how about some of that lemonade?" Darcy called out.

Vera Brinks put down her trowel and pulled off her work

gloves. "Yes, Mr. Darcy," she said, straightening up. "I do wish you'd occasionally say please." She poured them both lemonade and then returned to her garden.

Deborah drank hers quickly, eager to get on with the story. The mention of the witch had fired her curiosity. What did the old house have to do with witches? Had Ethan's great ancestor, living on that hill miles from Salem, played a part in the Salem witch trials? Could he have been one of its victims? The old root cellar she had explored might have belonged to a convicted witch, she realized, as well as the ring she had found inside it. She wondered if Ethan knew what had happened to his forebear. The whole prospect intrigued her. She didn't believe in the evil powers of witches, but the witch trials themselves were irresistably fascinating.

She tapped her pencil impatiently in her palm while the old man sipped his lemonade, smacking his thin lips between tastes. Finally he stretched a shaky hand forward and put his glass down on the table.

"Mr. Darcy," said Deborah.

He turned to her and seemed surprised to see her there. "Oh, yes," he said after a moment. "Where were we?"

"You were telling me about the witch and the house that was burned."

"Witch, witch," he repeated in a faded, searching voice. "Nobody believes in 'em anymore."

Deborah tried to help him focus on the story, but he seemed unable to pick up the thread of it. He was becoming peevish and she could feel her own frustration growing. It would probably be best to leave it for another day, she reasoned.

Reluctantly she put her notebook and pen back in her pocketbook and stood. She thanked Mr. Darcy for his time and told him how much she'd enjoyed listening to him and that she'd be back soon.

He smiled at her with the same benign smile and empty eyes.

She was at her front door rummaging through her pocketbook when the telephone started ringing. She found her keys and struggled to get the door open. She raced in and grabbed the receiver breathlessly.

"Don't tell me you've taken up jogging, too," said Edith.

"No, I just got in," Deborah replied. She'd managed to forget about Ethan for a few hours. At least until she heard the phone ringing. Now her disappointment came back in a flood.

"Overtime at camp?"

"Visiting a friend." She tried to sound cordial. She wasn't up to a quarrel.

"Listen, Deborah, the reason I'm calling is, Hal and I would like to come up and see you this weekend. If that's all right with you?"

Company for the weekend. She could even stand Edith if it meant company. "Great. I'd love it," she said with genuine enthusiasm. She could hear muffled words being exchanged and Hal took the phone.

"Hello, Deborah. You're sure you haven't made any other plans for the weekend?"

"No. None at all. It'll be wonderful to see you both again."

"Okay. We'll leave early in the morning. See you for lunch. Don't you fuss with anything. Do you understand?"

"Yes. I'll see you tomorrow."

Deborah was surprised at how happy she was that they were coming. "I'm in worse shape than I thought," she murmured to herself. "Wouldn't it be funny if Ethan just happened to show up tomorrow, too? Edith would flip. So would I." The prospect wasn't likely.

She went into the kitchen to make dinner. What if the apparition appeared while Edith and Hal were visiting, she realized with sudden horror. She had no control over it. Then she remembered her pledge not to worry in advance and tried to put the awful possibility out of her mind.

She sat down with her dinner. She'd think about Old Man Darcy instead. She wanted to go back to see him soon, maybe even Monday after camp. She'd have to be careful about pumping him for specific information. He wouldn't open up to her unless he believed she was interested in all of his stories. Which she was, to a lesser degree. She'd be the surrogate son. She'd let him ramble and tell her things as he remembered them. Just guide him with a remark or an observation. She chewed the last forkful, satisfied with her plan. She stood to clear the table and had to grab the back of the chair to steady herself. She was suddenly dizzy and her head was throbbing in a peculiar way. She took a few deep breaths and felt better. But as she was washing the dishes, the throbbing began again and her stomach was pulsing in rhythm with it. She reached for the dish towel to dry her hands. There was no time. She raced for the small bathroom.

Chapter Eighteen

Deborah felt limp the next morning. "Fine time to get a stomach virus," she groaned and pushed herself out of bed. She'd decided before falling asleep that she'd better try to keep Edith and Hal away from the house as much as possible. The less time they spent there, the less chance they'd see an apparition. If the weather held, a picnic at the common could occupy most of Saturday.

She looked toward the windows. Sunlight was streaming in around the edges of the shades. At least the weather was on her side. She pulled on a blouse and her jeans and she went downstairs to the kitchen. She made herself some toast, although she wasn't hungry, and she felt better after eating it.

She spent the morning frying chicken for the picnic, trying not to dwell on memories of another picnic, and straightening the house so that Edith wouldn't have too much ammunition for her complaints. In spite of her efforts, her mind kept returning to that Saturday three weeks ago when it had been Ethan she'd been waiting for. The longing ache for him seeped into every inch of her body, like a chemical carried in her blood.

The doorbell rang almost precisely at noon. Edith rushed in before the door was completely open, enveloping Deborah in a hug.

"Take it easy, Edith, you'll smother the poor girl," said Hal, walking in around them and setting down an overnight case.

Edith moved away, studying Deborah while Hal embraced her briefly.

"Are you all right, Deborah?" she asked, the fine lines across her forehead deepening. "You look awfully pale."

"I had a little upset stomach last night. But I'm fine today." Deborah said, trying to sound healthy. She turned to Hal. "How was your trip up?"

"Smooth once we got out of New York."

Edith crinkled her lips. "You ought to try to get a little sun," she said.

Deborah ignored the comment. "Come on, I'll show you your room and you can put your things away."

"House smells better than it did," Edith said, sniffing as they climbed the stairs.

Hal was sniffing too. "Smells like fried chicken, actually."

"You got it," Deborah grinned. "You always did have a perceptive nose."

"I thought we told you not to fuss," said Edith.

"I didn't fuss. I just thought we'd have a picnic. The town has a beautiful park. They call it a common up here. You'll love it."

"Sounds good to me," Hal said quickly.

Deborah stopped at the bedroom across from hers. "Here's your room. I put fresh sheets on this morning. The bathroom's just down the hall."

An hour later they were at the common. They spread the sheet they'd brought along and set out the food.

"So, Deborah, are you having a good summer?" Hal asked, opening a cold beer.

Deborah smiled. He always made Edith tolerable. "It's been a change, an interesting one. I've met some nice people. And I have one really good friend."

"Good, I'm glad you haven't been disappointed. It certainly seems lovely enough here, in spite of what your sister says." He gave her a "What can you do?" smile and finished his beer.

"Any men among those 'nice people'?" Edith inquired.

"One or two," Deborah replied evenly. Edith probably wouldn't agree, but then her yardstick was different. Jeffrey had turned out to be more of a friend than she'd anticipated. And Ethan. Well, even if she never saw him again, she wasn't sorry she'd been in Rachael Crossing to meet him. It was nice to know that the kind of man she'd always dreamed of really did exist somewhere.

"Oh?" Edith's eyes twinkled in their sun-parched sockets. "So tell me about him, them."

"There isn't much to tell. I'm not ready to register my silver pattern at Tiffany's." Deborah was sorry for the acidity of her tone. Edith's face had fallen like a tire deflating in slow motion. "I'm sorry. But I know how much you want to see me married, and I guess it's become a sore point."

Edith put her hand on Deborah's arm. "No, I'm sorry. It's like I say to the kids, 'If I didn't love you I wouldn't nag you.' " She smiled and sighed at the same time.

"If it's any help I could tell you I haven't seen one eligible man at the club so far this summer."

"Now that's a relief!" Hal said with mock sobriety. "Lord only knows what Deborah might have done if she'd let her big chance slip by."

Deborah laughed. Even Edith allowed a hoarse, half-hearted chuckle.

"Can you at least tell me a name or something? I promise not to mention it to anyone."

Deborah thought for a moment. There was no harm in giving her a few details. "Ethan. His name is Ethan," she said and she told Edith briefly about him. But as she talked she realized how little she knew him, how abruptly he moved in and out of her life, his presence all-consuming and hypnotic. Her attempts to describe him failed miserably, the ordinary words unable to capture the way his eyes and smile reached inside of her. She brought herself up short, hoping her emotions weren't as transparent as they felt.

"But he may be out in L.A. for good now," she concluded more evenly.

Edith shook her head. "What a pity. I'm glad to hear you're not upset. I guess it's a good thing you didn't get too involved with him." She started packing away the leftovers.

Deborah could feel Hal's gaze on her. She turned to him. She hadn't fooled him. He'd always been able to read her like a barometer. She smiled weakly. He nodded and stood up.

"Think I'll take a little stroll around the park, ladies. The common, I mean."

Edith seized the opportunity to launch into the latest gossip from suburbia. Deborah leaned back against the trunk of the maple, her eyes drifting closed. She didn't realize Carl was there until Edith's droning had come to an abrupt stop and she heard Carl's distinctive hello. No one else in Rachael Crossing sounded like that. Her eyes flew open.

Carl was standing next to her, a grin pushing up his clean-shaven jowls. His undershirt was covered by a red plaid sport shirt that was pulling open at his stomach. He bobbed his head. "How ya doin'?"

"Oh, hi, Carl." Deborah sat upright. "Fine, just fine." She introduced him to Edith and they exchanged greetings. "My sister and brother-in-law are up from New York visiting for the weekend."

"Long Island, actually," said Edith.

"That's nice."

Deborah wished he would just bob his head again and say good-bye before something slipped out about the house. But Carl wasn't picking up on her thoughts. He was pointing out his wife who was sitting about twenty-five feet away. Carl waved to get her attention. She waved back. Carl pointed to Deborah. She waved at Deborah. Deborah waved back, wondering why he hadn't just brought her over to introduce her.

"My kids are down by them there peddle boats," he said. "Can't get enough of 'em."

Deborah smiled. "Well, it's nice seeing you and your wife here." She hoped that hadn't sounded too much like "Here's your hat, what's your hurry." Apparently it hadn't.

"You got quite a sister here," Carl said to Edith, stuffing his hands into his trouser pockets as if he were preparing for a long chat. "Explores old root cellars, digs up stories to scare herself silly." He laughed. "But she's a nice gal all the same. Never forgets to offer me a cold drink."

"It's the least I can do," Deborah said quickly. "We've had some pretty hot days. How has it been on the Island?" she asked Edith.

"Hot enough. What's this about root cellars and scary stories? What does he mean, Deborah?"

"Oh, I found an old root cellar behind the house. That's all." Deborah sent Carl a furtive, pleading glance. "You know, the historian in me coming out."

Edith was about to ask another question.

"Carl," Deborah cut her off, "we shouldn't be keeping you. I think I saw your wife motioning for you."

Carl looked toward his wife. She was rummaging through a picnic hamper. "Yeah, uh, well," he turned back to them, "it's been nice meetin' you." He bobbed his head at Edith. "I hope you and your husband have a good time here. I've gotta be goin'. I'll see ya Friday, Deborah."

"Take care, Carl." Deborah didn't like being impolite, but the conversation had to be stopped. She'd apologize on Friday. She hoped he'd understand.

At that moment Hal returned from his walk, curious about who Carl was, and Deborah was spared any further questions about scary stories and root cellars.

She crawled into bed that night exhausted and grateful. The day was over. No one had seen a fire or heard a howling spirit. Edith had gone to her room, too. Hal was still dozing in front of the television in the living room. They planned on leaving before lunchtime on Sunday. Then, Deborah knew, she could really sigh with relief.

She turned from side to side, but as tired as she was, she couldn't fall asleep. Carl had reminded her of the root cellar and by association, the ring. She didn't like thinking about the ring. Whenever she did she had an uneasy feeling. It was like listening to a piece of music in which one note was wrong, and not being able to figure out which one. She tried to put it out of her mind, willing herself to sleep, when she heard Edith scream.

Deborah flew out of bed and down the hall, her robe

hanging from one arm tripping her, her mind conjuring up images of flames and charred bodies. She reached the door to Edith's room. Hal was running up the stairs. There hadn't been any screams after the first one. Deborah expected to find her sister in a fainted heap. But she was sitting on the edge of one of the twin beds holding her hand to her chest as if she were preventing her heart from leaping out.

Deborah quickly scanned the room. Everything seemed to be in its place. No grotesque forms or nightmare visions. But then she hadn't been able to see the ghost fire that scared Jeffrey either. She knelt beside her. "Edith, what happened?" Her voice was shaking. She was afraid to hear what her sister would say. Hal came up beside them.

"What the hell was that about? Are you all right?" He was staring at them with the wide, unfocused eyes of someone who was still half asleep and fighting to think clearly.

Edith nodded and pointed to the window. Deborah and Hal swung their heads in that direction, Deborah expecting to see an apparition staring back. The shade was still up. The window frames held empty darkness.

"I went to pull down the shade," Edith said between heavy breaths. "And I found myself staring into this furry face. I think it was a raccoon. Scared the daylights out of me, I can tell you that."

Chapter Nineteen

"What are you going to do?" Linda asked. She and Deborah were leaning against the window ledge in the large, all-purpose room while their campers worked on arts and crafts projects.

Deborah sighed. "I guess I could go on worrying for a while longer. Or I could go to see a doctor.

"Look, it's probably all because of nerves, but it couldn't hurt to see a doctor anyway. At least he'd be able to put your mind to rest."

"That's what I've been telling myself for the past two weeks, only I'm not so sure that what he's going to tell me will put my mind to rest. I've never skipped or been this late before in my life." She laughed uneasily. "I'm even half hoping I've just started going through my changes early." She turned away abruptly, struggling with tears.

Outside a patchwork sky of white, gray and black clouds spread a dull, uneven light that seemed as depressed as her spirits. Why did things in her life always work out by half measures? Why had she fallen so desperately in love with Ethan if it was just to lose him? And why, if she were finally going to have a child, couldn't the circumstances have brought her happiness and not the fear akin to panic that gripped her now?

"If Ethan were still here it would all be so wonderfully simple," she said, turning back to Linda with a rueful smile. The concern and sympathy that she saw on Linda's face were so genuine that tears rushed into Deborah's eyes again.

"He may still come back."

Deborah shook her head. "If you could have seen that look in his eyes. He was so sad."

"You mean like he knew he'd be leaving?"

"More than that—as if he knew it and had no control over it. I know it doesn't sound the least bit sensible," she added sheepishly. "And maybe I'm just trying to defend him. I love him so, I want to believe it's not his fault that he's gone." She paused for a long moment. "Do you know of a good doctor around here?" she resumed evenly.

Linda was relieved to hear Deborah's tone return to the reasonable one she knew. "Yes. My mother's used this one doctor over in Salem forever. She swears by him. I've been to him myself a couple of times for routine exams. He's a nice grandfatherly type."

"In my case make that fatherly type. If he were my grandfather he'd probably be in a nursing home."

Linda smiled. "I'm glad to see you haven't lost your sense of humor."

"I'll let you know after I see this doctor—what's his name?"

"Jansen. You really ought to call for an appointment as soon as possible. He's usually booked two weeks in advance."

"There goes relieving my mind," Deborah groaned.

"No, tell the nurse it's an emergency, she'll squeeze you in. In fact, why don't you go down the hall and call right now? The kids are busy and I can handle it alone for ten minutes."

"You're sure?"

"Go ahead. You'll be able to find the number in the book. Dr. Jansen."

She located Dr. Jansen's number in the directory. While

she was rummaging through her purse for change, she heard footsteps coming down the hallway toward her. She found a dime. The footsteps had become two distinct sets. The second a rubbery squish-squashing sound. She was beginning to pick up voices, too.

"Can you imagine," one was saying. "He actually told her what he'd seen and she refused to leave with him."

Deborah didn't hear any reply.

"The fire and the burning man, the whole thing," said the first voice again. "If I had any doubts before, I don't anymore. Some things are better left unexplored."

"She's either brave or crazy, the poor thing," a second, smaller voice remarked. "She'd have to be one or the other. . . ." The voice trailed off as Rose Bennington and Eleanor Sharpe rounded the corner and saw Deborah at the phone.

Deborah smiled sweetly, pretending she hadn't overheard them. They smiled and nodded and hurried off down the hall in silence.

Apparently everyone knew about Jeffrey's experience at her house. Well, there was no reason for him not to talk about it. And if he hadn't told everyone yet, Rose and Eleanor would surely take care of the rest. So I'll be the crazy lady, she thought humorlessly. I always did want to be distinctive and interesting. She inserted the dime and dialed.

After a few moments, Deborah was speaking to a receptionist with a cheerful, birdlike voice. Charging her voice with as much urgency as she could, Deborah explained that she wasn't feeling well, that she might be pregnant and needed to see the doctor. The receptionist was very sorry, but the earliest Dr. Jansen could possibly see her would be a week from Tuesday. Deborah calculated quickly. Twelve days.

"However, Dr. Jansen does have an associate now," the receptionist went on. "Dr. Gates. He could see you at ten fifteen this Saturday morning, if you'd like."

"Ten fifteen Saturday? Uh, yes, okay." Anything was better than two more weeks of waiting.

"And it would simplify matters if you could bring a urine

specimen to a lab on Friday. That way Dr. Gates will have the results when he sees you.''

"Does it matter which lab?"

"No. Just give them the doctor's name and they'll call us. And be sure the specimen is the first of the morning.''

Deborah thanked her and hung up the phone. Specimen, lab test. Suddenly the vague possibility of being pregnant was taking on a disturbingly concrete shape.

Chapter Twenty

Deborah checked to make sure she hadn't missed any buttons on her blouse and that her skirt was zipped up all the way. Then she let herself out of the tiny examining room. Dr. Gates had told her to come into his office after she was dressed. The room at the end of the corridor looked like an office. The door was open. Deborah walked toward it.

A nurse was sitting at a desk tucked into a corner just outside the office. She was writing on a form inside a manila folder, but she looked up as Deborah approached.

"Go right on in, dear," she said. "Dr. Gates will be with you in a minute."

Deborah sat in a chrome armchair. This is where you hear the good news or the bad, she thought, her stomach throbbing anxiously. She looked at the paintings on the walls and tried not to think about it.

The door clicked closed and Dr. Gates crossed the room. He came around the desk and sat in his leather chair. Deborah's folder was on his blotter. He opened it and glanced at the single sheet inside it.

Deborah's hands had been ice cold in the examining room. Now they were perspiring. She slid the palms along her skirt to dry them and tried to arrange her features into a serene, confident expression.

Dr. Gates looked up at her. "Well, Ms. Colby, your examination corroborates the test results. You are definitely pregnant." He paused as if to allow time for her reaction.

Was she supposed to act either jubilant or despondent? Actually she only felt stunned. As much as she had considered the possibility that she might be pregnant, she had never really accepted it.

"It's still very early in the pregnancy of course," Gates went on. "And I'm sure you're aware of the options open to you."

Deborah nodded.

"If you decide to have this baby, I would have to advise you that first pregnancies at your age can have complications. However, you appear to be in fine health and in all probability the risks would be minimal. I would want to perform an amniocentesis in order to rule out Down's Syndrome."

"Mongolism," Deborah murmured hoarsely.

Dr. Gates folded his hands together on top of her folder. "Yes; well the age of the mother does seem to be a definite factor in the incidence of Down's Syndrome."

"The alternative is an abortion," Deborah said in a thin voice, as if to herself.

"Yes. It's quite a decision to make and unfortunately you haven't much time to think about it. If you decide on an abortion I'd suggest you have it done as soon as possible."

Deborah tried to wet her lips, but her tongue was dry. She nodded again.

Gates closed her folder and stood. "Whatever you decide, give me a call Monday or Tuesday and we'll take it from there, okay?"

Deborah said she would and thanked him.

"Ms. Colby, Deborah, it's not the end of the world no matter what you decide."

She forced a smile, but only half of her mouth responded, as if she'd had novocaine.

Linda was sitting in the waiting room thumbing through a

magazine. She looked up the moment Deborah came through the door.

"I was beginning to think they'd sold you into bondage," she whispered.

"I think the nurse put me in an examining room and forgot where I was. It's like a maze in there."

They walked out through the halls of the single story medical building and out to the parking lot.

"So, how was Dr. Gates?" Linda asked.

Deborah shrugged. "He seemed okay. Competent, I mean. But there ought to be a law against gynecologists being young, tall, dark and reasonably handsome."

"Not the grandfatherly type."

"A good ten years my junior."

"I think I'll stick to Dr. Jansen in that case." Linda unlocked the car door and they slid in.

"Aren't you going to ask me what he said?"

"I was being polite and waiting for you to tell me. But I'm dying of curiosity."

"And I'll burst if I don't talk to someone," Deborah groaned.

"Now that doesn't sound like you. Is it bad?"

"That all depends on your point of view. I'm pregnant. He said it's definite."

Linda turned away from the road long enough to study Deborah's face. Her features were relaxed and expressionless, except for the troubled, dark-lashed eyes.

"Do you want to go someplace where we can talk?"

"Okay."

"We'll be passing Baynor's Inn. We can stop there for lunch. My treat. And if you argue you walk home."

"Did Dr. Gates recommend an abortion?" Linda asked when they were settled in the restaurant.

"I'm not even sure I heard all he was saying after he gave me the initial news. It was like getting thumped on the head with a blunt instrument and waiting to pass out. I was dazed."

"You didn't get the feeling that he was in favor of one option over the other?"

Deborah drank some water. Her throat was dry and hot. "He pretty much said the decision was mine, if I understood him correctly. Thirty-seven isn't exactly an ideal age to have a first child, not to mention my marital and financial status, which we didn't even touch on. But it's also not an impossibility since I'm basically healthy. He did say he'd do an amniocentesis to check for Down's Syndrome." Her lips bent up in a wry smile. "It seems the decision rests completely with me. I was kind of hoping he would say point blank, 'You're too old, forget it.' "

"Then it sounds like what you really want is an abortion."

Deborah shook her head. "Logically I know that's the only solution. Yet I can't accept it quite that nonchalantly. You don't know how much I always wanted children. But when I hit thirty without any prospects, I went through some rough times learning to accept the possibility that I might remain single and never have a child. I thought I'd made peace with myself on that score. And now this. I feel like a laboratory rat with a piece of cheese dangling in front of him." She paused while their food was served.

"I don't know if I'm strong enough to surrender this last chance." Deborah looked down at the pyramid of fruit and cottage cheese on her plate.

"You talk about strength," Linda said. "It's not easy to raise a kid today, let alone all by yourself. Are you strong enough to hack that?" she asked.

Deborah had dislodged a wedge of cantalope. She had the fork midway to her mouth, but she dropped it back to the plate. "You don't think I should have the baby, then."

"It doesn't matter what I think. To be perfectly honest, if you seemed bent on an abortion I'd probably be reminding you of the opportunity you were denying yourself. I'm trying to play the devil's advocate to help you see both sides. That's all I can do. I can't make the decision for you any more than Dr. Gates could. The only one who can legitimately help you decide is Ethan. Is there any chance of that?"

"You know as much as I do. I haven't heard from him. Not a word in four weeks. I don't even know where to reach him. And if I did I wouldn't try. To tell you the truth, and I know this is going to sound crazy, I was never completely sure he was even with me that night. At times I thought maybe I had dreamed it all." She laughed bleakly. "At least now I know I didn't."

Deborah ate quietly for a few minutes, chewing and swallowing without tasting the food, then she pushed her plate away.

"Isn't it any good?"

"It's fine. I'm just not very hungry these days," she said, a sob half hidden in her voice. She covered her face with her hands. "This kind of thing happens to teen-agers. Not to thirty-seven-year-old spinsters."

"You need some time to think it all through," Linda said gently. "You'll make the right decision, I'm sure of it."

Deborah moved her hands away. There were tears caught on her lashes. "Dr. Gates wants me to decide by Tuesday; the sooner the better for an abortion."

Linda nodded.

"Will you come with me if I have it done?" Deborah asked in a small, defeated voice.

"You know you don't have to ask."

They rode back to Rachael Crossing in silence, listening to the radio. Linda stopped the car in front of the old house and Deborah stepped out.

"I'll do you a favor," she said, "I won't invite you in."

Linda grinned. "Thank you."

"Thanks for everything, especially the ear."

"Sure. Listen, I don't want to bother you—you call me if you want someone to talk to."

Deborah nodded. "You'll be the first to know the momentous decision." She sighed. "I guess we both know it already." She pushed the door closed and watched Linda drive off. Then she turned and started up the cracked walk to the house. In spite of everything it had begun to feel like home. But today it seemed only vaguely familiar, locked in a strange silence like something seen in the shadows of a recurring dream. Her whole simple, straightforward life had been turned upside down. She hardly knew herself anymore. How could she be expected to make such a decision alone?

But she had to. No one could make it for her. Although Edith probably would, if she asked her to. Edith, New York, her teaching position. They seemed impossibly far away. As if they existed on a different plane entirely.

Deborah unlocked the door and was about to go inside, when she picked up a flash of movement. Ethan was coming around the side of the house toward her.

Chapter Twenty-one

She watched him approach, an unexpected anger subduing her initial excitement. She could see the easy, boyish smile curving his lips, so incongruous with the grave, penetrating eyes. She was angry that he could treat her this casually and expect her to be glad he'd returned. Maybe he had other women in other towns who would be. But he was wrong if he thought he could add her name to the list. All she had prayed for over the past weeks was to see him again. Now that he was here, part of her wanted to run to him and fall into his arms, and another part of her wanted to lash out at him. She waited, trying to compose herself. Her face felt like stone.

"Hi, I was about to give up on you," he called out while he was still several yards away. "I've been sitting in the backyard for hours."

"I was out . . . shopping," she said. She had no intention of telling him about the baby. At least not until she knew exactly where she stood with him.

Ethan came up to her, cocking his head to one side and studying her, the smile playing across his features. "You weren't too successful," he remarked.

For a second Deborah didn't know what he meant, then she realized she wasn't carrying any packages.

"I was browsing through antique shops actually. And what I liked I couldn't afford."

Ethan let it go and nodded to the open door. "Are you going to invite me in? I could use a cold drink."

"Yes, of course." Deborah walked in first and headed for the kitchen. "If you'd phoned to say you were coming I could have arranged to be here," she said pointedly.

"It was a last-minute decision. Some meetings I had for the weekend fell through. I packed a few things, hopped a cab to the airport and was able to catch a plane back. I got in at three this morning. Hardly the best time to call someone."

Deborah opened the refrigerator. "Is iced tea all right? That's all I have ready."

"Fine."

She filled two glasses and handed him one. "You're only in for the weekend?"

"Umhmmm," he murmured while he drank.

She watched him, absorbed in every subtle movement, in spite of herself. "Kind of a long trip for such a short stay," she said, fighting to maintain her reserve.

Ethan drained the glass and put it down on the counter. "I came to see you."

Her throat constricted, making it **hard** to swallow the tea. She cleared it as calmly as she could and sat down on one of the kitchen chairs.

"Forgive me if I don't take you too seriously. But it does seem a little strange that you would fly three thousand miles to see me, when you haven't even bothered picking up a phone to speak to me in a month."

Ethan straddled a chair next to hers. "I don't bother much with those things," he said.

"Well, I do," she replied petulantly, running her finger around the wet ring her glass had left on the table. "When I didn't hear from you I assumed I wouldn't see you again."

"You were wrong." He put his hand over hers. "I know you're angry, but don't ask me to leave."

She had been angry. Where was that anger now? It had

deserted her. Vanished at the first touch of his hand. She could feel herself being drawn irresistibly to him again, and she was losing the will to fight it.

She slid her hand out from beneath his, picked up her glass and took it to the sink. "I won't," she said, her back to him.

Ethan came up behind her. He put his hands on her shoulders and pressed his cheek against the back of her head. Then he turned her around to kiss her. Tears glistened in her dark eyes, but she managed a weak smile and tilted her chin up to him, the tears weaving between their cheeks and into their open mouths.

They sat on the couch in the living room. Deborah had her feet tucked up and was leaning against him, her head resting on his chest. The pressure of his arm around her, his breath on her hair, the rhythm of his heart soothed her. She wished she could preserve the feeling. Laminate it and hang it from a key chain, she thought, and suppressed a giggle.

"Well, that sounds better," Ethan said, kissing the top of her head. "What are you thinking about?"

"It's silly. Just a silly thought. When do you have to go back?"

"Monday morning."

She suddenly didn't feel silly anymore. "Are you going to stay with me until then?" she asked timidly.

"Is that an invitation?"

She nodded, rubbing her head up and down against his chest.

"Good. Because I don't have anywhere else to stay."

"How did you get here? Where's your car?"

"The car is in the garage in Boston. I've been using taxis to and from the airports. My suitcase is out back."

"Will you be gone a long time again?"

"I can't say. I'm still trying to sign a few of the big companies. You know," he said dryly, "for a quiet girl you have an awful lot of questions." With his free hand he angled her head back and kissed her. "I hope we're not going to spend the next day and a half talking."

Deborah was about to defend her curiosity, but he put his mouth over hers again.

* * *

The early morning sun lit the room with muted colors. Deborah opened one eye and looked at the clock—six. She'd forgotten to draw the shades last night. She lay on her stomach, the sheets at an angle across her bare back. She could feel the warmth of his body inches away and hear the peaceful, even sounds of his breathing. She remained very still for a long while, reluctant to disturb the contentment she felt, allowing her hazy mind to wander through the memories of the night.

They had stayed on the couch, talking, kissing, touching until evening. They'd snacked on cheese and fruit and then gone upstairs to Deborah's room, where they'd made love on the soft old mattress. The memories lingered with such intensity that she could still feel the touch of his hands, his lips on her, as if they'd made indelible impressions on her flesh. If that first night he had been gentle and restrained, catering to her needs, this time he had nearly overpowered her with his own. Engulfing her in his arms, crushing his mouth against her as if he couldn't get close enough to her. But instead of being frightened by his passion, Deborah had found it exciting. Proof that he had missed her and needed her too. She'd fallen asleep in his arms awakening a short while later to the sweet luxury of his caresses. She had come close to telling him about the baby then, but the words had stuck in her throat. He had a right to know, but in spite of the love he had shown her, she was afraid of his reaction. Afraid of seeing annoyance constrict his features, or irritation flash in his eyes. Afraid, at the least, that the unexpected disclosure would hang between them, making them awkward with each other. So she'd left it for the morning, unwilling to spoil the night.

Now, with the sunlight strengthening, she tried to formulate the words in her head. Should she be casual, apologetic, tearful? No, that was ridiculous. She'd be matter-of-fact and let the rest depend on him. Her stomach contracted painfully. Morning sickness or nerves? Probably both. She'd better get it over with.

She turned toward Ethan and pushed herself up on one elbow, drawing the sheets up to cover her.

He was lying on his back, his hair tousled, his features

softened with sleep. He looked younger, vulnerable. Deborah realized she didn't even know how old he was. And he had never asked her age. In spite of their intimacy, they knew incredibly little about each other. Edith would have thrown her hands up in despair. She was probably right. But Deborah knew she couldn't worry about filling in all those details until after she'd told him, if there was still anything left between them to build on.

Ethan stirred as she watched him. He opened his eyes and smiled at her, dimples creasing his cheeks.

"Good morning," he whispered. He stretched out his arm and she nestled down into the crook of it, burrowing her head beneath his chin. She was tempted to postpone the discussion. But it was a reality that had to be faced. She took a deep breath.

"I have a confession to make."

"You're a hatchet murderer wanted in twenty-six states," Ethan murmured.

"I think I'd find that easier to tell you."

"This is beginning to sound serious."

"I wasn't shopping yesterday. I was at the doctor's."

Ethan stroked her head, waiting for her to continue.

"I wasn't sure until yesterday." She paused and swallowed. "I'm pregnant."

He didn't respond immediately. His hand rested, immobile on her head. Deborah realized she was holding her breath. She exhaled slowly, wishing he would say something, anything. Finally she drew her head out from under his and leaned up on her elbow again.

Ethan had been staring at the ceiling, but he turned to her now, his long, blue-green eyes tranquil, as if she hadn't said anything unusual.

"Why did you wait to tell me?" he asked.

Deborah shook her head. "I didn't want to upset you, make you feel trapped. Besides, I've just about decided to have an abortion, so there was almost no point in bringing it up at all."

Ethan's face went taut, the boyish look gone completely. "An abortion?" He pushed himself up against the headboard abruptly, nearly knocking her over. "You would have made that decision without even asking me?" His voice was sharp, accusing.

Deborah was startled. She hadn't expected the distress and anger that had met her last remark. She sat upright, too. "Let's face it, until yesterday I didn't have the vaguest notion of where you were or how to reach you," she said, her voice rising defensively. "As far as I knew it was a decision I had to make on my own. And I'll tell you, I wasn't thrilled either about being in that position."

Ethan's expression softened. "You're right, of course. What I meant was, you thought of not telling me now that I am here."

Deborah looked down, absently smoothing and resmoothing the sheets over her legs. "I was afraid of chasing you away."

Ethan ran his palm along her bare shoulder. She shivered.

"Is that really what you think of me? Do I seem to care so little?"

"I don't know, honestly. I think a lot of men might feel manipulated, roped in."

"I guess they might. But that's certainly not giving me the benefit of the doubt. Hey," he shook his head, "you don't think I flew all the way back here for a one night stand, do you?"

Deborah shrugged and smiled.

"I'd nearly given up on ever finding someone like you. I love you." He leaned forward and kissed her. "And this baby's mine too, you know. As much as if we were married. Don't destroy it, Deborah, please."

"Are you sure?" You can't decide something like that on a whim. It's a lifetime commitment. That's what made me consider the abortion in the first place. I didn't think I could handle it on my own."

For the breadth of a second Ethan seemed to hesitate, his eyes clouded by some inner conflict. But then as quickly his composure returned and Deborah wasn't sure that she had seen anything there at all but the reflection of her own anxiety.

"I think you're wrong. You're strong enough to handle almost anything. But you don't have to worry about that. We'll get married."

"It's funny," Deborah said, her heart soaring. "I always assumed I'd be married first and pregnant second."

"Does that mean you don't accept?"

She shook her head. "Not a chance. I'm very adaptable." She could feel the tears welling up in her eyes. She tried to blink them back, but they spilled over her lashes and down her cheeks.

"If I have this baby," she hiccuped, "I'm afraid you'll have to spend the next eight months listening to me cry. That's all I seem to do lately."

Ethan reached out and folded her into his arms.

"You came back just in time. By next weekend it would have been too. . . ."

"I know." His arms tightened around her. "I know."

They sat in the center of the bed with the sheets tangled around them. Then Ethan held her away and smiled.

"So, what will it be? A quick ceremony today at a roadside minister's, or something more formal in a month or two, when I finish up my business in L.A.?"

"You're a sweet romantic," Deborah laughed. "But I don't think there's any way we could be married today, not without the license or blood tests."

"Is all that really necessary?"

She studied him for a moment. "I guess I'll have to be the practical one, it's obvious you're not." But she didn't feel very practical. She felt exhilarated, heady, and impulsive, barely able to grasp this new turnaround in her life. So little had happened to her in the past thirty-seven years and so much in the short space of this summer. She'd virtually fallen in love at first sight, swept away by feelings as intense and irrational as they were new to her. If indeed there was such a thing as destiny, it had drawn her here to Rachael Crossing for this summer, and the thirty-seven years that she had waited were a small price to have paid.

"Besides," she went on, "I'd like Edith, Hal and their kids to be there. They're my only real family. Edith would be devastated if she missed my wedding. She's been looking forward to it more than she did her own. And Linda. She's been such a good friend. I want her to be there, too."

"Then I guess we wait. Are you sure you won't be bothered by raised eyebrows over a very premature baby?"

She shook her head. "I'm not exactly a free thinker, but one thing that never made much sense to me is how much weight some people give to a piece of paper. It's not the license I want. It's you. If I have that, their eyebrows can lift right off their faces for all I care."

"Even Edith?"

"She'll survive it."

"One more question then," Ethan said solemnly.

"What's that?"

"Can you make us some breakfast—I'm starving."

Ethan suggested a quiet, lazy day in the backyard and dinner at a little restaurant he'd discovered the year before during his travels through the area. Deborah asked if he meant Baynor's Inn.

"No," he said. "That's become too common and crowded. I'm sure you'll like this place better."

She said she was looking forward to it and tried to mask her disappointment. She had hoped that at Baynor's Inn she might bump into someone she knew and have the chance to show him off.

While they relaxed beneath the oak tree, she filled in details about herself. Things she thought he'd want to know, although he'd never asked. He seemed only mildly interested, as if he were content with his limited knowledge of her. She had thought that if she initiated the exchange he would do his part, but he didn't offer anything new about himself. And when she asked specific questions, his answers, while not evasive, were insubstantial.

"Growing up in a small town like this I imagine your early childhood must have been very different from mine," she said, trying once more to draw him out.

"Yes, very different."

"Did you like it?"

"I don't remember. It was so long ago." He laughed uncomfortably.

"So long ago," Deborah chided him. "You'd think you were old and senile." Old and senile. She was reminded of Darcy. "So long ago that you were around when your family home was first built?"

The transformation that swept over his face was as dark and sudden as the first time she'd mentioned the old root cellar. It was as if a black cloud had covered him, blotting the sun out of his eyes.

Even though his mood had changed so drastically, she couldn't stop herself. "Ethan," she went on, "was your family involved in the Salem witch trials in any way?"

"Why?" His tone was ominous.

"I . . . I've heard some stories, that's all."

"Tell me," he demanded. "What stories?"

Deborah saw no way to retreat. "I heard that a witch had something to do with the fire that burned the house down," she said reluctantly.

"Witches," Ethan snorted. "Do you believe in witches?"

"No. No. I don't think so."

"Then why do you listen to old stories about them?"

"I was just curious about how the stories, the witch trials started."

"How they got started? They hatched in dark corners and fed on ignorance and fear. The past has no place here." As he spoke the tension in his face eased, his eyes brightened noticeably.

Deborah was struck by the dichotomy between Old Man Darcy and Ethan. One lived to recount the past, the other couldn't bear to speak of it. She found Ethan harder to understand.

Empty answers, dark moods, would she ever really know him, even after years of marriage? Or would there always be an intangible separateness to him? But she couldn't dwell on it. Ethan was kissing her, pulling her down onto him, and her need for him overshadowed her misgivings.

She awakened to hear him whispering her name. The sun had descended toward the horizon, the air was slightly cooler. She stretched languorously. "How long was I asleep?"

"An hour or so."

"You should have gotten me up sooner. You must be stiff from lying in that position for so long."

"That's okay," he grinned. "You needed the rest. Especially since I plan to keep you up again tonight."

The restaurant was as small and quaint as Ethan had promised. Miniature covered lanterns glowed dimly on each of the thick oaken tables, creating the atmosphere of an old-fashioned inn. Deborah saw only one other couple as they were led to their booth.

It was extraordinarily quiet. No clinking of glasses or silverware, no muted thumping of swinging doors. Deborah couldn't even hear the other couple talking.

A waiter appeared noiselessly at their table, took their order, nodded, retrieved the menus and was gone.

"It's so quiet," Deborah couldn't help remarking. Her voice rang out sharply in the stillness.

"I know, that's why I like it."

She lowered her volume several degrees. "How do they make any money if it's always this empty?"

"Oh it's not. Sundays are usually slow though. But it never gets terribly noisy in here anyway." He extended his hand across the table to her, palm up, and she lay her hand in it, touching the gold band of the signet ring. She was glad he was wearing it. She hadn't bought it for him, but in a sense she had given it to him. She was no doubt imparting more meaning to it than he did.

"You never had a guard put on the ring," she observed.

Ethan shrugged. "I always wear my rings loose. I hate it when they get stuck going over the knuckle. That's probably why I lose most of them."

The waiter reappeared with two wine glasses and a bottle. After they had gone through the tasting ritual, Ethan raised his glass and Deborah touched hers to it.

"To our son," he said.

Deborah laughed. "Or daughter."

Ethan said nothing. He just smiled indulgently and brought the glass to his lips.

Deborah sipped her wine and wondered if she were marrying a male chauvinist.

Ethan set his glass down. "Getting back to more immediate matters," he said, "when does your lease on the house run out?"

"In a couple of weeks. I'd almost forgotten about that."

"You'll have to see about renting it for longer, since I don't know exactly when I'll be back."

"I'll try to get into town on Monday right after camp." She sucked in her breath, "Oh my God, I must be in a daze."

"What's wrong?"

"I'll have to call Joel, he's my department chairman, and tell him I'm not coming back when school reopens. I'll try to get a maternity leave, just in case. We don't know definitely where we'll be living. I hate doing this to him on such short notice. He'll probably be furious."

"Do you really care?" Ethan asked.

The alarm rang at seven thirty Monday morning, wrenching Deborah from a deep sleep. Her eyes flew open, but she closed them quickly. She was dizzy and disoriented. Too much wine and too little sleep. Her stomach was bouncing around discontentedly. She turned her head to see if Ethan was awake. But he wasn't there. She sat up abruptly, the room swimming around her. Could he have left again without awakening her?

"Ethan," she called out, her voice high and nervous.

"Good morning," he said from the doorway. He was already dressed in a light blue shirt and white chinos that emphasized his slim hips and long legs. He sat on the edge of the bed and kissed her lightly. "I put up the water for coffee, but you look as if you'd do better with tea."

"I do feel a little green around the gills," she admitted sheepishly. "Are you going soon?"

"I called for the taxi. It should be here in fifteen minutes." Her lips drooped. She was on the verge of tears again.

"You have to get ready for camp, don't you?"

She nodded, not trusting her voice.

"Okay, you get dressed while I pour the coffee and tea." Deborah sipped her tea despondently.

"Hey," Ethan said, putting down his cup. "You've got

lots of plans and things to take care of now—the time will pass quickly."

She forced a smile. "I know. It's just that—I miss you already." She stared at the tea, stirring it over and over. "Can you leave me the name of the hotel where you'll be staying?"

"I don't have any reservations. I can't say exactly where I'll be."

"Will you call me then?" She looked up, her eyes overly bright with tears.

"Deborah, please don't cry. I don't think I can stand to leave you crying."

"I'll try not to. But you didn't answer me."

"If I say yes, will you promise not to cry anymore?"

She nodded.

"Okay then."

A horn beeped outside.

"I guess that's for me," he said, standing.

Deborah rose too.

He came around the table to her. "Let's say good-bye in here, alone." He kissed her, holding her against him and ignoring the second, more impatient blast of the horn.

"Just remember above everything, I love you," he said, moving back from her.

"I love you too," she whispered hoarsely.

Chapter Twenty-two

"I can hardly believe it!" Linda exclaimed, glancing from the road to Deborah and back to the road again.

Deborah was beaming. "I wouldn't have believed it myself if I hadn't been there," she said. "At first when I saw him I thought I'd conjured him up. That my hormones had me hallucinating."

Linda let go of the wheel with her right hand and squeezed Deborah's arm. "I'm so happy for you. And doubly glad because you'll be staying on a while longer. It's sure going to make at least part of my last year here more bearable."

"Your last year—then you've decided to go back to Boston?"

"Yeah. I do love it here. I always will; it's home. But there's really nothing here for me, for my career or socially. I'll stick out the year because I made the commitment to Mrs. Baily. But after that it's off to the bright city lights."

"Sounds like a realistic decision," Deborah agreed.

"Meantime though, it gets pretty lonely here and I'm glad you're not leaving just yet. Am I being terribly selfish? I know you're counting the days 'til he comes back for you."

Deborah shook her head and smiled. "Who could complain about being wanted? But the days are going to drag for me once camp is over."

"Have you thought of subbing while you're here?" Linda suggested. "If you apply in Rachael Crossing and in Salem you'd probably get at least one or two calls a week."

"That's not a bad idea. And I've been toying with another one." She told Linda about her second visit to Darcy. "I thought I could try writing up a few articles or short pieces based on his stories and see if I could sell them to magazines in the New England area. Local color type stuff. Even if I don't succeed in selling anything I'd enjoy the background research."

"You're ambitious."

"No," Deborah said wryly, "desperate. If I don't have something to do I'll spend all my time crying. And wondering if he's real."

"Oh come on," said Linda. "You're not serious, are you?"

Deborah smiled weakly and shrugged. "No. I guess not. It's just hard to explain how I feel. When I'm with him everything seems to make sense. But when he's gone I start seeing so many loose ends. Questions keep popping into my mind. I feel uneasy."

"Just the normal jitters of a future bride and expectant mother."

The Rachael Real Estate Office came into view. Linda pulled over to the curb. "Here we are."

They found Mrs. Hopkins tucked into her chair watching television.

"Hello girls, hello," she greeted them without rising. "Love a good comedian. Brightens up the day. What can I do fer ya?" She switched off the set.

Deborah explained that she'd decided to stay on in Rachael Crossing a while longer and wanted to know if she could continue to lease the house by the month.

"Don't see why not," said Mrs. Hopkins. "Don't have no waiting list for it." She smiled as if it were an inside joke. "Have yaselves a seat and I'll find the kind a' lease we'll be needin'."

Deborah and Linda arranged themselves in the two chairs

in front of the desk. Mrs. Hopkins rummaged through first one and then the other of the bottom desk drawers. She paused once to look up and rub her neck. "Never can find what I need when I need it," she complained amiably, and went back to searching. "Aha," she said after another minute. "I think I've found it now." She pushed the drawer in with her foot and placed the stapled form on her blotter.

"All nice and standard, don't ya know. We'll jest fill in the amount of rent and any other particulars." She looked up at Deborah. "Ya say ya don't know how long you'll be wantin' to stay on?"

"That's right. It depends on some, uh, personal matters."

Mrs. Hopkins stroked down the prickly ends of her short silver hair. "Seems to me I heard ya say ya have a teachin' job back in New York City," she remarked.

"Yes, well I'll be taking a leave of absence."

"Uh huh. It'll sure be nice havin' ya stay on a bit longer."

Deborah knew the woman was angling to find out more. And she would tell her more, but not yet. After Ethan returned and the baby had passed the first three critical months. Now she felt anxious talking about it to anyone but Linda. She knew it was just superstitious nonsense, but too many things could still go wrong, and she had the feeling something would. Of course she would have to tell Edith. She'd take care of that after dinner.

She and Mrs. Hopkins agreed on the rent and Deborah signed the lease.

"I'll send Carl round to check out the heatin' system," said Mrs. Hopkins. "And if somethin's not workin' that he can't fix, I'll call in a man knows what he's doin'."

"Fine, thank you." Deborah stood and shook her hand.

"Glad to see ya decided not to take notice a' them stories any more 'n I do."

Deborah smiled and nodded and they said good-bye.

"You know, it's strange," she remarked once they were on their way out of town. "I'd completely forgotten about those stories and Jeffrey's ghost fire until Mrs. Hopkins mentioned them."

"I wouldn't call that strange, I'd call it good."

"No, it's strange. The whole time Ethan was here I never

once worried about the apparition appearing the way I did when Edith and Hal were visiting."

"You were wrapped up in Ethan, that's all. And from your description of him that's not hard to understand. Besides, having him there probably made you feel safe."

"Maybe," Deborah conceded reluctantly.

"It's not maybe, it's certainly. Now stop looking for dark meanings in perfectly ordinary situations."

"There's something else," said Deborah. "Something I haven't told anyone because I was afraid they'd think I was really paranoid. Ever since I started living in that house I've had this weird feeling, as if someone were watching me. The feeling is so intense I can't even walk around undressed. And once, once I could have sworn there was somebody behind me. I spooked myself so badly I slipped and fell down the stairs. I can't even blame it on hormones or nerves. It goes back to my first days in the house."

"It probably goes back to the horror movies you saw when you were a kid," said Linda. "If I were a psychologist I'd do a study on the long-term effects of those movies on our young."

After a light dinner, Deborah sat on the front step, taking in deep breaths of the cool air. When she felt she couldn't put it off any longer, she went into the living room to call Edith, rehearsing her speech and imagining the conversation that might follow. After fifteen minutes she still hadn't reached for the receiver. It had been a long day. She was tired. It was hard to believe that Ethan hadn't even been gone twenty-four hours. She went upstairs and in the dresser found stationery she'd brought along and never used. She'd take the coward's way out and write to her sister. At least that way she could explain everything without exclamations and interruptions.

Chapter Twenty-three

Edith's call came at five thirty Thursday evening, two days after Deborah had sent the letter.

"Hello, Deborah," Edith said tartly. "I received your letter this morning."

"Oh," said Deborah. "The mail's pretty good, then. I only sent it two days ago."

"Don't you think I at least rate a phone call with this kind of news?"

"I apologize for that," Deborah replied, determined to be courteous and still stand her ground. "But I just didn't know how to tell you. Maybe because it's so new and overwhelming for me. It was easier to explain it in a letter. Please don't be angry."

"I'm not angry," Edith sniffled. "I'm hurt."

"I thought you'd be happy," said Deborah, wishing she hadn't answered the phone.

"I'm not sure if I am happy," Edith was saying. "Less than two weeks ago you told me you'd probably never see this Ethan again and you weren't even disturbed about it. Now you not only tell me you're going to marry the guy, but that you're already pregnant by him. I mean, I keep up with the soap operas and all, but you're moving too fast even for me."

"I guess my mistake was not letting you know how much he meant to me from the beginning," Deborah said gently. "Then maybe you could understand this better. Please be happy for me, Edith. I'm happier than I've ever been." She hoped she was convincing. She could picture her poor sister in her hand-wringing pose.

"I don't know," Edith muttered. "When is the wedding going to be?"

"We haven't set a date yet. It depends on when Ethan gets back."

"Well then, you'll be coming back here after camp ends next week, right? You've told him you'll wait for him back here?"

Deborah explained that he expected her to wait in Rachael Crossing and that she'd already signed a month by month lease with the real estate agent.

Edith tried to change Deborah's mind and when she saw that she wasn't making any progress she announced that she'd be up for the Labor Day weekend.

"Edith, don't be ridiculous," Deborah said firmly. She had to end this conversation. "The traffic on Labor Day is horrible and you were just here. I promise to call and let you know more as soon as I do. Now calm down and go shopping for a dress. I'm thinking of a Sunday afternoon ceremony."

When Edith finally seemed placated, Deborah hung up the phone and went to make herself dinner. At least now Edith was taken care of. She had called Joel on Tuesday and he had actually been pleased for her, although he didn't know where he'd find another history teacher on such short notice. Now if Ethan would just call she could relax. She had the uncomfortable feeling he wouldn't, but she was determined not to dwell on it. She'd go to see Old Man Darcy tomorrow after camp and get started on those articles she was going to write.

They were coming out the front door when Deborah turned onto Carriage Drive. Darcy was leaning over on his cane, feet set apart, slightly bent at the knee for balance, while Vera Brinks locked the door. Then she turned and took one of his arms and they proceeded slowly down to the sidewalk, Darcy staring fixedly at the pavement as if to search out hidden traps.

"Hi there," Deborah called, hurrying toward them.

Vera Brinks looked up, took a moment to recognize her, then waved. Darcy didn't appear to have heard her at all. Vera had to pull back on his arm to make him stop and wait for Deborah to catch up.

"Hi," she said again when she'd reached them. "Hello, Mr. Darcy. I was going to stop by for a visit, but I can see you're on your way out."

Darcy glanced up finally and nodded, pursing and unpursing his lips at her.

"It's good to see you, Deborah," Vera said brightly. "Actually we're not going far. Just up and down the block so Mr. Darcy can have some exercise. Perks up his appetite a bit. You're welcome to join us if you like."

"Thank you, I think I will." She fell in on Darcy's other side and the three of them started down the street. Their progress was haltingly slow and Deborah found herself pausing every third step in order to keep pace with them. Darcy walked like a mechanical toy gone stiff with rust. His pants flapped shapelessly around nearly skeletal legs and veins snaked across his arms, protruding through the translucent skin. All of his concentration seemed to be focused on coordinating his body and cane. She doubted if he would be able to carry on a conversation as well.

"Soon we'll be needing sweaters," remarked Vera Brinks. "Autumn comes quickly enough up here."

"It must be a magnificent season with all these trees turning."

"It certainly is. Autumn's my favorite time of year."

"Do you like autumn, Mr. Darcy?" Deborah inquired, trying to draw him into the discussion.

"Nope. Too cool. And winter just behind it. Can't take the cold," he muttered without looking up.

He sounded coherent. Mrs. Brinks had probably insisted he wear his dentures out in public.

"Do you feel up to telling me more about the story you started last time?" she asked hopefully.

"What story was 'at?"

Encouraged, Deborah took out her pad and pen. "You were telling me about the first house on Foxton Lane. Something about witches. Do you remember?"

"Ah, witches. Nobody believes in them anymore."

"You were saying that a witch had something to do with the burning of the house. Did a witch live there? Is that why they burned it down?"

Darcy's eyebrows twitched together over his eyes with the effort of remembering. "No. 'Twas more the doin' of Emily Hawkins and her dreams. Now there was a true witch fer ya."

"Emily Hawkins," Deborah repeated, trying to write as she walked. "You say she was convicted of witchcraft because of her dreams?"

"Let's cross over to the other side to walk back," interjected Vera. "More sun and less shadow."

"She claimed to have dreams of the future," Darcy continued, after navigating the curbs with the help of the two women. "The devil's own gift. And she used it to his purposes. Even killed a man. A good honest, God-fearin' man, name a' Purvey." He paused to catch his breath.

"I'm afraid walking and talking are a little too much for him," Vera explained in a hushed voice to Deborah.

"Stop talking about me like I was a freak a' some kind," Darcy grumbled. "And don't look so damned surprised I heard ya. I keep tellin' ya I ain't deaf. I jest hear what I want t' hear."

Vera was smiling, blue eyes dancing with amusement. "Glad to hear you're feeling so chipper, Mr. Darcy. Shall we go on?"

"What connection did this Emily Hawkins have with the fire?" Deborah pursued, eager for him to finish the story before he lost track of it.

"They found out she was in cahoots with the feller who lived there. Both a' them servants to the devil. He never did have a trial. They just burned the whole place down around him."

Deborah was gripped by a sudden image of what the dark hysteria of that time must have been like, and an involuntary shudder flashed through her body in spite of the warm sunlight. Her pen shook so that she had to put it away and trust the rest to her memory.

"Are you cold, dear?" Vera asked. "We're almost back to the house. You can come in and I'll fix you a nice cup of hot coffee. Or tea if you prefer."

"Huh? Oh, no. No thanks," Deborah stammered distract-edly. A man who'd been burned alive in the original house. The man of the ghost fire. Was he more than rumors and imagination then? And why had she been spared this awful vision so far? Her head felt light, making her stomach spin and pitch. They had crossed back over and were standing at the foot of the walk up to the house.

"You're sure now you won't come in?" asked Vera. "You're not looking real well."

Deborah managed a smile. "Just a little tired. I'll be fine. The fresh air is probably the best thing for me."

"If you're sure. Take care, then, and thanks for stopping by."

"Good-bye, Vera. Mr. Darcy."

Deborah started to smile, but another wave of nausea swept over her.

Chapter Twenty-four

    The noises had started soon after the end of camp. At least Deborah was fairly sure they had. But there was the possibility that she'd been too tired and busy to notice them before that. They weren't particularly ominous noises. Sometimes a dull thud as if some animal had bumped into the side of the house, a scratching against glass, or the sound of a rock-like object striking the roof and rolling down. What disturbed her was that she couldn't find any source for the noises. She'd go outside, anxiously scouting the perimeter of the house hoping to find a small animal, a tree limb hitting the window, a bird or squirrel dropping acorns onto the roof. She never found anything. She looked at the ground for tracks. But the grass was shorn low, resistant to imprints, and the ground was firm since there hadn't been any rain for a week.

    She finally made up her mind to ignore the noises. If she could become accustomed to the sensation of being watched, she could learn to tolerate innocuous noises as well. It wouldn't be for much longer. Then she would be leaving with Ethan and the house could wait for new tenants to play with.

She didn't mention the noises to anyone. Linda was already too spooked by the house to venture inside. And everyone else thought she was crazy to be staying there in the first place. Besides, she felt she was coping with the situation well enough. At least until that one Friday evening.

She had eaten dinner, cleaned up the kitchen and was sitting on the living room couch, reading. It was just past nine o'clock and fully dark outside. At first the noises were more or less what they had been all along, scratchings, objects rolling on the roof. Deborah looked up when they started, wagged her head, more with annoyance than fear, and found her place again. Then she heard something new, a low humming that started in a rolling undercurrent like distant engines or a muted power generator and built on and on to a throbbing intensity, as if it were echoing itself. At its harshest, rumbling peak it was suddenly pierced by a single high-pitched whine that lasted for a minute or more and shot through Deborah's head like bolts of cold steel. She clamped her hands hard over her ears, but the shrill sound penetrated her fingers. Then, as abruptly as it had started, all the sounds stopped. The air was empty and light. Deborah let her hands fall into her lap.

Although it had seemed to come from the direction of the backyard, she was too terrified to investigate in the dark. Afraid of finding whatever had created those noises. Afraid of finding nothing and having to doubt her sanity. She sat and waited, a sheen of tears filming her eyes as she prayed it wouldn't start again. Seconds passed that felt like hours. There were no new sounds. She swallowed, relief beginning to unlock her muscles, and retrieved her book. Her hands were shaking and she couldn't concentrate. She read the same sentence over and over without absorbing the meaning. Then the humming filled the air again. Deborah turned the book over in her lap and listened, her own heart sounds thrumming in her ears. The noise didn't come from any clear direction. It appeared to emanate from around the entire house, or from within it, as if the walls themselves were vibrating, murmuring to her, ominous whisperings that taunted and threatened. It seemed to Deborah that something, something intelligent, was playing with her, orchestrating the noises to shatter her nerves.

Would flames soon start crackling around her, the burning apparition materialize, screaming in its eternal anguish? Did she believe in witches, or ghosts? She was no longer sure what was real, what imaginary, or what she believed in. She thought she ought to leave the house, but fear had frozen her into a barely breathing statue while her skin remained strangely sensitive, tingling from the touch of the very air. She was straining so hard to pinpoint the origin of the noise that she jumped when a loud thrashing began. It sounded like huge tree limbs sweeping across all the first floor windows with such force that the glass rattled in its frames. But there were not many trees close enough to the house to make that much noise and no wind that night to blow them.

She debated calling the police, but wondered if they'd consider it a crank call. Would they shake their heads and ask her what she expected if she lived in a haunted house? What could they be expected to do against supernatural forces? While she was deciding what to do, the thrashing stopped as abruptly as it had begun and the humming resumed. Then there was a loud crack as something slammed into the roof, followed by a cascade of what sounded like rolling hailstones, accompanied by a high, whining noise.

Deborah's heart was hammering against her ribs, her hands balled into fists so tightly that the nails dug into her palms. She wanted to cry, to run, but she was trapped inside. Surrounded. Imprisoned by the noises. Suddenly a voice called out. A human voice. She couldn't tell if it were male or female. Almost immediately it was joined by others, shouting.

"Watch out!" "Oh my God!" "Over here!" Then she heard screams. Not the strange whine she'd heard earlier, very real human screams. Followed by the muted patter of footsteps over grass, and the dying away of all sound into absolute silence.

Deborah remained motionless, paralyzed for fifteen minutes waiting for the cacophony to begin again. She forced herself off of the couch and tiptoed, trembling, to the front window. The moon was a pale, hollowed arc low in the sky. A street light further down the road threw an eerie glow, making only the large shapes of trees and bushes distinguishable from the murky landscape.

"It's over," she kept telling herself. It's over. She went mechanically into the kitchen and put the kettle up for tea. The voices she'd heard were human, but perhaps from human beings no longer alive. How could she continue to stay in the house now? This last episode had been too much for her. She sat at the kitchen table, absently stirring her tea. The doorbell rang. She jerked her hand so violently that she upset the cup and righted it with her other hand, burning the tips of her fingers.

"Ghosts don't ring doorbells," she told herself, shaking her hand to ease the pain. By the clock above the sink she saw that it was nearly ten o'clock. Late for ordinary visitors. Maybe Ethan was back. The bell rang again. Deborah pushed back from the table and ran to the door.

She started to turn the lock then stopped. "Who's there?" she called out.

"It's Carl," came the thick, nasal reply.

She pulled open the door.

"Hi," she said. "I'm surprised to. . . ."

"Sorry to disturb ya this hour," Carl interrupted. His face was set grimly, his lips pressed together, his eyes flitting uncomfortably from her to the house and then to the ground. "But there's somethin' needs clearin' up right now. Can we come in?"

It wasn't until he used the plural that Deborah noticed the other black silhouettes lingering several yards behind him. She was becoming frightened again, but she trusted Carl.

"Yes, I, I guess so," she stammered and stepped aside.

Carl turned and waved to the other figures. "Aw right, c'mon you guys," he said gruffly. He came in first, stopping in the foyer. Four boys in their early teens slouched in after him, heads down, glancing furtively at Deborah and at one another. Their faces were ashen in spite of their deep, summer tans.

Deborah recognized two of them as Carl's sons. The other two looked familiar, but she couldn't place them.

"Do you want to sit down in the living room?" she inquired, still trying to figure out why they had come.

"No," said Carl. "This here's just fine. These boys got somethin' to say to ya and then we'll be leavin'."

"Okay." Deborah looked at the boys. None of them returned her glance.

"Git on with it," Carl snapped. "You, Danny," he poked a stubby finger into the shoulder of his older son. "You tell Ms. Colby."

The boy chewed on his lips for a moment, his discomfort tangible. "We're the ones that've been making all the strange noises," he said dully, staring at his feet. "We didn't mean nothin' by it. Just a little harmless fun."

"Yeah, that's all," echoed the boy who stood beside him.

"Everyone's always sayin' you're crazy an' all to stay here, so. . . ."

"Danny!" thundered Carl.

Danny shoved his hands into his pockets and glanced sheepishly around the foyer. "What I mean is, well, nothin' ever seems to scare you. We wanned to see if we could. We had this little bet goin' with some of the other guys."

"We're sorry, really we are," said Andrew, Carl's younger son. The other boys murmured their apologies.

Deborah nodded silently, a smile threatening to curve her lips. Her relief was too pervasive to leave room for anger.

"You succeeded boys," she said sternly, adding to herself, more than you'll ever know!

Carl pushed past the boys to face Deborah. "Seems they first got the idea for this here prank when I asked them about the stories for ya. Who would have thought . . ." he left off, wagging his head miserably.

"It's all right, Carl. It's certainly not your fault. And I think these boys have learned their lesson." She fixed each one of them with a reproachful gaze. They hurriedly assured her that they had. And she noticed that they kept looking at the door as if to be certain it was still there and open.

"I'm afraid that ain't all," Carl went on. "Now, I can't guarantee the rest a' this to be a hunnerd percent true, but judgin' by the state them boys was in when they charged into my house tonight, I'd have to say it ain't all a tall story."

"What's that?" Deborah's brows drew together. What else could there be?

"They say they saw it. That fire and the burnin' man."

Her pulse quickened again.

"It's true. I swear it," whined Andrew. "We were trapped in it."

"Yeah," said Danny. "It came on so sudden. One minute we were throwing cans of pebbles onto the roof and the next we're standing in a ring of fire."

"And then that thing, that man," said another boy who sounded close to hysteria. "All burned and his skin hanging off and screaming."

"Just like the stories," said Danny, his eyes wide, his voice trembling.

"Ya see," Carl resumed. "Could be partly imagination. But if all a' them seen it, there must a' been somethin' there."

Deborah took a deep breath to steady her own voice. "Yes, you may be right."

"Well," said Carl, "I just thought ya oughta know."

"You did the right thing by telling me. Thank you."

There was an awkward silence. Then Carl shrugged and said, "Anythin' I can do fer ya before me and the boys go?"

Deborah shook her head. "No. That's okay. I'll be fine. Now that I know what those noises were," she added with a soft, nervous laugh.

The boys were already filing quickly out the door. Carl hung back a moment. "You're gonna stay on, then? Even with the fire an' all?"

"It's not the first time someone's seen it," she replied evenly. "Maybe if I'd seen it I'd feel differently. But it doesn't seem interested in me. So nothing's changed. I'll be fine." She gave Carl what she hoped was a confident smile.

He shrugged again. "Okay. You know where ya can reach me if ya need to. Take care. Good night."

"Good night." Deborah closed the door and locked it. She went into the kitchen to make sure the back door was also locked, but she knew if something malevolent were at work, locks would not keep her safe.

It was so dark and quiet, the world seemed drugged into a deep sleep. She lay on her side, her body stretched against the length of his, sunken into the soft warmth of the mattress and quilt, her fingers nestled in the gently curled hair of his chest. His arm was beneath her neck and shoulders, palm upward in the ease of sleep.

Her mind drifted in peace. Fears and questions that had tormented her had been dimmed as if by years. He had that power over her. To draw her from the world and from herself. She wondered languidly if love was this way for everyone. Although her eyelids longed to close, she kept them open, unwilling to sleep, each moment too precious to lose. Curiously the realization that he would leave again did not trigger tears. It was as if the ability to feel pain had been suppressed.

He awoke before first light. Without a word he ran his hand through her hair and kissed her, then moved away and out of bed. She wanted to hold onto him, beg him to stay, but her arms wouldn't obey and when she opened her mouth no sound came. She watched helplessly while he dressed and started to walk from the room. The pain of losing him pierced her calm. She called to him again and again, choking on the silence. Finally a sharp, desperate cry ripped from her throat, striking the air. He turned back in surprise.

Deborah sat up, awakened by her own scream and bewildered. A dark shape moved near the doorway.

"Ethan? Ethan, is that you?"

There was no response.

"Ethan!" Deborah leaned over and turned on the light. It stung her eyes for a moment as she struggled to take in the room. No one was there. The side of the bed where he had lain was smooth and cool. No footsteps sounded in the hall or on the stairs. Even so, she threw herself out of bed and ran through the house turning on lights and calling his name. Finally, in the hazy gray light of dawn, she sank into a kitchen chair, buried her head in her arms and cried.

Chapter Twenty-five

Camp had been over for three weeks. Ethan had been gone over a month again and Deborah still hadn't heard from him. She kept herself as busy as possible, spending much of her time with Linda. She had applied as a substitute teacher in Rachael Crossing and Salem. Dr. Gates had given her instructions on diet and activity. He also set up an appointment for an amniocentesis. Deborah explained that she might not be in Rachael Crossing for the full term of her pregnancy and he made her promise to have the test done wherever she might be. He estimated her due date as April 11.

Having a specific date in mind lifted her spirits. It was the only concrete thing she had. The baby was still just an idea to her. She hadn't felt it move yet, and if not for the nausea she would have doubted that she was actually pregnant. Even Ethan had begun to seem like an abstraction. She talked about his return and their marriage less frequently. Linda seemed to understand and avoided the subject.

Edith, on the other hand, harped on Ethan's absence every time she called, which had become more often since Deborah's letter. When had she last heard from him? When was he coming for her? Didn't he want to be with his fiancée

194

at a time like this? Finally, Deborah, worn down and dispirited herself, told her that Ethan had called and was sure to be in by Thanksgiving, the latest.

Edith considered the length of time irresponsible and declared that she'd have a hard time accepting such a man into her family. Deborah let the comment slip by, afraid that Edith might never have the option of rejecting him. But even at such pessimistic moments, she would recall how genuine his love had seemed and how important the baby had been to him. The nagging doubts lingered, but at least they were balanced by hope.

All of her acquaintances in Rachael Crossing reacted with surprise when they learned that she was staying on. They had raised eyebrows and remarked that they had thought she had a teaching position in New York City. She had smiled and said she'd decided to take a leave for a while. She didn't mention the baby. They'd find out soon enough. And she didn't mention Ethan, who was becoming harder to accept as part of the real world, even for her.

With the school year under way Linda was occupied until late afternoon and often needed her evenings for planning lessons. She tried to make time for Deborah nearly every day, but Deborah understood and was determined not to be a burden. She had gone to see Mr. Darcy again, but learned that he was not feeling well. Mrs. Brinks had asked her to come back another time.

Deborah knew she needed to get out of the house. She decided to start on the research she'd been talking about and found the library easily from the directions Linda had given her.

She found several musty-smelling volumes that dealt with New England in the seventeenth century and two that were specifically about Salem. She took them to one of the long wooden tables and sat down. The library was nearly deserted. She opened her notebook and started working.

She read the more general books first, taking copious notes since she wasn't sure what would prove useful. She was quickly caught up in the flavor of the period. After nearly three hours she closed the last of the general books and flexed her right hand, stiff from holding a pen. She glanced at her pages of notes. She hadn't written this much since her college days. Her eyes were burning, too. She'd see about obtaining a library card and checking out the last two books on Salem.

She walked the last block from the bus stop enjoying the dry, mild air, so refreshing after the stuffy library. She paused at the curb to check for mail and noticed that the sun was already beyond the roof of the house. Soon the clocks would be turned back and the nights would be long. Did she really want to spend the cold, dark winter here alone? She sighed and glanced through the few letters she'd received. A thick envelope from Joe. Probably the application for maternity leave. A check from the people who had subleased her apartment in the city. The address on the third envelope was handwritten. She flipped it over. No return address. She took it inside and sat down at the kitchen table.

The writing was elaborate and difficult to read. Her eyes skipped to the signature at the bottom of the page. "Ethan." "Ethan," she said aloud, her heart suddenly racing, the paper shaking in her hand. She went back to the beginning and read it slowly. He hoped she wouldn't mind him writing rather than phoning, although he gave no explanation. He was still trying to sign on accounts and would be back as soon as his business was concluded. He gave no specific date. He reminded her more than once that he loved her and then closed rather formally, "With deep and enduring affection, Ethan."

"He never even asked how I'm feeling," she murmured incredulously once her initial excitement had dissipated and she'd reread the letter for the sixth time. But then she realized that she wouldn't know where to write to answer him even if he had asked. She picked up the envelope again and checked it both front and back. It was strange that he hadn't used the stationery from the hotel where he was staying. She thought the postmark would give her a clue but the letter bore no post mark or cancellation. Well, she sighed, what was important was that he had written to her and that he loved her. She refolded the letter and put it back inside the torn envelope.

Chapter Twenty-six

"What do you think?" asked Deborah. She and Linda had planned a leisurely Saturday afternoon lunch.

Linda shrugged. "No postmark? I've seen it happen, too. Why should it concern you? Look at it this way, you get to use the stamp over."

"I guess so. It just struck me as strange. No hotel address, no postmark. I don't know what difference that should make. As long as I received it."

"Right," Linda said emphatically. She stopped at a red light. "How about telling me where we're going. I don't mind being surprised, but I'm the one who's driving."

"You have to bear with me. I'm trying to remember. It's the little place Ethan took me. Just keep going on this road a few more minutes. Then you'll have to make a left."

Linda laughed. "Something tells me we should have brought along a picnic lunch, just in case."

They rode for twenty minutes stopping at every intersection so that Deborah could peer down the side roads and see if they looked familiar.

"I think maybe we should turn back and investigate some

of those side streets," she suggested finally. "I know it was before Salem and we're almost there already."

"Good enough. I'm starving." Linda found a straight section of road and swung the car in a "U" turn. "I'll make a deal with you. If we don't find your elusive restaurant before we get back to Baynor's Inn, we stop there to eat."

"It's a deal," Deborah agreed with a sigh. "But it's so frustrating. I just know it was around here somewhere. Wait!" she cried. "Make a right here. This looks like the street."

Linda had been halfway past the narrow road. She made a wide turn onto it, her tires spewing the pebbles that covered it. "Are you sure?" she asked skeptically. "This looks like an old farm road that hasn't been used in years."

"I know." Her eyebrows were drawn together as she strained to remember. "Somehow it just seems right."

The car bounced over low matted weeds that had encroached on the roadway.

"I think it was bumpy that night, too," she murmured with less certainty.

"I think we ought to turn back," Linda proposed after they'd gone a quarter of a mile with nothing in sight but rolling hills of weeds.

"Look," Deborah said excitedly, pointing ahead. "I just caught a glimpse of a building over that next hill."

"If that's it, I can tell you why it's never crowded or noisy."

They came over the hill and around a curve and Linda stopped short. The building Deborah had seen was on their right. She stared at it out of her side window. It was a small barn, its gray, splintered walls sagging, most of the roof gone. It seemed to be eroding as they watched. One more storm would flatten it to the ground completely.

Linda grinned. "I don't think this is it."

"No. But I could have sworn—it seemed like the right way."

"Baynor's Inn?"

"Yeah, I guess so," she said absently, unable to shake the feeling that they were in the right place, but the restaurant wasn't.

Linda turned the key in the ignition.

"Wait," said Deborah. "I want to tell you about something before we go, okay?"

"Sure." Linda let the engine die again. "What's wrong?"

"I'm not certain. I had a dream a few weeks ago. The night those boys scared me half to death."

"A nightmare?"

"No. As a matter of fact it was one of the most lovely dreams I've ever had. Until the end anyway. Ethan was with me in bed. And it was so real that I could actually smell him and feel his breath on me. But then he got up to leave and when I tried to talk to him my voice wouldn't work. Finally I managed a scream and that woke me up." She paused and exhaled a deep sigh.

"I've done that too. Woke myself up laughing or crying out loud. Is that what bothers you?"

Deborah shook her head. "Just as I awoke I saw Ethan for a second. Then he was gone. I looked all over the house for him. I know I saw him."

"You must have been half asleep. The dream was still working in your mind."

"That's what I've been telling myself. It's rational and it makes sense. But there's still a part of me that knows he was there like I know the restaurant was here."

"Deborah," Linda said firmly. "You've been so reasonable and realistic in spite of all the stories and goings on. You've never let your imagination run wild. And I'm not going to let you give in to it now. There is a perfectly good explanation for this change in you, you know," she added with a playful laugh. "Some women lose their self-control with food, you lose yours with your imagination. Now we're going to get you some food, before low blood sugar does a number on you."

Deborah smiled, wishing she could convince herself that what Linda said was true.

Chapter Twenty-seven

It was nearly two weeks since the amniocentesis had been performed. The physical discomfort had been minor compared to the psychological agony of waiting for the results. Her friends made every effort to see that she kept busy, and the day she was scheduled to find out the results the O'Neils unanimously demanded that she wait with them.

Marge O'Neil made her comfortable, with her feet up on the plaid high-backed colonial sofa in the living room, tucking an afghan around her and propping throw pillows behind her, although Deborah protested that she felt fine.

In spite of their warmth and hospitality, Deborah found it hard to maintain an optimistic attitude. A steady rain beat against the house from the low steel gray sky, and the fir trees scratched the living room windows whenever the wind gusted. Linda prodded her father to build the first fire of the season, hoping it would cheer everyone.

"I love fires," said Deborah. "Ones that stay in fireplaces, that is," she added with a wry smile.

"Me, too," Linda agreed. "They're hypnotic. How are you feeling?"

"Anxious. What time is it?"

"Four," said Marge. "One more hour." She was sitting in a chair crocheting a sweater. She looked up at Deborah. "It's going to be all right, you know. I have premonitions about this sort of thing."

Deborah chewed on her lower lip. Premonitions. Dreams of things to come. Wasn't that why Emily Hawkins had been convicted of witchcraft? And why Ethan's ancestor had been burned alive? But she didn't voice these thoughts. Instead she said, "I wish I believed that. But nothing else has turned out right, why should this?"

"Don't be such a pessimist," Linda scolded.

"Pessimists don't get disappointed as often. I guess I must really want this baby," she added, patting the mound of her stomach through the afghan, "or I wouldn't be so afraid of losing it."

Linda pushed herself up from the floor. "I'm going to make us some hot chocolate with a pile of whipped cream," she said. "Hot chocolate goes with cozy fires and damp October days. Mom, Dad?"

"Not for me," said Marge, "but you go ahead if you like."

Bill sat down with the newspaper. "I think a beer would suit me better in spite of the weather."

"Sure."

Deborah didn't bother saying she wasn't hungry or thirsty. Linda would make it anyway, just in case she felt like it later. She'd been a perfect friend all along and her family like a second family. She watched the shifting colors of the flames and tried to lose her thoughts in them.

Linda returned with the beer for her father and two steaming mugs capped with swirls of whipped cream. She handed one to Deborah.

"Don't tell me you don't want it," she said firmly, "just drink it." She sat in the armchair across from her.

Deborah smiled and obeyed.

The room was quiet except for the occasional crackling of the fire and the muted tattoo of the rain. Bill was immersed in his newspaper, Marge was crocheting and Deborah and Linda were absorbed in the fire and their own thoughts. When Marge announced that it was five o'clock, Deborah bolted up, swung her feet onto the floor and pulled off the afghan that was tangled around them. The half empty cup of cocoa was cold in her hand. She set it on the end table beside the couch.

"Why don't you go into the kitchen," Marge suggested. "We'll wait here."

Deborah nodded, grateful for the privacy. She needed to be alone, if only for seconds, to assimilate the news herself before passing it on.

She dialed the number with an unsteady finger and asked for Dr. Gates. There were several endless minutes before he came on the line. She kept clearing her throat and trying to ready herself for the answer, whatever it might turn out to be.

"Hello, Deborah?" Dr. Gates' voice was businesslike and gave no hint of what would follow.

He must bluff well at poker, the thought flashed through her mind. Her own voice was tight and high with anxiety.

"Hello, Dr. Gates. Do you have the results of my test?"

"Yes, we just received them as a matter of fact. The lab was running somewhat late today. The test shows no abnormalities."

Deborah let out the breath she'd been holding. "Everything's all right?"

"It certainly seems to be."

Deborah thanked him and hung up. Tears were washing over her eyes. She took a tissue from the box on the counter and went back into the living room.

Linda and her parents looked up expectantly.

"The baby's okay," she sobbed. "I don't know why I'm crying."

Chapter Twenty-eight

      Deborah pulled off her bathrobe, kicked off her slippers and slid quickly between the icy cold sheets. She lay on her back, tense and shivering, with the quilt pulled up to her chin, waiting for her body heat to seep into the covers and rewarm her. It was mid-November and although there was yet no sign of snow, the weather had turned sharply colder. She'd had Edith send up the winter clothes she thought she might still fit into and she'd bought several warm maternity outfits and a coat that left room for expansion. Although she hadn't gained much weight, she had entered her fifth month and she was clearly "showing."

      With the bed warming around her and her muscles relaxing, she felt the baby begin its nightly thumping. It moved the most when she was still, reminding her that she was no longer alone. She ran her hand over the fluttering as if to communicate with the tiny being that shared her life. And she was filled with a sense of wonder at how much she already loved this child—this child who was all of Ethan that she might ever have. To think that she had even considered an abortion horrified her. The baby was no longer an idea, but a reality, the central reality of her life and future. She counted the weeks until she would be holding her daughter in her arms. Her daughter. She believed the baby would be a girl, perhaps just to spite Ethan who had seemed so sure it would be a boy. She spent hours thinking of names. Only girls' names. Saying them aloud and writing them. They had to sound right with Colby, too. She'd all but given up on Burke.

Since that one letter in September she hadn't heard from Ethan again. At one point in early November she had convinced herself that he had been killed in a horrible accident and no one knew that she should be notified. In a state of panic she had called the police departments in Los Angeles and various adjacent cities. No one fitting Ethan's description had been in such an accident. She wasn't sure if she was relieved or not. She considered calling hotels to try and locate him. But there were so many in Los Angeles alone that the task seemed overwhelming. Besides, she reasoned, if he didn't care enough to contact her, what would be the purpose of finding him at all? After that she concentrated on the one reality left to her, the baby. She willed it to be a girl.

Because she'd made no attempt to hide in the house, all of Rachael Crossing knew that she was pregnant. And with the exception of Linda's family, who had nearly adopted her, and Mrs. Hopkins, who seemed largely immune to all extreme emotions, they were all distinctly uncomfortable around her.

No two reactions had been the same, yet Deborah knew they all stemmed from the same basic inability to deal with something they couldn't understand. A woman who lived in a haunted house and had a baby out of wedlock was simply unfathomable to them. Even Carl, who came by now only to check on the heating and to see if anything was in need of repair, was unusually taciturn and uneasy. Though it might have been because he didn't like being inside the house.

Deborah believed that, given time, the town would come to accept her again. In spite of everything, she had no desire to return to New York. She felt that she had found her niche in Rachael Crossing. And while she had made peace with herself about Ethan as best she could, there was perhaps one tiny part of her that still held out the hope he would return someday. But she kept that hope tucked deeply away, choosing instead to look to the baby for her happiness.

As the holidays approached, Deborah found it harder and harder to keep her spirits high and not indulge in daydreams. In the middle of a class she'd catch herself thinking how wonderful it would be to spend Christmas with Ethan. The festive holiday season stretched ahead of her like an endless desert.

She tried to keep herself as busy as possible. She took out her notes and pad and set to work on the articles she'd planned to write, but her initial enthusiasm had fizzled. She thought she might be able to rekindle her interest if she visited Darcy and listened to more of his stories.

Vera Brinks answered the phone breathlessly and Deborah inquired if she would be able to visit Mr. Darcy in the next day or two.

"Oh, my, I guess you didn't know," she panted. "The poor dear man is in the hospital. He was trying to get to the bathroom by himself last Wednesday night. Said he didn't want to disturb me. He slipped and broke his hip. Just between you and me," she added in a confidential tone, "he hates having anyone take him to the bathroom."

"I'm sorry," said Deborah. "I hope he's going to be all right."

"Yes, well, the doctors say he should be okay. Just going to take him a while to mend. Bones are brittle at his age and healing can be very slow. They want to keep him in the hospital until after the holidays. Nothing to worry about, they want to watch him, is all. So I'm going back to Boston to visit family meanwhile."

"I don't want to keep you," said Deborah. "Have a happy holiday. I'll speak to you again after New Years to find out how Mr. Darcy is doing."

Deborah hung up and slumped miserably onto the living room couch, sinking into its formless cushions. Now all she had to look forward to was Edith's visit over the weekend, an unappealing prospect.

She had tried to convince her sister that she wasn't lonely.

She just preferred to stay in Rachael Crossing for the holidays. Although the morning sickness had miraculously abated by the end of the third month, she didn't feel up to the long train or car ride back to New York.

Away from the family for the holidays? Edith was horrified. Deborah assured her that she wouldn't be alone, that she'd be spending the holidays with the O'Neils. Edith relented, but she insisted on spending a long weekend before Thanksgiving with her sister in Rachael Crossing.

Deborah was no longer concerned with the possibility of the apparition making an appearance. No one had seen the ghost fire since Carl's boys. She was becoming convinced it was a phenomenon akin to mass hysteria. She still frequently had the sensation of being watched, but she had learned to live with it as one would with a mildly annoying allergy. What she did dread was two full days of fielding questions about Ethan. For some strange reason, whenever Edith began one of her tirades against him, she felt compelled to defend him. Maybe it wasn't so strange. She still loved him.

The first snow of the season fell two days before Edith and Hal's visit. Peering at the scene from her bedroom window, Deborah sucked in her breath with pleasure. It looked as if a skilled pastry chef had spent the night decorating the world in a snowy confection. Snowfalls in New York were nothing like this. There the flakes coming through the polluted air turned a dull gray before they ever hit the ground.

She thought how beautifully her red geraniums would have punctuated the stark whiteness. But they had died in October and Carl had dug them out. She wouldn't think about what was past, she told herself. Only what lay ahead. She ran her hand over her stomach where it swelled beneath the flannel nightgown. Then she pulled on her long bathrobe and went downstairs to listen to the radio. Maybe the storm would discourage Edith from making the trip.

By Friday morning the snow had formed a hard crust that crunched underfoot. Deborah had called Edith to tell her how conditions were, but Edith assured her that the main roads were clear.

When Edith and Hal arrived in the afternoon, Edith

picked her way up the walk, looking haggard and irritable. Hal followed, balancing himself between a suitcase and an overnight case like a tightrope walker. Edith was thoughtful enough to leave her sermons for later.

Saturday morning Edith took over the kitchen. As soon as they had finished breakfast, Hal excused himself to take a walk.

Deborah got up to clear the table.

"Sit a minute," said Edith. "I want to talk to you." Her voice was mild and conversational, but Deborah's defenses were triggered. She took her seat again.

"Okay. More coffee?"

Edith shook her head. "Who do you think you're fooling, Deborah?" she asked. "Surely not me. Maybe only yourself."

Deborah opened her mouth to reply.

"He's not coming back," Edith went on without pausing. "You're going to have to face that fact. I know it's painful, but it's necessary. He is not coming back."

"I know," said Deborah.

Now Edith's mouth hung open. "Then why haven't you come home?" she asked.

"I don't want to."

"But there's nothing for you here."

"I have nothing in New York either."

Edith bristled. "You have us. At least we'd be with you. You could come and stay with us until the baby's born. Longer if you want to."

"It's nice to know I'm wanted," Deborah smiled, trying to be understanding of her sister's need to control and protect. "But I'm happy here. Rachael Crossing feels like home to me now. Linda's the best friend I've ever had. Everything's so much quieter here. I don't feel like I'm on a treadmill moving on overdrive all the time."

"It's quiet on Long Island, too," Edith said, her voice becoming quarrelsome.

"I know," Deborah replied gently. "I've just sort of found my niche here. I wish you would accept that."

Edith changed tactics. "Let's be practical, Deborah. How

will you live with no income, especially once the baby's born?"

"I've saved quite a lot over the past fifteen years. We'll be able to live off that for a while. I can't think of a better way to use the money. And when it's gone I'll go back to teaching and find someone to watch the baby. It'll be all right. I'm not worried. So don't you be."

Edith clucked and sighed with frustration. "What kind of a man is he anyway?" she muttered.

"Let's not go into that again, Edith, please." Deborah stacked the plates and carried them to the sink.

In spite of the tension between them, Deborah was sorry to see them leave on Sunday. The house was overwhelmingly quiet, tucked into its bed of snow that outside noises seemed unable to penetrate.

Deborah walked aimlessly from room to room and stopped outside the doorway to the room she'd chosen as the nursery. She spotted the three paintings that she'd bought at a yard sale on the floor next to hooks and a hammer, waiting for Carl to come and hang them. Deborah supposed she should let him do it, but it seemed like such a simple job. She didn't see why she couldn't handle it herself.

She pulled a rocking chair over to the wall where she intended to put the baby's dressing table and she kicked off her shoes. She picked up one painting and clambered onto the chair. She stood upright and gently hammered the hook into the wall.

With the third painting, she was more confident. She didn't wait for the chair to stop rocking completely before she stood straight and started hammering. With the first hammer stroke she felt her balance falter. Her fingers clutched at the wall and for an instant she clung to the painting until it came away in her hands. Her only thought was to protect the baby as she tumbled wildly to the floor.

Suddenly she was encircled in strong arms. She looked up to see Ethan's face above her, drawn with concern.

"Ethan," she cried out, the sight of him almost painful with the need it evoked. Emotions she'd fought so hard to deny raged through her again.

"It's all right. You're okay now," he whispered, brushing her hair back with his lips.

She turned her face into his shoulder and clung to him fiercely. She didn't care where he had come from; all that mattered was that he was there. She wouldn't let him leave again. Her mind was drifting, her thoughts beginning to blur. She could feel herself slipping away.

Chapter Twenty-nine

The ringing was coming from a long way off. She was rising toward it like a diver returning to the surface light as she opened her eyes. She was lying on her side on the wooden floor in the nursery. Ethan was gone. This dream had left no fragments to torment her, only a hollow ache because it had not been real. She glanced down at her watch. She must have lain there for more than an hour and a half.

She heard the ringing again. The doorbell. She sat up gingerly, not sure how she had landed or where she might be hurt. The baby shifted and kicked as if it, too, had just awakened. At least you're all right, she thought with relief. And it didn't seem that she had hurt anything either. She pushed herself to a standing position and took a few tentative steps. Still no pain. But if she hadn't been hurt, why had she been unconscious for so long? Puzzling over this she walked downstairs to the front door.

The bell rang a third time as she reached for the knob. She pulled the door open to find Mrs. Hopkins' squat form enveloped in a dark tent-like coat.

"Just thought I'd drop in to chat," she bubbled as Deborah let her in.

They had come into the kitchen and Mrs. Hopkins lowered herself onto a chair, sitting with her feet planted apart, as if the chair needed steadying. She wore the same blue flowered dress that Deborah had seen on her in the summer, her fleshy arms bulging out of the short sleeves.

"Was there something in particular you wanted to see me about?" Deborah asked. She set the kettle up to boil.

"Not 'specially. Jest haven't seen ya around in town lately. An' I wanned to see if ya was doin' okay. What with the snow we had, see if maybe ya needed milk or bread or somethin'."

"Thank you. That's really very thoughtful. But everything's fine here."

"Tole ya it would be," Mrs. Hopkins nodded. Her chin, resting almost directly on the swell of her chest, gave her the appearance of an owl. "Don't pay to listen to rumors. Heat's been workin' okay?"

"Carl has it under control." The kettle whistled. Deborah poured the hot water and took a seat.

"So, when is it your baby's due?" Mrs. Hopkins asked while she added milk and stirred her coffee.

"Mid-April."

"How ya been feelin'?"

"Better now. I never thought the morning sickness was going to end."

"Ain't that the truth," said Mrs. Hopkins and she launched into a detailed account of her own three pregnancies. "Not that I mean to frighten ya, don't ya know. I'm sure you'll have a nice, easy time of it from now 'til April."

Deborah took a swallow of her coffee and grimaced. It was cold. She'd been listening to Mrs. Hopkins for forty minutes, and she couldn't help wondering when she intended to leave.

"Just think," she was saying. "Yours'll be the first baby born in this house, old as it is."

"It does seem strange for a house to have been around for a century and never to have seen a baby," Deborah agreed. "I guess no one stayed long enough. There must have been families with children, though."

Mrs. Hopkins set her cup down. "Oh and plenty of 'em. It was mostly families that lived here. With children. Only twice that I recall did I ever rent to a single before you. One was a writer. Too much imagination to live in a house that attracts ghost stories," she chuckled. "He left before the first week was out."

"Was the other also a man?" Deborah asked.

"Come to think of it, it was. Moved out right fast, too. Guess that makes ya the only eligible woman this house has ever known. That's two firsts for ya. Goes to show that a woman can be more sensible 'n a man, don't ya know."

Deborah smiled politely, but for some reason the compliment didn't please her. She felt uneasy without knowing why. She offered Mrs. Hopkins more coffee, but the woman declined.

"No one tends to the office if I don't," she explained.

Deborah couldn't imagine what needed tending to there, but she nodded and walked her to the door.

"Remember. Should ya need anythin', you're more 'n welcome to call on me, m'dear," she said.

Deborah thanked her and reminded her to be careful going down the walk.

Chapter Thirty

Deborah was glad to see the holidays over. The O'Neil's had been especially gracious, insisting that she stay over on Christmas and New Year's Eve. There were even several beautifully wrapped gifts for her and the baby underneath their tree. At another time she might have enjoyed the small town, old-fashioned Christmas. But this year the holiday was just another few weeks to be lived through.

Lying in bed Christmas Eve, Deborah wondered what next year would be like. She imagined herself decorating the tree while her little girl watched transfixed from her playpen. She thought of the toys and stuffed animals she'd buy for her. A red velvet dress and bows for her hair. And if Ethan was missing from her visions, the love he'd awakened in her was not. It was invested instead in their child.

But the pleasant images had been overshadowed by deep misgivings. For the first time since she had decided to have the baby, Deborah doubted her ability to raise it alone. How could she be father as well as mother? She felt terribly inadequate. She drew her arms protectively over the swell of her abdomen. For all those years that stretched ahead the burden and the responsibility would all be hers. No one to help with the decisions or to share the sweet moments.

Didn't Ethan know how much the baby would need him? Oh, God, who was she kidding? She needed him too.

On the first clear morning after the holidays Deborah decided to get back to her research. She found the library nearly empty. In the index file she looked under witchcraft and quickly found the volumes listed.

Deborah settled herself at one of the tables and started reading. *Witches?*, by Amanda Jennings, covered different attitudes toward witches throughout the centuries. It was provocatively written and the theories advanced in it intrigued her. She checked out the book, eager to discuss it with Linda that afternoon.

"So," Linda began when Deborah dropped in. "Tell me about this fantastic book you've discovered."

"It was written by an Amanda Jennings. Her premise is basically that there was good cause for the people back in the seventeenth century to believe that there were witches among them."

"Oh? I always thought the Salem witch hunt was just an adolescent lie that got out of hand."

"Not according to this book. She contends that there have always been people with extrasensory perception. Psychics. Stories about them go all the way back to soothsayers of ancient Greece. Even the legendary Merlin was supposed to have had precognitive powers."

"Okay."

"Well, if you accept that, then it's logical to assume that there were physics in every century, including the seventeenth. Chances are that at least one or two of the victims of those witch hunts in Salem were actual psychics. They must have displayed some sort of psychic power. Precognition, telepathy, maybe even levitation. They were probably as much in awe of their own powers as anyone. Who knows, maybe they even considered themselves witches." Deborah paused. "So, what do you think of her theory?"

"I guess it's another question of the chicken versus the egg."

"What do you mean?"

"Were there people with witch-like powers to begin with, as this Jennings says, or just baseless accusations that produced so-called witches?"

"I tend to go along with her theory. Look, there probably were one or two psychics whose powers resembled witchcraft and gave rise to a panic in which lies could proliferate. She even refers to a diary of one of the accused witches that has survived since that time and is on display in a museum in Boston. I'd like to take a trip there one day and see if I can talk the curator into letting me read it."

"You ought to ask Old Man Darcy what he thinks of this theory. If it's compatible with the stories he knows."

"You're right," Deborah agreed. "I'll have to call to see if he's out of the hospital yet." Then she fell silent.

"You're awfully pensive," Linda remarked after a moment. "What happened to that enthusiasm?"

"It's what you said about the chicken and the egg," Deborah replied. It keeps rolling through my mind. I don't know why." She shrugged and tossed her head. "I'm chalking up peculiarities rather quickly."

"Speaking of which," Linda grinned, "don't forget to call Darcy. I expect to see an article of yours in print someday."

Deborah tried Darcy's number as soon as she got home. Vera Brinks told her that Mr. Darcy wasn't due to be released from the hospital for another two weeks. His hip was healing nicely but he'd developed pleurisy. She promised she'd contact Deborah after he was home.

Deborah hung up the phone. All she seemed to be doing lately was waiting. She knew she shouldn't take every setback personally. But sometimes it was hard not to think that fate was working against her.

She crawled into bed early that night. Lying in the darkened room she thought again about Linda's comment about the chicken and the egg. Why had that idea made such an impression on her? It was just an expression—cause and effect. She started to doze. Then her eyes flew open. The signet ring. That's what had bothered her about it. The question of sequence. She had put the ring in the palm of her hand to show it to Ethan, intending to explain where she'd found it, but he'd anticipated her and recognized it as his

great ancestor's before she'd had a chance to tell him.
Before he'd even had time to see the ring up close. She'd
been so flustered by his proximity that this incongruity had
eluded her completely. Or almost completely, pricking at her
thoughts like the tip of an iceberg. There was no way he
could have known that ring was a family heirloom just by
glancing at it. He had to have seen it before. Yet supposedly
it had lain in the old root cellar since his forefather had
dropped it there three centuries ago.

Deborah's brows knit together and she stared at the dark
ceiling as if the solution were written there. The more she
tried to figure it out, the more tangled and confused her
thoughts became. Now that she knew the reason for her
restiveness about the ring, she was more perplexed than
ever. She thought of Ethan's ancestor burned alive. Was the
ring his, a symbol of that merciless time that had survived to
haunt her with insoluble puzzles? Had his crime been knowing a woman with precognitive powers? The clock read two
a.m. before she finally fell asleep.

She thought she'd been buried alive. The musty odor of
earth was overwhelming, the darkness so deep she couldn't
tell if her eyes were opened or closed. She wanted to cry out
for help, but as she opened her mouth she heard shouting,
muted, from somewhere above her. She listened. The volume swelled, as if it were drawing closer, threatening. She
suspected she should stay hidden in this subterranean place.
Within a minute the voices were directly overhead and
distinct. A man was giving commands. A faint flickering light
penetrated her hideout. With a start she realized where she
was—in the old root cellar. The light was passing through
the chinks in the wooden door. What was she doing here?
Who was waiting above her? Were they her rescuers or her
captors?

The light was illuminating nearly the whole of the root
cellar now. Instinctively she glanced down at the place
where she had discovered the signet ring. It wasn't there.
Why should it be? Then her eye caught the flash of gold on
her finger. She was wearing the ring. Or was she? The finger.
The hand. It wasn't hers. It was a man's hand.

Two black shapes were coming down the ladder. One reached out to grab her. She swung her arm and knocked him to the ground, amazed at her strength. She was grabbed roughly from behind by another. As she struggled to free herself she could feel the ring slipping down on her finger. The man on the ground pulled himself up and took hold of her, too. She was half pulled, half dragged up the ladder. The ladder's last rung was intact. From the top step she could see the night sky. A man held a torch up to her face. He was dressed in a costume—a three hundred year old costume. In the distance a sharp, insistent bell was peeling.

Deborah awakened to the clock's alarm. She lay back in bed trying to comprehend what had happened. Her dream, had been terrifying, but her heart wasn't racing, she wasn't perspiring or distraught. Its impact had been buffered, like something seen on a movie screen, realistic yet removed. It was as if the dream had not been hers. As if she had relived someone else's memory, someone else's nightmare.

Chapter Thirty-one

Deborah was reading with her feet up on the couch. Dr. Gates had instructed her to stay off her feet as much as possible.

She shifted her weight, trying to find a more comfortable position. She was bored and restless. The last person she'd seen was Carl when he'd come by two days before to shovel the latest snowfall off her walk.

She looked at the telephone, longing for some human contact. But Linda was at work and she didn't have the patience for Edith. When the phone rang it startled her.

"Miss Colby—Deborah—Vera Brinks here."

"Hello, Mrs. Brinks," she said, "It's good to hear from you. How is Mr. Darcy?"

"That's just the reason I'm calling. Mr. Darcy is home from the hospital and feeling pretty well. All things considered," she added with a confidential chuckle. "So I wanted to let you know you're welcome to come for a visit anytime you'd like."

"Oh, I'd love that," Deborah replied, forgetting the weather and Dr. Gates' warning. "How about today?"

"Well, it's quite all right with us, dear, but the weather is pretty awful. Maybe you'd be better off waiting a few more days."

Deborah could hear the wind buffeting the house, resculpturing the snowfall and sweeping it back across the walk, but she needed to get out of the house. There had been too many empty days recently and troubled nights. And she had another, more practical reason for wanting to see Mr. Darcy. She hadn't been making much progress with her article and she hoped that he would provide a different perspective. One that she could contrast with Ms. Jennings' theory.

"Deborah, are you there?" Vera Brinks' voice came over the phone again.

"Yes. Yes, I was just trying to decide what to do. I think I'd like to come by today anyway."

"Like I said, it's fine with us. We'll be expecting you."

She moved cautiously down the slippery path, her feet planted widely apart, waddling like all the pregnant women she'd ever seen. She was cold by the time she had gone the few blocks from the bus to Darcy's house on Carriage Drive. Her nose felt frostbitten and her eyes were tearing from the wind.

The house looked better in the snow than it had in the summer. The mailbox still hung open but the dead lawn was cloaked in elegant white, and spindly icicles hung decoratively from the porch roof. She thought wistfully of the warm sun and lovely rose garden and wondered what Mrs. Brinks did for a hobby during the winter.

As soon as she stepped inside it was clear what that hobby was. The house was filled with the smell of warm cinnamon and brown sugar.

"I was just baking a coffee cake," said Vera Brinks, taking Deborah's coat and scarf. She showed no surprise at Deborah's maternity outfit. She'd no doubt heard the news months ago.

Deborah stooped awkwardly to pull off her boots.

"Don't bother, dear, they're hardly wet and it's not worth the effort. You look positively frozen. Let me take you in to Mr. Darcy and I'll fix you some tea. My cake should be out of the oven any minute."

Deborah followed her into the living room, where Mr.

Darcy was sitting across from the television, a blanket draped over his lap. The room was sparsely furnished, and although it was in no way luxurious, Vera Brinks kept the floors shining and the furniture dustless.

"Make yourself comfortable, dear. Just tell him you're here. He's expecting you. I'll see to the cake and tea."

Deborah went over to the couch and eased herself down. She wondered how loudly she should call his name in order to attract his attention. But he turned his wizened face toward her before she could decide. He had lost a considerable amount of weight since she had last seen him. His face looked like a drawstring purse too tightly tied. His eyes, yellowed and dull, flashed with light when he recognized her.

"Hello, Mr. Darcy," she said. "I'm glad to see you're home again.

"Nice to see you, uh, Miss. . . ."

"Deborah. Just call me Deborah."

He smiled, displaying the overly white dentures. "You can turn that thing off," he said, waving his hand in disgust at the television. "No decent shows on to watch anyhow."

Deborah turned off the television set and returned to her seat. "How are you feeling?" she asked.

"Lousy. But what can you expect at my age," he grumbled. He was staring at her stomach. "You expectin'?"

"Yes, I am."

He thought for a moment and opened his mouth, but whatever he'd been about to say eluded him, and he closed it again like a fish drawing air.

"I was hoping you might be up to telling me some stories," Deborah proposed.

He nodded. "Have a good 'un all set in fact. Came back to me when Brinks said you was comin'. Mighty fine one." He licked his lips eagerly. "As good as any a' them soap operas nowadays. Only this 'un is true. Happened back about eighty-five years ago."

"Before you begin, Mr. Darcy," said Deborah, taking out her pad and pen, "I wonder if I could ask you a specific question that crossed my mind?"

220

Darcy eyed her suspiciously. "I thought you came to hear my stories."

"Well, it's related to your stories," Deborah hurried to assure him. "You're the only one who would have the information to answer this question."

"All right. Let's hear it."

Deborah rephrased the question first in her mind. Sometimes he was harder to deal with than a child. "Based on your knowledge, is it possible that some of the people who were executed during the Salem witch trials were not actually witches, but only what we call psychics today?"

"They was witches," he replied sharply. "I don't care what folks call 'em today. I'm talking about near three hundred years ago. Could be some innocent people were killed, but not the ones I know of. An' I learnt about 'em from my granddaddy who learnt from his granddaddy and direct like that all the way back."

Deborah was nonplussed by the hostility that had penetrated the thin, reedy voice. He obviously wasn't open to any new psychological theories like Amanda Jennings.

Vera Brinks had come in with tea and the coffee cake.

"Them, like Emily Hawkins, was evil through and through. An' I won't stand for no one white washin' such as her with fancy scientific talk." He reached for his cup with a shaking hand, rattling it so hard against the saucer that Deborah thought it might break.

"I'll tell ya somethin' else," he said more mildly.

"Please go on." Deborah helped herself to a wedge of the cake.

"It was the minister's fault from the beginning."

"In what way?" she asked between bites. She remembered having read something similar in one of the books in the library.

"Well now, not directly. But it was him brought that slave woman into the country. Tituba was her name. An' the way I heard it, she was the head of them witches. Came here with all her spells and magic. Brought the devil right into Salem, and all with that preacher's help." He paused and took a piece of the coffee cake, eating it with the same sideward grinding motion as a cow chewing grass.

Deborah was busily jotting down notes.

"Is there anything else you can tell me about the man that was burned, the one who worked with Emily Hawkins?"

"Not much more t' tell," said Darcy, licking the crumbs off his lips. "He hid in the root cellar. Had 'em fooled for a while, too. But they found him. Marched him back inside the house and burned it down."

"Oh, my God," Deborah murmured. It had actually happened just as she'd dreamt it. But how had she known? If a spirit created the ghost fires, could it also pass on its nightmare to her? She shuddered, feeling oddly violated.

Chapter Thirty-two

The large, brown envelope was folded over and jammed into the mailbox. Deborah's stomach lurched and dropped. Her article had been returned, rejected again.

After her last visit to Old Man Darcy, the article had begun to take shape in her mind, consuming what little extra strength she had. She drew out a comparison between Amanda Jennings' views and Darcy's stories, with the final conclusions left to the reader. But she had to admit, on reading the finished copy, that it did seem rather slanted to Jennings' more modern, scientific approach. She felt enormous satisfaction when she completed the article. But now that she was down to the last magazine she wasn't so sure anymore. She tugged roughly at the envelope, tucked it under her arm and went inside.

Leaning back against the arm of the couch she stretched her feet out and closed her eyes. Thank goodness the month was almost over. The teaching had helped the time pass more quickly, but she was worn out. Dr. Gates had seen it, too, and had told her she could finish out the month, but then she would have to refuse future jobs and allow herself total rest. The thought appealed to her.

She yawned and opened her eyes. The envelope lay beside

her. She ought to open it she supposed. Maybe some sympathetic editor had written a personal comment of advice or encouragement. She tore away the envelope. Her article was not inside. Deborah pushed herself up to a sitting position. There was a stapled form and a letter. Something smaller dropped out from between the pages and fluttered to the floor beside the couch. She groped for the check with excitement. She read the letter over and over. They liked her article. They wanted to use it.

Deborah held the check up again. It wasn't a large amount, but it meant acceptance and approval of her work. And as soon as the month was over she would start working on her next piece. She could lie in bed and write to appease Dr. Gates. It would be a short story this time. About an old man who told tales like minstrels of the Old World.

The phone awakened her. She must have fallen asleep on the couch. The room was dark, the curtains still open to the night. How long had she been asleep there? She pushed herself off the couch and turned on the lamp. By her watch it was five a.m. The phone shrilled again. She stumbled awkwardly across the room to answer it, her heart pounding, her stomach tumbling. Only bad news came in the dark hours of the morning.

"Hello?" she whispered, her voice hoarse with sleep.

"Deborah?" It was Vera Brinks. Why would she be calling at such an hour?

"Yes?" she said.

"I really must apologize for disturbing you." She sounded rattled for the first time since Deborah had met her.

"What's the matter?"

"Nothing to worry about, dear. It's Mr. Darcy. He took this notion and insisted I call you immediately. The poor man was so agitated. I've never seen him quite like that before and I was just afraid he'd work himself into a stroke or a heart attack. So I gave in and called."

"I don't think I understand," said Deborah, hugging herself and shivering. The house was cold and she'd been asleep all night without even a blanket.

"Well, last night, out of the blue, while Mr. Darcy and I were sitting in the living room he turned to me and started asking all these questions about you. Now he hadn't even mentioned you since the last time you were here, about a month ago. I thought he'd completely forgotten about you. Goes to show you how erratic his memory is these days. Anyway, he wanted to know where you were living and if you were going to have a baby. Then he, uh, he asked me your husband's name and I, well I said I didn't think you were married. After that he dropped the subject. The next thing I know he's yelling for me at four o'clock this morning. I jumped out of bed thinking Lord knows what was wrong with him. And when I got to his room, there he was, sitting up in his bed, as fine as could be.

'Brinks,' he said to me, 'what is the name of that baby's father?' At first I didn't even know what he was talking about. I mean, at four a.m. Well, he kept repeating the question and finally it dawned on me that he meant your baby. So I said I didn't know, which I don't, and I asked him to please go back to sleep. But he refused to. He insisted he had to see you, right away. The more I tried to calm him, the more agitated and hysterical he became, until I thought for sure he'd have a stroke. So I called. To placate him. And I apologize again for the intrusion."

"He wants to talk to me? Now?" Deborah repeated in bewilderment.

"If you don't mind," Vera Brinks said meekly.

"No, I guess not," murmured Deborah. But she was suddenly overcome with a terrible sense of foreboding, as if this phone call held bad news after all. She listened while Vera Brinks told Darcy she'd be right over. Then she heard the old man's voice, high pitched and excited in the background, the nurse trying to calm him and finally coming back on the line.

"I can't quiet him down," she said distractedly. "I don't even understand what he's babbling about."

Deborah felt somehow responsible. "Tell him I'll be over as soon as I can get dressed and catch a bus."

"I don't know if you should, dear, in your condition and all," said Mrs. Brinks, but her voice didn't hold much conviction. She was worried for the old man's life and for the first time ever, she found herself unable to cope with a situation.

"Try to calm him down until I get there," Deborah said firmly. "I'm afraid I can't move very fast these days."

Upstairs she grabbed her warmest pants and tunic out of the closet, ran a brush through her hair and clipped it back.

The sun was just beginning to lighten the sky in the east when she locked the front door behind her. Her feet throbbed in the tight boots and her coat, only belted above the swell of her abdomen, kept blowing open, the wind probing her body with icy fingers.

The stillness was dense and eerie, broken only by the slap of her steps on the pavement. She strained to catch the distant hum of a car's engine or the rustling of a winter bird in the fir trees. Something that would make the day ordinary.

She arrived at the bus stop before the first bus at six o'clock. She stamped her feet, exhaling smoky cones of air and shivering. She was crazy. She would wind up with pneumonia. She could hear Edith yelling at her. But that old man knew something. And maybe he could finally unravel some of the mysteries that had plagued her since she'd first arrived in Rachael Crossing. She wasn't shivering from the cold alone.

By the time she reached Darcy's house the sky had lightened to a dismal gray. The thin living room curtains were still drawn. No soft glow of light shone through them. She pressed the bell. She could hear it ringing inside the house. Almost immediately Mrs. Brinks pulled open the door and let her in. She was wearing a short, pink quilted robe, much of the stitching pulled in loops. Her hair was disarrayed and her blue eyes were puffy and tired behind the blue framed glasses.

"You really are a dear girl to come here at this ungodly hour," she chattered anxiously. "Let me take your coat and bring you right in to him. Once we've gotten all this nonsense settled I'll make you a nice big breakfast."

She led Deborah into the living room. It was dark except for the feeble sunlight that penetrated the curtains. The furniture and walls merged in shades of gray. Darcy was sitting on the same couch where Deborah had last seen him. His shoulders were hunched forward and he was staring into space. His mouth was working noiselessly and his thin, gnarled fingers were contracting spasmodically in his lap.

"Sorry I can't put on the light," said Mrs. Brinks, "but Mr. Darcy's been having a hard time with his eyes these last couple of weeks. The light causes him a great deal of pain. Can barely watch television anymore, poor man."

"That's okay," Deborah replied, but she stood at the doorway, reluctant to enter. She had dreamt about this darkened room. A dream she'd dismissed as pure imagination after visiting Darcy in the sunny rose garden. Now here it was. All that she really remembered of it was the horrible desperation it had left her with, but that was enough.

Mrs. Brinks was looking at her queerly. "You can go on in," she said.

Deborah nodded and walked slowly to the couch next to Darcy. She looked back to see if Vera was still in the doorway. She was gone. Deborah could hear the click of kitchen cabinets opened and closed and the running of water. She felt better knowing she was nearby.

She lowered herself onto the edge of the couch and tried to take a deep breath to steady herself.

"Mr. Darcy," she said. "It's Deborah Colby. I'm here."

The old man jerked his head toward her. His face was ashen, the muscles in his neck straining against the thin, loose flesh. He squinted at her with eyes sunken deeply into their sockets.

"Who is your baby's father, what's his name?" he demanded. "I must know."

Deborah was startled and she swallowed hard. What difference could that make to this shrunken old man? But the way he was looking at her compelled her to answer.

"The baby's father," she hesitated. "The baby's father is Ethan Burke."

"Ethan Burke died nearly three hundred years ago," snapped Darcy. "In the house that stood on the hill on Foxton Lane before yours."

Deborah shook her head and broke into a short, nervous laugh. "Well, we're obviously not talking about the same

Ethan Burke. Maybe the one I know is a descendant of the other. He did mention that his family. . . ."

"He had no descendants," Darcy interrupted. "They made sure of that."

"I don't understand what you're trying to say."

"Ethan Burke lived in the house on the land where you are living now. He was the one killed when the house was burned down around him. He left no family."

"Okay," said Deborah gently, trying to humor him and keep him calm. "But why? Why was your Ethan Burke killed? Just because he knew Emily Hawkins?"

"My Ethan Burke?" A grim smile twitched Darcy's thin lips. "Mine and yours are the same. You want to know why he was killed? I'll tell you. Before they hanged Emily Hawkins she told them that he was to have a child who would bring destruction to all a' them. So, as the children's verse at the time went:

> Marlowe went and found him,
> In his house he bound him,
> Burned it down around him,
> And now we're safe from harm.

"The ghost fires," Deborah said to herself.

Darcy cocked his head. "What's that?"

"You're saying Ethan is the one in the ghost fires?"

"Oh yes, and they all seen it. Everyone that's stayed in that house of yours."

"Except me."

"Seems as how he didn't want to frighten you away."

"Who?"

"Ethan, or his spirit. He's been waiting for someone like you all these years. Waiting to have that child of his. They thought they destroyed him, but the fire only destroyed the human form. His spirit is stronger than they ever imagined."

"This is crazy," Deborah said suddenly. "Are you actually trying to tell me that a spirit fathered my baby? How do you expect me to believe something like that? I mean, I like your stories and all, but I draw the line at your trying to terrify me with your fantasies. The man who fathered this child is a man like any other."

"Or so he had you think."

She stood up. "That's absurd. I didn't drag myself here at this hour to be taunted and upset."

"Who else saw your Ethan?" Darcy hissed at her.

Deborah searched her memory. No one. They had always been alone. No, that wasn't true. "A cab driver and a waiter in a restaurant where we ate," she said triumphantly.

"What restaurant was that?"

"I don't know the name. It was off the main road not far from Baynor's Inn. It was. . . ." Her words trailed off. She remembered looking for it with Linda and how all they'd found was a disintegrating old barn.

"There is no restaurant," said Darcy. "Sit down."

The room was spinning. Deborah reached for the arm of the couch and sank down. All the mysteries that had perplexed her flooded into her mind. The feeling of being watched. Ethan's sudden appearances. No phone calls. Just a letter with no postmark. The ring that he had recognized but supposedly had never seen before. His reappearance just before she was going to have the abortion, and his horror when he learned that she might have gone through with it. It all made sense if she accepted what Darcy was telling her. But how could she accept it? It was a tale, a ghost story, a witch story, passed on as entertainment for three hundred years.

"You must not have the baby," Darcy said shrilly. He wasn't rambling and he sounded more lucid than she'd ever heard him.

She tried to shake off the hysteria that was threatening to close in on her. She had to think logically. "This baby is perfectly normal," she insisted. "The test I had proved it."

"I'm sure it did. The baby will be perfectly normal and grow up to fulfill its awful destiny."

"No," Deborah screamed. "No. You're just a crazy old man. And you have no right to try to frighten me like this. No right." She stood up and started to the door.

"What makes you think you know and understand all that

there is in this world and beyond it!" Darcy called after her. "Think about what I've said."

Deborah rushed down the hallway straight into the arms of Vera Brinks who had come out of the kitchen to see what all the shouting was about.

"My dear, what's wrong? What's happened?"

Deborah pushed away and ran past her. She found her coat draped over the bannister, and stumbled out the front door, catching hold of the door jamb to keep from falling.

Chapter Thirty-three

Deborah walked into the empty waiting room. She went straight to the receptionist's desk, moving with difficulty. The baby seemed to be pressing lower and heavier, making it hard to lift her feet. Once she reached the desk she collapsed onto the chair beside it. The girl looked up, thin penciled brows arched in surprise.

"Ms. Colby, are you all right?"

Deborah shook her head and tried to catch her breath.

"I have to see Dr. Gates. Is he in?"

"Why didn't you call? You don't look well at all. You shouldn't have made the trip."

"Is he in?" Deborah repeated, gulping mouthfuls of air.

"Yes. Yes, he's here. But he's in with a patient now, and then he's got to rush over to the hospital to perform surgery in a little while."

Deborah heaved herself out of the chair. "I have to see him before he leaves."

"Well, uh, not right now. I mean, I don't know. Let me buzz him." She reached for the intercom.

Deborah walked out toward Dr. Gates' office. She felt sorry for the girl, who obviously didn't have much experience handling emergencies or insistent patients. Generally

231

Deborah went by the rules, but in this instance the rules had to be set aside.

"Wait, Ms. Colby," the receptionist called after her desperately. "Please wait."

Deborah ignored the plea and made it halfway to Dr. Gates' door before being intercepted by one of his nurses. She'd no doubt been alerted by the receptionist, because she didn't seem surprised to see Deborah there.

"I have to speak to Dr. Gates," Deborah announced.

"All right, Ms. Colby, you will. Just calm down now. There's no need to get yourself all worked up. Why don't you go into his office and have a seat and I'll send him in to you as soon as he's finished examining his patient."

Deborah nodded and went into the office, trying to compose her thoughts. She had to make Dr. Gates see the situation as clearly as she did. At home after her confrontation with Darcy she had tried to think through the bizarre things the old man had told her. But all that she'd succeeded in doing was convincing herself that they were true. Everything slipped neatly into place if she accepted his theory. Especially the ring. It had been Ethan's very own, lost in the old root cellar before the fire. And there were more coincidences, she realized with a chill that shook her body. The fall that should have injured her and didn't leave a mark. The ghost fires that had scared Jeffrey and the others off. Ethan had been there, watching over her and then over his child. Darcy was right. The baby must not be born. She had to see to it.

She wondered if Ethan could stop her. Just how much power did he have? He could obviously assume a physical form at will and create realistic illusions. But perhaps there were limits to that power. She'd come to Dr. Gates knowing he was her only hope.

Deborah stiffened in her seat. She could hear a door open and close and the low voices of the nurse and doctor speaking in the hall. She couldn't make out what they were saying. Then the office door clicked open and Dr. Gates came silently across the room to his desk.

"Deborah," he said, sitting down, "what seem to be the problem? Aren't you feeling well?"

"Yes. No. I mean that's not exactly why I'm here. I have something to talk to you about. I know this is going to sound strange. And it might be hard for you to believe at first. It was hard for me. But it is true. I have no doubts anymore." Keeping her voice as even and unemotional as possible, she went on to describe all the inexplicable incidents she could recall, concluding with Darcy's explanation and his admonition that she must not have the baby.

Gates listened, mildly amused at first, and then with increasing concern, his eyebrows inching together until they formed a dark line over his eyes, his hand massaging his chin.

The telephone buzzed. He reached for it, but his eyes remained fixed on Deborah. "Yes, yes, I know. Tell them I'll be there in a minute." He put the phone down and considered her for a moment. Her hands were clasped tightly in her lap, dark eyes intense and anxious.

"Deborah," he said, "you're a mature, reasonable woman. And although this old man's story seems to make sense to you, I'm sure there is still a part of you that understands that that kind of supernatural thing doesn't really exist, and that there are other, more mundane explanations for all these, uh, mysteries you've mentioned."

"No, Dr. Gates, there aren't," Deborah protested urgently. He didn't believe her and he had to. "Don't you see, even the ring. . . ."

"Deborah," Gates interrupted, "you've known me for quite a while now and I think you know you can trust me. There is nothing evil or supernatural at work here. You're a normal, healthy woman who is going to have a normal, healthy baby in a little over a month. Even if there were extraordinary medical factors involved, there is no way I could condone an abortion at this point. It would be tantamount to murder." His voice was firm and measured and hypnotic.

Deborah wanted to believe him. She wanted to escape the panic that was engulfing her. She wanted to lie down and rest. Sleep. Wake up and laugh it all off as another crazy nightmare. But he was wrong. With all his education and training, he was wrong this time. She said nothing more. It had been a waste of time to come here. She'd have to handle matters herself.

"Now I want you to be a good girl and go on home," he was saying. "Miss Crane will call a taxi for you. No more expeditions." He wagged a finger at her as if she were a disobedient child and she wondered what she had ever liked about him. "Get into bed and get some rest. I'd love to give you a mild sedative, but it's not advisable. So have some warm cocoa and try to relax. I think you'll see things in a different light after a good night's sleep. And I want to hear from you in the morning. Okay?"

Deborah nodded mechanically.

"All right then. You go and have a seat in the waiting room until the taxi arrives."

Deborah mumbled a thank you. Gates helped her out of the chair and held the door open for her. Then he returned to his desk and pressed the button on his intercom. "Pull Deborah Colby's file," he said tersely. "I want to know if she has any family around here."

Chapter Thirty-four

Deborah lined up the bottles from the medicine chest. Aspirin, antacid, mouthwash and an over-the-counter sleep aid. Not a very impressive selection, she thought. She picked up the bottle of sleeping pills. It was full except for the two tablets she'd taken at the beginning of the summer. She'd probably have to swallow all of them to be sure. There was no cup in the bathroom. She took the bottle downstairs with her.

She filled a glass with water, opened the bottle and poured the contents into her hand. She didn't have Ethan, she couldn't have the baby. Life wasn't very precious anymore. Then why couldn't she lift her hand to her mouth? She stared at the small mound of white pills for several minutes. It should be a simple matter of swallowing. The same act she'd performed countless times since she was born.

"Pretend they're mints," she told herself, but she couldn't be tricked. "Start with just one and the rest will be easier." She dropped one of the tablets into her mouth and washed it down with the water. "See, nothing to it." She reached for another.

The doorbell rang. Deborah tried to ignore it. But it rang again and a third time before the first chimes had faded

235

away. She put the pills down on the counter and went to see who was there.

Linda stood in the doorway, her coat wide open, the wind whipping her hair and her skirt. She was chewing on her upper lip and reaching for the buzzer again.

"Oh, Deborah, thank God you're all right."

"What do you mean?"

Linda walked past her into the living room.

"You're actually coming inside my house?" Deborah said dryly. "Shouldn't you still be in school?" She pushed the door closed.

"Yes, on both counts. But your Dr. Gates scared the hell out of me."

Deborah came into the living room. "Dr. Gates?"

Linda studied her. "Are you sure you're all right? You seem, I don't know, distant." She pulled off her coat and tossed it onto the couch.

"I'm fine."

"Could I have some coffee? I'm freezing. I got someone to cover for me and I rushed over here. No gloves, I didn't even wait for the car to warm up. It stalled out three times." She was walking toward the kitchen.

"Sure, I'll go put on the water," Deborah said quickly, blocking her path. "Why don't you sit down in here?"

"I'd rather sit in the kitchen."

Deborah pivoted and reached the kitchen first. She slid the pills off the counter and into her palm and was spilling them back into the bottle as Linda came in.

"What's that?" she asked stopping beside her. "Do you need some help?"

"No, I, uh, I just spilled these when the doorbell rang. That's all."

Linda noticed the glass of water. She took the bottle out of Deborah's hand. "Oh my God, Deborah." She grabbed her arm. "How many of these did you take?"

Deborah sighed and pulled away. "Just one. You interrupted me. But I don't think I could have gone through with it anyway."

Linda held her by the shoulders. "Tell me the truth," she demanded. "How many?"

"One. You can count them if you want to. There are three missing. The two I took in the summer and the one today. There were twenty-five to begin with."

Linda let her go and started counting the pills. Deborah sank onto a chair, powerful sobs racking her body.

"Gates said he was worried about you, that you might be experiencing a mild, temporary psychosis, but I don't think he expected anything like this." Satisfied with the number of pills, she poured them back into the bottle and closed the lid.

"He's going to win," Deborah whimpered. "I'm not strong enough to fight him."

"Dr. Gates?" Linda asked in confusion.

"Ethan."

"You're going to have to explain all this to me," said Linda. "Dr. Gates wasn't too clear and I feel as if I walked in on the middle of an Alfred Hitchcock movie."

"What's the use. You're not going to believe me either."

"I'll try to be open minded. I've always been in the past." She led Deborah into the living room and settled her on the couch. "Besides, I know you and what you've been through better than Dr. Gates does."

Deborah poured out the story again, punctuating it with sobs and hiccups. The more Linda heard, the more concerned she became. Deborah sounded far from rational. This was not the Deborah she knew. But she fixed her face with an impartial expression and nodded, encouraging her to go on. Toward the end Deborah doubled over.

"What is it?" Linda put her arm around her shoulders.

"I don't know," she said faintly. "I'm not feeling very well."

"Here, lie down. You've had quite a day." She helped lift Deborah's feet onto the sofa. "Is that better?"

Deborah nodded, but a few minutes later she was bent over again. "I think I'm in labor," she gasped as the pain subsided.

"No, you can't be. The baby isn't due for six weeks yet."

"I wouldn't take any bets on that. I think you'd better call the doctor."

*   *   *

Dr. Gates met them at the hospital emergency room. Linda waited outside while he examined Deborah. He reappeared after ten minutes.

"I'm admitting her," he said, his mouth set in a grim, straight line.

"She's really in labor then?"

"And dilating."

"What about the baby?" Linda asked. "She's still in her eighth month."

"I know. We'll just have to hope for the best. In any case, my first obligation is to Deborah. Does she have any family?"

"A sister and brother-in-law in New York. I can contact them."

"Fine. Don't alarm them. There's no reason to believe this won't be a perfectly ordinary delivery. But they may want to be here with her. In case there are problems with the baby afterward. In a premature birth like this the first concern is that the baby's lungs be adequately developed to function and sustain life."

"I understand."

"Good." He turned to go back in to Deborah.

"Dr. Gates," Linda called after him.

He stopped and looked over his shoulder at her.

"I'll be staying here. Please let me know how she's doing."

He nodded. "There's a maternity lounge on the third floor. Why don't you wait there. I'll keep you posted."

An orderly rolled a wheelchair into Deborah's room. Linda waited near the door for a glimpse of her friend.

Deborah looked disheveled, but she smiled at Linda.

Linda squeezed her arm. "Everything's going to be fine. Dr. Gates told me. The baby, too," she added brightly.

The smile vanished. "No. It won't," said Deborah. "It mustn't."

Linda opened her mouth to reply, but the orderly had whisked Deborah down the hall to the elevators before she could respond.

*   *   *

Deborah lay on her back in a small room that was bare except for the bed, a large clock and an eight-by-ten color photo of a baby hung high on the wall. The nurse had explained that the photo was used as a focal point for women in labor, but Deborah closed her eyes and tried not to look at it. Her baby was premature. It couldn't survive.

She felt another contraction and tried to breathe evenly. Wasn't that what she had read somewhere she was supposed to do? She wanted to turn onto her side and draw her knees up to ease the pain, but there were two belts across her abdomen attached to machines that were monitoring the fetal heartbeat and her contractions. If she moved they would dislodge and the nurse would come rushing back in to reattach them.

Deborah clenched her teeth. Her controlled breathing wasn't helping. The contraction relaxed and she glanced at the clock. They had come every two minutes for hours. Dr. Gates came in frequently to check on her, and had told her he was satisfied with her progress. But as far as she was concerned, the only thing that had progressed was the intensity of the pain.

Sometime after eight that night the pain became unbearable. Deborah lurched onto her side, ripping apart the velcro straps that held the belts. She screamed. The nurse appeared almost immediately and Gates was at her side telling her to relax. The pain wasn't subsiding this time, but consuming her in its shock waves. The nurse was holding her, urging her to lie still. She felt an acute pain in her back as the local anesthetic was injected, then a man's voice told her she wouldn't feel any more contractions. Miraculously the pain was fading. It was gone. She opened her eyes and the nurse eased her onto her back again. Dr. Gates was standing at the foot of the bed with a short, stocky man who was also wearing a white coat.

"This is Dr. Paulson. He's an anesthesiologist. The best."

Dr. Paulson beamed at her through steel-rimmed glasses.

Deborah started to smile back, but then her mouth went slack, her expression frozen. Behind and to the right of Dr. Paulson stood Ethan. "Oh, my God," she gasped, "he's here!"

239

"Who's here?" asked the nurse.

Deborah pointed and tried to sit up, but she couldn't. The lower half of her body was paralyzed. "I can't move," she cried out.

"That's what I've just been explaining to you," said Dr. Gates. He came to stand beside her. It's from the epidural Dr. Paulson gave you. It'll last a few hours and then wear off. There's nothing to be concerned about. We use it all the time. Now who is it you think is here?"

Deborah looked beyond Dr. Gates. Ethan was gone. "Ethan," she said, fear and confusion blending in her voice. "He was here, but now he's gone. Darcy was right. I told you he was right. Ethan was standing there. Right next to Dr. Paulson, and now he's gone."

The two doctors looked at each other. The nurse shrugged and wagged her head.

"Take her into delivery," said Dr. Gates. "Dr. Paulson and I will be along in a minute."

"Deborah," he said as the nurse wheeled her bed past him, "everything will be all right."

Deborah closed her eyes. Tears trickled down the sides of her face and onto the pillow.

Deborah wouldn't watch the baby being born in the large mirror the nurse had angled for her. She turned her head away when her son was wheeled past. She heard the muffled comments that passed between the nurses and the doctors and was grateful to be finally left alone in the recovery room.

Dr. Gates stopped in to see her before leaving the hospital for the night. Seeing that she was still awake he ordered a mild sedative for her. He didn't mention the condition of the baby, and although she was aching to know, she didn't ask.

Chapter Thirty-five

She opened her eyes. It was still night, but in the diffused light coming through a partly open bathroom door she realized she was no longer in the recovery room. While she slept she must have been transferred to her own room. A private one, she noted. The doctors must be concerned about her, but the thought didn't disturb her. It was as if her emotions were suspended. She felt herself drifting, her eyelids closing again. It was good to sleep. She was so tired and she didn't want to think.

"Deborah." The voice jarred her back to wakefulness. She hadn't noticed anyone there. She turned her head to the side.

"How are you feeling?" Ethan stood in the dim light beside her bed.

"Please leave me be," she whispered. "It's over. You don't need me anymore."

He reached out to touch her cheek. She pulled back. "Don't be afraid. I would never hurt you. I just want to talk to you." He pulled a chair close to the bed.

Deborah watched him warily, no longer sleepy.

"You have a buzzer right near your hand," Ethan said. "You can call for the nurse at any time and I'll be gone."

Deborah lifted the cord and pulled it through her hand until she felt the button under her thumb. She didn't press it. She didn't know what was real or not anymore. She knew only that she didn't want him to go. Not yet.

"I won't have this opportunity again," he said. "I shouldn't even be here now."

"Why are you here?" she asked stiffly.

"Because you have a right to the truth."

"I know the truth."

"No. You know a story that an old man believes is true." His eyes were steady and engaging.

"All right. I'm listening. Tell me your truth," she said with irony. "But I don't promise to believe it."

"Part of what Darcy told you is correct," he said. "Emily Hawkins was convicted of witchcraft. But she wasn't a witch. She did have the ability in certain instances to predict future events. What your scientists today call precognition. She was psychic."

Deborah thought of the Jennings book. What he was saying seemed to support her theories. "But that's no reason to assume it's true," she warned herself.

"About a month before her arrest," Ethan was saying, "she had come to see me. To offer condolences on the death of my father. We'd lived up on the hill where your house is now, my father and I. We were miles away from Salem and never had much to do with the people in town. We spent our time raising a small summer crop and reading. Most of them didn't understand us anyway and consequently left us to ourselves. Emily was one of the few who ever bothered to come by. A sweet, fine lady she was, too. But I'm digressing. As I said, she'd come to see me to pay her respects. But also to try to cheer me by telling me of a dream she'd had. One of her psychic dreams. As I understood her, I was to someday sire a child, a son, whose achievements would help the world."

Deborah pushed herself up on her elbows. "No," she cried. "That's not true. Darcy said the child would only bring evil." Her head was wobbly, her arms weak. She fell back onto the pillow.

Ethan reached out to touch her, but withdrew his hand in

midair. "Please Deborah. I don't want you to hurt yourself. Just be still and hear me out." His eyes were anxious, his brows drawn together.

Deborah wondered why he had bothered coming and why he needed to talk to her. The baby was already born. Whether or not it survived was in other hands, not hers. A small gleam of hope flickered in her thoughts.

Perhaps Darcy had been mistaken. "Don't be beguiled too easily," she cautioned herself. "He's not what he seems."

"If what you're saying is so, then how did Darcy's story come about? It's obvious he believes it's true."

"A miscalculation on Emily's part. For which I bear her no malice. You see, before they hanged her she told them that one who lived among them would have a child who would bring destruction and evil to all of them. She only sought to frighten them with the lie and thereby have some small revenge. She had no way of knowing it would lead them to me. And it wouldn't have, except for a precocious young girl by the name of Sarah Danby. She had seen Emily come to visit me that day and she convinced the crowd that it was I whom Emily meant. To be fair they didn't take much convincing. If the finger were pointed at me, they would each be safe from a similar accusation. Everyone looked out for himself. It was a mean and terrible time then, Deborah. They came to my house that night. I hid in the old root cellar that's still behind your house. But they found me and dragged me out. And the rest you know."

"The ring was yours all along," Deborah murmured.

"It fell off during the struggle in the cellar."

"The dream. It was yours, too."

Ethan nodded. I didn't mean to scare you with it. I only wanted you to understand what happened, so that in the end you might understand me."

Deborah didn't say anything more for a few moments. There was too much to absorb, too much to try to accept. Seeing him so close again, so real, she found it hard to believe he was a spirit, a ghost. It was strange even to think it. Shouldn't she be frightened by him? She wasn't. She was once again powerfully drawn to him. And having him there she felt as she had before, as if they were suspended in a world that turned around them alone. Perhaps for her there were two realities. One in which she moved with the rest of the world. And one which she shared with Ethan.

"All these years you've been waiting to have that child?" she asked finally.

He nodded. "In a very lonely limbo. Neither alive nor dead. And I kept thinking that whatever good my son was to have done couldn't possibly matter anymore—so much time had passed. But once I met you I realized that it had all been meant to happen just as it did, all of it—the dying, the waiting, and you. Although we were separated by three centuries, you were always intended as the mother of my son."

"Three hundred years," said Deborah, shaking her head. "That's so hard to accept."

"Accept?" Ethan repeated with a weary smile. "We accept what we have to. Our will is less our own than we know. And three hundred years are nothing in the entire pattern of life."

"Even if what you're saying is true, I don't understand why it should matter to you if I believe it or not."

"Because I love you," he said with urgency. "I thought I'd feel nothing but peace and relief when it was over. But there is no peace. Not yet. I don't want to be separated from you. I keep thinking about how it would have been to spend our lives together, in my time or in yours. Yet since there is nothing I can do about that, I hope at least to make it less painful for you by explaining everything. Then I must let go of you. Let go of the thought of you."

"I want to believe you," Deborah whispered, touched by the emotion in his voice. "But there's just no proof one way or the other."

"Yes, there is," said Ethan. "Emily Hawkins kept a diary where she noted all of her predictions. Her friend Anne Thorndike saved it, hid it and passed it down to her grandson. It stayed in their family until fifty years ago when they donated it to a museum in Boston. The diary will prove that what I've told you is true."

Deborah could see the blue-green of his eyes more clearly and she realized the room was no longer dark. The sun had risen and was stealing through the slits between the blinds. She could hear small noises in the hallway outside her room. The muted patter of gum-sole shoes, objects moved and set down, low voices. The world was moving in on them. She thought of the baby, so tiny and fragile in the isolette. For the first time since his birth she was afraid of losing him.

"Will the baby survive, Ethan?" She reached for his hand. "He's early. I know the doctors are worried. You should have seen him."

Ethan smiled and closed his hands over hers. "I did. He'll be all right. He was meant to, now wasn't he?"

Deborah nodded.

"What will you name him?"

She remembered all the time she'd spent selecting girls' names. She suppressed a smile, wondering if he had been there watching her. "What was your father's name?" she asked.

"Eli."

"Then I'll name him Eli."

He leaned over her and kissed her gently. "Thank you. I know it's not going to be easy for you alone with a baby, and I can't make it any easier. We never had a chance to be married properly. I never even gave you a ring. But I want you to have this one." He pulled the signet ring off his finger and slipped it onto hers "You'd better have a guard put on it, so you don't lose it," he said, the dimples appearing in his cheeks.

Deborah's mouth turned up in a crooked smile, her lower lip trembling.

"I love you Deborah." He kissed her again. "Take care of yourself. And since I can't be here, love him for both of us." He laid her hand back on the covers.

"Will I see you again?"

"I don't think so."

"Ethan," she reached out to him. It seemed so final.

"Sleep now," he said.

"Ms. Colby," the nurse said briskly. "Time to get the day started. We have to take your temperature. And breakfast will be along shortly. Ms. Colby?"

245

Deborah opened her eyes and looked around her. Ethan was no longer there. Had he ever been? Could she have dreamt it all?

The nurse crossed the room and pulled open the blinds, letting in the full sunlight. Then she came back to Deborah and whipped out a thermometer. "Open, please," she said and tucked it under Deborah's tongue. This was a different nurse than last night. She was tall and broad with a stern, unapproachable face.

She withdrew the thermometer. "Normal. Now we'll have to get you into the bathroom. Have to make sure all systems are functioning. Here, give me your hand."

Deborah raised her hand off the blanket and felt something heavy slip over her knuckle. She picked the ring up and put it back on, caught between sadness and joy. Ethan had been there. It wasn't a dream. She maneuvered herself to the edge of the bed.

"Nurse?"

"Yes?"

"How is my baby doing? Do you think I'll be able to see him this morning?"

The nurse's harsh expression softened. "I don't see why not," she said, an approving smile flickering around her mouth. "He seems to be holding his own. The doctors are very optimistic. He's some little fighter, your son."

August 2010

Deborah smoothed a drop of light makeup under each eye. She hadn't slept well the night before and dark hollows framed her eyes. She knew her restlessness wasn't due to the unfamiliar hotel bed. She hadn't slept properly for weeks. No, it was months now that she awakened to some inner clock close to three every morning, the endless, unanswerable questions stalking her mind. At times she would fall back into a fitful sleep before dawn. But more often she would sit at the bedroom window and watch the sun rise. She'd gone to a doctor who'd prescribed a medication intended to help her sleep. It had worked for two nights, then her body had fought off its effects and resumed its early morning vigil.

She screwed the cap on the makeup bottle and stared at herself in the wall-to-wall mirrors with dissatisfaction. She could still see the dark smudges beneath her eyes, but because of the makeup they seemed more gray than black. Not much of an improvement. Even until a year ago she had been pleased with the graceful way she had aged. She was an attractive woman. Several widowers had persisted in asking her out, but although she was flattered, she had declined all their invitations to dinners and shows. Deborah hadn't been interested in any man since Ethan, as she hadn't been interested in any man before him. It was as if her life had been uniquely planned around him. She preferred to continue living as she had been. In fact, she thought wearily, she would be glad to get back to Rachael Crossing and the comfortable routine she had established over nearly thirty years. At least there her days were too busy for the rambling of her private thoughts and torments. She still taught in the high school, a position she'd assumed when Eli was only two years old. She had no wish to retire, and the board, well pleased with her performance, saw no reason to ask her to step down. In her spare time she continued to write articles and short stories; she had sold close to a hundred pieces over the years, and not just to local publications.

Her social life revolved around her friends, especially Linda and her husband, who'd moved back to Rachael Crossing to raise their children. She and Linda were still the only ones who knew the identity of Eli's father. Eli himself had been told that his father had died in an accident before he was born, which wasn't really that far from the truth.

Deborah was treated like a native in Rachael Crossing and she felt like one. It was as if the first thirty-seven years of her life had belonged to someone else. Someone she had only read about in a novel. The house on Foxton Lane was home. The mysteries resolved. At least she had thought them resolved until last March, six months after she first learned of Project Prometheus.

"Just what is this Project Prometheus you're working on?" Deborah had asked Eli over coffee and cake during a rare weekend visit that September.

Eli, who was tall and slender like his father, with the same high, wide angled cheek bones, chose his words carefully while he sipped his coffee.

"It's essentially a space station that will generate energy for us by collecting solar radiation and transmitting the microwaves to a receiver on Earth. For as long as our sun lives, an inexhaustible supply of energy." His tone was even, controlled, but just behind the words Deborah could hear the enthusiasm and involvement she had heard when he'd explained his first junior high science project to her. "Eventually there will be a whole network of these stations in space. But Prometheus will be the first. It should be operable within a year."

"The final solution to all our energy problems." Deborah shook her head incredulously. "It's almost too much to believe. And yet I seem to remember having heard something about using microwaves as far back as the seventies."

"You've got a good memory. They did consider the possibility back then. But they couldn't overcome some problems intrinsic to the idea, and they let it drop."

"So, tell me how you got the project off the ground," she pursued. "Pun intended."

"I'll forgive you anyway," Eli grinned, his father's dimples creasing his cheeks. Then he shrugged. "I worked out the mechanism that enables the beam to be transmitted accurately and without drift to the receiver."

Deborah stared at her son with a mixture of pride and awe. "Then the entire project owes its existence to you." She had always known his life's work would be important, but she had never come close to imagining its true magnitude. An unlimited source of energy for the entire world.

"Listen, Mom," said Eli soberly, "I have to ask you not to mention this to anyone until it's released to the news media in about a week."

Deborah had promised to keep her excitement contained until then. As it happened, within days of the public announcement, the protestors had set to work. They called Project Prometheus a doomsday machine, a space age game of Russian roulette, a death ray. They caricatured Eli as a mad scientist, a young apprentice of the grim reaper.

At first Deborah ignored the protestors. There were always protestors when something innovative was proposed. Usually they were alarmists, groupies of causes. But as the project's date of completion loomed closer, a prominent, aging actress and her son joined the protestors. They became better organized, more vociferous, more violent. The age of passive protest was long past. They carried knives, sometimes guns. Police and civilians were injured, a few killed, in the skirmishes that ensued. And Deborah had started listening to their arguments. She couldn't help but listen. They were everywhere. Many of her own students were among them. They claimed that nothing was fail-safe. That even the conventional microwave beams had been known to cause blindness, deafness, genetic damage and cancer. An accident with Project Prometheus, they said, would result in widespread and hideous death, its victims fried from the inside out. A death preceded by unbearable abdominal pain, vomiting and shock, the gastrointestinal tract, eyes and bladder being especially sensitive to the internal burning.

The people who had been her friends and neighbors throughout the years in Rachael Crossing were suddenly distant. Other teachers spoke in whispered conversations that ended abruptly when she entered a room. Shopkeepers kept their greetings terse, eying her with suspicion, as if she were other than what she appeared to be. As if she were somehow responsible for her son's work. Was she? she'd wondered aloud to Linda. After all, she'd borne him. Emily Hawkins had been held responsible just for having visionary dreams. Linda had tried to console her, assuring her the hysteria would die down once Prometheus was activated and shown to be harmless. But Deborah couldn't be calmed.

She wished she could see Eli. He would quiet her concerns. But during the last hectic months she'd only heard from him with hurried, sporadic phone calls. During one of those brief conversations she had tried to ask him about the protestors' claims, but he had cut her off abruptly, saying he was late for a conference.

For the first time Deborah realized she shouldn't necessarily trust the answers he might give her anyway. That realization had shaken her to the core and sent her back to the museum in Boston that she had first visited after Eli's birth. She wanted to see Emily Hawkins' diary again, reread the words that had once reached across three centuries to reassure her of Ethan's love and sincerity and had made bearable the sometimes lonely, difficult years of raising Eli alone. Words she could no longer remember exactly, clouded as they were by her fears about Project Prometheus.

On a cool, blustery day at the end of March she made the second trip to the museum. Again she leafed through the fragile pages of the diary until she located the reference to Ethan. The words were small and cramped, blotches of ink obscuring some letters. Deborah squinted at them through her reading glasses. When she looked up from the diary her heart was thumping fiercely. Oh, my God, she thought. She must have uttered the words aloud, because the curator jerked up her head and inquired if she were all right.

Deborah had swallowed and tried to steady her voice. "Yes, I'm fine," she replied. The curator had shrugged and gone back to work.

Deborah focused again on the entry halfway down the brittle, yellowed page that began with the date and Ethan's name. It was just one sentence:

He will father a son whose life and work will bear great significance beyond our own time.

The words could not have been more ambiguous. How could she have ever taken them to be proof of Ethan's claim? The answer was plain. She had needed to. The baby had been born, and from the first moment she held him she had loved him. She had needed to believe in order to survive. She wondered what words Emily had used when she had related her prophecy to Ethan. Had they been as ambiguous? Had he misinterpreted them?

She closed the old book gently. Her hands were trembling. Stop it! she ordered herself. Those words are not a condemnation. Significance can be either good or bad. She would continue to interpret it favorably until shown differently.

She pulled on her coat and gloves and thanked the curator. Outside in the raw March wind she wished Emily Hawkins had chosen her words more carefully.

Deborah shook her head as if to be free of the clawing fears that had been threatening to overwhelm her since that day. She picked up her brush and pulled it roughly through her hair, scratching her scalp so hard that she winced.

There was a double knock on the door. She tucked the brush into her travel case and flicked off the lights in the dressing room. She glanced at her watch. Eli was early. She tried to relax her face into a natural smile and opened the door.

Eli wasn't smiling. He strode in quickly, purposefully. "Good, you're ready," he said, without any greeting. "We're leaving a little earlier than we'd originally planned." He walked to the window as he talked, then turned back to her abruptly and met her in the middle of the room.

"Do you have everything packed?"

"I just have to throw my cosmetics into the overnight case," said Deborah. "The big suitcase is closed and ready." She motioned to the unmade bed where she had left it. "Has something happened? Is anything wrong?" She tried to engage his eyes, but he was already walking past her. She thought how distant he'd grown from her, each step of his education and career widening the gap, until he was hardly more than a nice young man who came to visit infrequently and called her Mom.

"Nothing's wrong," Eli was saying, his back to her. "Just some adjustments to today's schedule. Out at Prometheus control they're afraid we'll be late. Administrative jitters." He gave a terse chuckle. "Can you get that other case together?" He swung the suitcase off the bed.

"It'll only take a second." Deborah went into the dressing room. Administrative jitters maybe, she thought, but not over our punctuality. We're already supposed to arrive an hour before the ceremony.

They'd been in San Francisco for two days attending dinners and presentations in Eli's honor. A limousine was to take them from their hotel to the airport. Then a private jet would fly them out to the small, recently constructed airport in central Nevada and another limousine would carry them to the control center itself. The weather was warm and dry, the customary fog having burned off earlier than usual. Deborah could see no reason for the schedule to have been altered. But she decided not to press Eli on it just now. She wasn't sure she wanted to know anyway.

"Ready?"

She nodded. "Are we checked out?"

"All taken care of, Mom." He held the door for her. Deborah turned left toward the elevators. Eli took her elbow with his free hand. "No, we're going this way," he said. "The service elevator."

"Why?" she asked as he propelled her down the hallway in the opposite direction.

"It'll take us out through the staff quarters and back entrance. There are some protestors out front. The police think we should avoid them."

Deborah swallowed. Her throat was tight and dry. The chiefs at Prometheus weren't worried about timetables. They were hoping to avoid trouble with the protestors by moving everything more quickly.

She'd expected to see some protestors at the gates to Prometheus control, maybe even at the airport. But at their hotel? Was their anger so specifically aimed at Eli? She clutched his arm as they entered the elevator, not because she needed support, but because she was afraid of losing him.

There were several policemen waiting for them when they emerged from the elevator and they were escorted to the waiting limousine without incident.

The scenes at the airports in San Francisco and Nevada were worse. The hostility of the protestors was tangible as they screamed obscenities and hurled objects. But what Deborah saw on their faces were the contortions not only of anger, but of fear, a fear that was a reflection of her own.

She was exhausted by the time the car roared out of the small airfield for the last leg of the journey to Prometheus control. She and Eli had hardly spoken during the flight. He had patted her hand from time to time and she had smiled back unconvincingly. But in the silent cave of the limousine as it rushed through the Nevada desert she turned to her son.

"Eli," she said. "How safe is Prometheus? Could they be right, all those people?"

Eli's face relaxed into a smile. The same smile she had

seen whenever he was dealing with something he understood. There was confidence in the smile. Control and confidence.

"It's safe, Mom," he said. "I created it and I know it's safe."

"They thought nuclear power plants were safe, too," she reminded him gently, "until that quake outside of San Francisco in '86 and the meltdown in the Soviet Union in '95."

"You can't compare the two," Eli replied comfortably.

"Except that where human work is involved so is the possibility of an accident. Could there be an accident with Prometheus?" She watched her son's face for signs of dissimulation. Although he was no longer smiling, he was regarding her frankly. His eyes, shaped like Ethan's, but brown like her own, stared back at her as openly as when he was a boy.

"An accident is virtually impossible," he said.

Deborah nodded. Virtually, she thought, but not actually. Suddenly she found his composure unsettling. She turned away from him to stare out the window. Somewhere high above them, hidden by the brilliant August sunlight, Prometheus was hovering. Waiting for Eli's finger to press the button that would activate it. Inexhaustible energy for a fuel starved world. Maybe Eli was right. She wanted to believe him. In any case it was beyond her control. "Our will is less our own than we know," Ethan had said to her the night Eli was born. Now she finally understood. It had never been up to her. Not at any time.

She sighed deeply. She was still afraid, but the burden of responsibility wasn't hers. She watched the flat, pebbly desert rush past her. Even the hardy scrub brush was browned and shriveled by the harsh sun. A barren, desolate landscape. She wondered if it, too, were a prophecy.